The More Things Change…

The More Things Change...

Maeve Maddox

HYPATIA PRESS

Published by Hypatia Press in the United Kingdom in 2025

ISBN: 978-1-83919-618-8

www.hypatiapress.org

To the people of every century who were driven from their place of origin by natural forces, enslavement, economic distress, religious oppression, corrupt government, or war.

And to the people who were kind to them in their suffering.

Plus ça change, plus la même chose
The more things change, the more they stay the same

Part One
Milan (Mediolanum)

December, 411 A.D.
Milan, Italy

In the reigns of Honorius, Emperor of the Western Empire (393-423) and Theodosius II, Emperor of the Eastern Empire (402-450).

Chapter One

A Call in the Night

Shifra left her maidservant Dacia in the kitchen preparing the evening drinks and hurried across the open peristylum to the main house. Her long-sleeved tunic did little to protect her from the December chill.

Inside, she moved quickly past the door curtain into the welcoming warmth of the tablinum, the cozy little office off the atrium where Benjamin kept his books and worked on household and business accounts. The room was warm, not simply from the two charcoal braziers, but also because of the heat rising from the floor, fueled by the hypocaust below. Tiptoeing behind her seated husband, she put her arms around him and kissed him on the side of his face. "Aren't you glad now that we bought the house with the hypocaust?"

Benjamin took her hands in his and kissed them. She pulled away and moved to her own chair facing the desk. He laughed. "You'll never let me forget, will you?"

As natives of Alexandria in Egypt, they'd found the winter temperatures in the northern Italian city of Milan hard to get used to. After that first winter, in frigid rented quarters near the synagogue, they'd gone looking for a house to buy. At the top of her list of wants, Shifra had placed central heating. Benjamin objected to the expense. After a second winter in the apartment, he relented.

"Yes, my darling, you were right to insist on the hypocaust. It's especially nice now that we're getting older."

Older. Shifra picked up her spindle from the table next to her chair. Older indeed. Three decades now since—a bride of sixteen—she'd come to Milan with her brand-new husband. So much had happened in those thirty years. Her mind flew back to a devastating memory. "Miriam would have been twenty-eight this year."

Benjamin nodded. "And the child, ten years old." He shook his head. "The same age as our Eastern emperor, the second Theodosius."

Shifra felt tears rise. Their beautiful daughter, dead in childbirth and the baby, a little girl, stillborn. Her emotion turned from sorrow to anger. So totally unnecessary. She prayed that the doctor whose fault it had been was burning in his Christian hell.

The curtain separating the tablinum from the atrium swayed as Dacia entered with two fragrant mugs of steaming wine flavored with honey and cinnamon. She placed one on Benjamin's desk and the other on the low table beside Shifra's chair.

"Thank you, Dacia. You may go to bed now." Poor Dacia. After all these years, still so self-conscious about her appearance that she wore a face covering even in the house. A slave, the girl nevertheless held a special place in her mistress's heart, having come into the household at the age of ten, in the weeks following the loss of Miriam. Damaged by abuse, she'd provided an outlet for Shifra in her sorrow, a living child who needed the care she could not give to her own flesh.

Dacia's forehead furrowed. "What about the lamps, Domina?"

Shifra patted her hand. "We can manage with the lamps, dear. You go on now." Dacia nodded reluctant acquiescence and left the room.

Benjamin put down his stylus and took a sip of wine. "Delicious as usual. Dacia never fails to make the *muslum* just as I like it. Not too hot and just the right amount of honey."

They sat in comfortable silence, the drinks warming them within. Shifra loved this time of night—Benjamin at his desk, her in her chair, the servants in their beds, or at least out of sight. Still, at the back of her mind, lurked the dread of a knocking at the door that would summon her husband into the night to attend some medical emergency. It hadn't been like that in the early years. She looked over at Benjamin. "I liked it better when the emperor's court was headquartered in Milan."

"What brought that into your head?" Benjamin replied. "It's been years since the court moved to Ravenna."

"I was just thinking how nice it was when you worked at the palace with Augustine and your other Gentile friends and had regular hours. Not like now, when we don't have any friends outside the congregation and you never know when someone is going to drag you out at all hours."

Benjamin stood, grabbed a folding stool and set it up beside her chair. Sitting, he took her hands into his. "I wasn't going to tell you until tomorrow."

"What? What were you going to tell me?" Shifra stared. He was smiling, but his words set her heart racing with fear. Far too many times in the past, he'd been reluctant to share more bad news about edicts against the Jews.

"It's good news, dearest. Something that I think will please you. I told you that Milan has a new Roman prefect. I met him years ago, during the troubles with the usurper Maximus. He says he's never forgotten how I handled the influx of wounded. He's asked me to be the official physician for the prefecture. The duties will be similar to the job I had when we first came here, when the first Theodosius was sole emperor and held his court here in Milan."

"But, doesn't he know that you're a Jew?"

Benjamin laughed. "Believe it or not, he's one of the few pagans who has managed to hold onto office without converting. The fact that I'm not a Christian is of no importance to him."

Shifra threw her arms around his neck. "That's wonderful. What will you have to do?"

"In addition to seeing to the medical needs of the prefect and his household, I'll be responsible for the health of about two hundred municipal slaves and employees. I'll receive a set stipend, plus additional fees for supplies and to pay for patients requiring ongoing treatment."

A terrible thought occurred to her. "Will we have to move?"

He smiled. "No. You get to keep your hypocaust. The job includes transportation. They'll send a litter when they need me. I won't even have to walk across town to get to the prefect's palace."

"What about night calls? Will you have to attend at night?"

Benjamin shrugged. "If an emergency comes up in the night, of course." He waved a document he'd been holding. "According to the agreement, in the case of a call between sunset and sunrise, the prefect will send a closed carriage and an escort of two municipal guards."

"That is wonderful! I'm so worried every time you go out after dark. Even in the daytime, when you have to go to one of the Gentile neighborhoods near the east gate, I fear for you. Now I won't have to worry. When do you begin?"

"Tomorrow. I've already put the word out that I'm no longer available for general practice."

Shifra sighed. Life had not been easy during the past few years. "The Lord be praised." She grinned mischievously. "This is especially good news, now that we're getting older." She stood and pulled him up after her. "Let's go to bed, noble physician."

As they moved into the atrium, a loud knocking at the front door shattered the silence. Ordinarily, Linus, the porter, would answer, but tonight he'd complained of a fever and Benjamin had permitted him to sleep away from the drafts of the vestibule. He moved to answer the door himself. Shifra clung to him.

"Don't answer," she whispered.

Benjamin took her outstretched hand and kissed her fingers. "I'm a doctor, remember? Someone may need me." He disengaged her fingers. She followed him to the door.

The bad feeling only grew stronger when she saw the rough-looking young man framed in the doorway. The torch in his hand lighted a gaunt and unsmiling face. The tattered clothing too filthy and ragged to belong to any urban slave. A wretch from the Sicilian mines might look like that perhaps, but not a respectable household slave in Milan—Milan, the elegant city that had once been the seat of a Roman emperor. Shifra pulled Benjamin aside.

"He could be one of those ruffians who attacked Reuben the banker while he was closing his shop last week."

Again, Benjamin pried her fingers loose. "I know the lad and his mother. His name is Spurius and he's no ruffian. Besides, Reuben had something to steal. Who would want the herbs and trifles I carry in my bag?"

The young man looked pleadingly at Benjamin, his face shiny with sweat and what may have been tears. "Please, Medicus, my wife is in childbirth and having a terrible time. She'll die for sure if you don't come."

Shifra turned on him "Why come for the medicus? What's wrong with a midwife?"

"Please, Domina, the midwife has been with her all the day. She says she's done all she can. She says the baby is at an odd angle and she can't shift it."

Benjamin took up his cloak and bag from a table in the vestibule, kept there for just such an emergency. Louder now, panic forcing the words, Shifra grabbed at his arm. "Please, don't go, Benjamin, or at least take Linus with you."

"Linus is ill." He turned to the man. "Will you light me back on my way, Spurius?"

"Yes, yes, certainly."

Benjamin turned back to Shifra. "Don't wait up, dearest. I'll be back as soon as I can." He followed Spurius into the night.

Dacia, having heard the knocking, entered the vestibule and barred the door after them. Then, taking Shifra's arm, she guided her back into the atrium. "Come, mistress. I'll help you to bed."

Shifra changed into night clothes and lay down. Sleep, however, eluded her as her mind seethed with images of Benjamin in the dark streets, beset by dangers of the night.

***

Benjamin followed Spurius through silent streets. A wintry moon cast some light, and a few householders kept torches burning at their entrances, but for the most part, the lad's torch was the only thing permitting Benjamin to see where to step. Despite his miserable appearance, Spurius was a Roman citizen. He worked as a roofer's assistant and lived in a rundown insula near the forum. Benjamin shook his head at the irony. His household slaves had better food and clothing than this free working man.

At the entrance to the building, Spurius doused the torch in a tub of sand and placed it in a holder by the door. As they mounted the stairway, Benjamin gasped at the overwhelming fishy odor of garum and a lingering smell of urine. The only light was moonlight from the open side. He ran his hand as lightly as possible along the inside wall to remain oriented. By the time they reached the fifth floor, he was panting for breath. Spurius stopped at the first door on the corridor.

"Here it is, Medicus."

The apartment consisted of one room, lighted with four small clay oil lamps. A brazier gave off a little glow as well. A figure rose from the floor as they entered—the midwife, who had been squatting beside the mat where Spurius's wife lay, moaning. Spurius pushed past her and knelt beside his wife, but Benjamin gripped his shoulder. "No, Spurius. You need to wait somewhere else." Slowly, the young man got back to his feet and backed away.

The midwife shifted from foot to foot. "The babe's turned, Medicus. I can't budge it."

Benjamin set to work, removing his cloak and instructing Spurius and the midwife to boil water. He would need to sterilize the speculum. A breech birth was nothing new to him. Among his most precious medical texts were the gynecological works of Soranus of Ephesus, a physician renowned for his knowledge of childbirth and female diseases. He and Shifra had spent many an evening reading and discussing it. Perhaps he should have brought her with him. More than once, she'd assisted him with a birth.

He took a vial of vinegar from his bag, poured some into a bowl and cleansed his hands before kneeling to examine the woman. The cervix was fully dilated. He inserted his right hand and felt for the feet. There. Gently and firmly, he maneuvered the fetus until the feet were in place. The woman shouted and pushed and there it came. He tied off the cord in two places before cutting it. Then he cleaned the infant's eyes with olive oil and handed the wailing morsel of humanity to the midwife to bathe. "Be sure to use warm water." He knew that some midwives still followed the barbaric practice of bathing newborns in cold water, "to make them breathe."

The new father stood huddled by the doorway. Benjamin smiled at him. "Congratulations, Spurius. You have a son."

The young man threw himself at his wife. "Nona, darling Nona, how do you? My brave, brave Nona."

Benjamin dipped some of the boiled water into a bowl, laved his hands and dried them on a cloth the midwife had laid ready. He replaced everything in his bag and put on his cloak.

"My work is done, Spurius. I'm ready to return home." He waited expectantly.

Spurius tried to stand, but his wife clung to him. "Please, Nona. I must go. I've promised to light the medicus back to his house. I'll be back as quick as I can." Nona wept piteously.

Benjamin sighed. The woman was young. It was her first birth. *Miriam.* His mind flew to that terrible time when his own daughter lay in childbirth. He should have been there. Her husband should have been there, but they'd been at the bishop's palace, answering to charges of blasphemy. By the time they got to her, Miriam and the child were dead. The doctor Shifra summoned had been slow in responding and botched the delivery when he did arrive.

Nona continued to weep. Benjamin knew from Soranus that a new mother needed more than medical help. She required comforting. He picked up his bag. "Never mind, Spurius. I can make my way back on my own. I will, however, require your torch."

Spurius disengaged himself long enough from Nona's grasp to accompany Benjamin to the ground floor where he rekindled the torch he'd used before. Benjamin took it and headed back the way he'd come, but, this time, alone.

The sense of wonder he always felt when delivering a child never palled. Physically tired as he was, he stepped briskly through the dark streets. After three decades in Milan, he knew his way around.

Thirty years ago, Rome was, as now, the nominal capital of the Empire, but Milan was the actual capital of the Western Empire. It was from Milan that Emperor Constantine issued the edict that transformed Christianity from an illegal superstition to a permitted religion. When Benjamin and Shifra first settled there, it was a city of many religions. Now, the orthodox form of Christianity dominated most aspects of life.

Raucous laughter brought Benjamin back to the present.

A knot of revelers emerged from a side street, jostling one another and blocking his path. Two or three of them carried torches, and he recognized the soup-seller's son, a lad of seventeen or so, one of dozens of Milanese children he'd brought into the world. He greeted him.

"Greetings, Lucius."

Lucius nodded and moved to let him pass. The boy's companions, however, encircled Benjamin, preventing him from moving forward.

One of the torchbearers leaned in, close to Benjamin's face. "Who's your friend, Lucius?"

Lucius mumbled something unintelligible. A tall man, older than Lucius, shoved himself close enough for Benjamin to smell the cabbage and stale wine on his breath. "I know him. He's the Jew doctor."

Icy fingers of fear ran up Benjamin's spine. He tried to push past them, but they hemmed him in. Others took up the shout. "Jew doctor, Jew, Jew." Rough hands tore his bag from his grasp. Someone seized his torch. And then the cries changed from "Jew" to "Christ-killer," and fists hammered him to the stone-cold street. Boots smashed against his ribs, triggering an explosion of splintering pain. His last thought—Shifra—begging him not to go.

Chapter Two

The Master Returns Home

Dacia woke with a start and scrambled to her feet. During the night, when she believed that her mistress had finally gone to sleep, she had unrolled her mat and lain down. Shafts of morning light streaked the empty bed. Heart pounding, she raced to the front door. Seeing the bars still in place, she took a breath and directed her steps to the atrium.

Shifra sat on the low marble wall that edged the pool under the opening in the ceiling. She jumped to her feet when she saw Dacia. "Is he back?"

"No, Domina. Not yet." Her mistress sank back down onto the ledge.

A heavy sense of dread clamped Dacia's heart. Even a difficult birth should not have required so much time. Feigning cheerfulness, she went to her mistress, intending to draw her to her feet. "He'll be back soon enough and you'll want to hear all about it. Come, lie down until he returns."

"No!" Shifra pulled away and walked to the far side of the pool. "Leave me, girl. Go about your duties! I'll decide when to lie down."

Dacia recoiled. She was not used to being spoken to as a common slave. She'd been in this household nearly half her life. And though the master never freed her, he and the mistress had nurtured her like a daughter, dressing her like a lady and teaching her to read. She studied Shifra's face, noting the fatigued darkness around her eyes. It was the fear talking.

Shifra returned to where Dacia stood. "Where is he? What can have kept him away all the night?" The imperious tone had vanished. Anxiety had reduced her to helplessness. Dacia realized that she must take charge.

"I'll send Haluk to look for him, Domina."

Dacia left Shifra seated in the atrium and fetched Haluk from the slaves' dormitory. A skinny youngster with an acne-covered face and a habit of cowering when addressed, as if expecting to be beaten, he'd been with them only a few months. Dacia didn't know the details, but she suspected that Benjamin bought him from an abusive master. As he had her, all those years ago.

"The master did not come home last night, Haluk. You must go look for him. I saw him leave with Spurius. I think he lives somewhere near the Via Porticata." She went with him, expecting to have to bar the door after him and was relieved to see that the porter had returned to his post. One less thing to worry about.

With Haluk on his way, Dacia went to the kitchen, told Cook to prepare a pitcher of sweetened wine for their mistress, and returned to the atrium with it. Shifra sat now where she could look into the vestibule. Dacia set the tray on the ledge beside her and commenced to pour. Sounds from the street, the heavy tread of boots and the clink of metal on metal, brought Shifra to her feet, jostling Dacia's hand, sending cup and ewer flying to shatter on the marble tiles.

***

Shifra raced to the vestibule ahead of Dacia, anticipating the sight of Benjamin, standing on the threshold, weary, but safe at home. Instead, the door opened on Haluk, clutching his master's medical bag, and flanked by two soldiers of the city watch.

The man on Haluk's left looked from Dacia to Shifra, uncertain which to address. Dacia stepped back a few paces.

The shorter soldier addressed Shifra and elbowed Haluk. "Is this your slave?"

Speechless with dread, Shifra nodded.

First shoving Haluk into the house, the soldier then turned and shouted. "Bring it on in."

Two municipal slaves, identified by green headbands, carried a litter into the house and lowered it to the floor. Shifra threw herself down after it.

Crusted blood caked the beloved features. No care had been taken to clean him up before bringing him home. He looked as if he'd been dragged from a midden. Bits of eggshell were caught in the threads of his tunic, and cabbage leaves stuck up in his hair. His thick warm cloak was missing. Shifra looked up at the men, shaking.

"Where did you find him? Who has done this to him?"

"Found 'im in an alley lower part of the Via Porticata. Not where I'd expect a Jew doctor. No rich patients there."

Shifra did not wonder how the ugly little soldier knew that Benjamin was a Jew. The Jews of Milan were not required to wear any distinguishing article of clothing, but the Gentiles all seemed to know who was who. She drew a deep sobbing breath. "My husband is a physician," she said. "He goes where he is needed."

The soldiers stared at her blankly and shifted their feet. The slaves withdrew to the street. Shifra turned back to the ruined remains of her husband. What had she said?

My husband is a physician.

Is.

My husband is.

My husband is…dead.

The shriek seemed to come from far away, but then Shifra realized that it was coming from her own throat, a ragged, soul-shattering keening without end. Benjamin, her husband of thirty-two years was dead. Tearing at the neck of her tunic, she felt it rip as she sank across Benjamin's body.

Hands lifted her from the cold body of her husband.

Mind splintered with shards of consciousness, she felt herself being led away. Someone removed her outer garments and sandals and put her to bed. She lay in the darkened cubiculum, the little room where Benjamin would never again take his place beside her. Never again would he nuzzle her hair as they talked about the day's events or about their absent children or simply chose to lie touching in comfortable silence. She lay on the lonely bed like one in a tomb, praying that Hashem—Adonai—the Lord God of the Universe—might take her too.

***

Dacia looked down upon her mistress, pleased that she'd managed to get her to drink some of a valerian mixture that would help her sleep. She wanted to remain in the room, but with the master dead and the mistress too distraught for coherent thought, Dacia knew that she must take charge of the household, at least for a time. She returned to the vestibule.

Linus sat perched on his stool, looking paler than normal. Haluk knelt beside the master's body, heaving with weeping. Dacia wanted to send him to notify the rabbi of Benjamin's death, but she could see the boy was beyond obedience. She knew from her own experience

15

how much he must have loved the man who rescued him from cruel and abusive owners. She would have to go herself.

After looking in once more on her sleeping mistress, and sending the girl of all work to clean the spilled wine in the atrium, Dacia hurried to the rabbi's house to deliver the news to the rabbi and his wife.

On her return, she found the household servants, with the exception of Haluk, gathered in the atrium. Shaken out of her usual subservient manner by the enablement of grief, Dacia spoke sharply. "What is the meaning of this? Why aren't you at your duties?"

Cook, rarely seen outside the kitchen, stepped forward, stirring the air with his usual greasy odor. Taller and wider than any of the men in the household, he appeared to be the designated leader.

"We want to know what the master's death will mean to us."

Dacia struggled to control the urge to wake her mistress and make her take charge.

The household lacked a major domo to supervise the servants and accounts. The master had himself performed such duties, assisted by the mistress. Dacia needed to collect her wits and try to keep things running smoothly until the rabbi could notify the people who would know what to do. There was a family lawyer, Atellus Vibius. Meanwhile, she had to do what she could to maintain the household.

Every set of eyes bored into hers. So silently they stood there, Dacia could hear their anxious breathing. She knew that the greatest fear of slaves following the death of a kind master was that they would be sold. She spoke as authoritatively as she could manage.

"The mistress will speak to you as soon as she can. Right now, she is deep in grief, but she has a strong spirit. As soon as the funeral is past, she will let you know her plans and how the master's death will affect you." Dacia looked from face to face, reading the anxiety. Most wore expressions of uncertainty and fear. Cook, by contrast, displayed hopeful anticipation. Sometimes, in the will, the master freed a favored slave. The master often praised Cook's work, although as far as Dacia could tell, no more than he praised any of the other servants. He had been a considerate master. Cook was no more likely to be freed than any of the others.

Putting as much authority into her voice as she could, Dacia addressed the group.

"For now, go about your assigned duties. If you need me, I will be with the mistress in her cubiculum. Come to me if you are unable to make a decision, but only on a very serious matter."

Dacia remained in the atrium until all the servants had gone. Glancing into the vestibule, she saw that Haluk still knelt beside Benjamin's body. He'd stopped weeping and was saying something over and over. Praying in his native tongue, probably. She wondered fleetingly what foreign god or gods he worshipped. She shuddered. Her mistress was a Jew and all the other servants pagans of one kind or another. Sometimes it was frightening being the only person in the house who practiced true religion.

Dacia had settled herself beside the bed when the little pot girl she'd sent to clean up the broken wine ewer appeared. "Please, Dacia, Linus sent me to tell you someone is wanting to come in and he don't know if he should let them. There's a lot of them."

Dacia drew a deep, suffering sigh, sent the girl back to the kitchen, and headed again to the vestibule. Dreading more unwanted decision-making, she was relieved to see Varda, the rabbi's wife.

A squat, plump, motherly woman, wearing a faded, once-stylish yellow palla over a brown stola, Varda stood fuming on the threshold, her way barred by the porter. Dacia could make out more visitors behind her. She stepped around Haluk and the body.

"It's all right, Linus. You may stand aside and let her in."

Varda bustled into the house of mourning, followed by a train of women carrying food, fabric, and all else needful for preparing the dead and comforting the living. Bringing up the rear was a bearded man carrying a scroll.

Varda took immediate charge. "You Linus, and you, Haluk, carry your master's body to the triclinium." The men remained stationary and looked toward Dacia for confirmation.

Realizing they expected her to say something, Dacia spoke to the porter and Haluk. "Do as she tells you. The mistress wishes to leave the preparations to Domina Varda."

With a sharp clap of her hands, the rabbi's wife repeated her command. "To the trinclinium. *Velox!*" As Linus and Haluk lifted the body, Varda turned to Dacia. "I'm having them take him to the dining room because it's a big room and has plenty of work surfaces." She patted her on the shoulder. "Don't worry, dear. Everything's under control. You go back and tend to your mistress. I'll send for you when I need you."

No stranger to the house, Varda led her entourage to the triclinium and Dacia returned to her mistress.

***

Shifra was still sleeping. Her dark hair lay spread on the pillow, framing her face, paler than its usual olive cast. Dacia felt her heart swell with affection for the woman who had taken her in and cared for her when she had needed help. She adjusted the bedclothes and drew a stool up to the side of the bed to keep watch, thanking the Savior that she could now repay the loving care she'd received. In her mind, Dacia traveled back to that terrible night.

Pain, dreadful, tearing pain below and burning pain on her face plunged her into merciful unconsciousness. When she again became aware of her surroundings, her face felt better. Something cooling had been placed on it. The other pains, the ones below, were still there, but dulled. She kept her eyes squeezed firmly shut. If the younger Ulpius and his friends were still there, she did not want to see them.

Someone standing close to her spoke. A man's voice, unfamiliar, speaking not to her, but to others in the room. "She will need stitching, below. And the dressing on her face must be changed hourly for the first twelve hours. Then less, but she will need constant care until the burned tissue heals."

"Zeus's balls!" Another man's voice, one she knew too well. Her master, Faustus Ulpius. "You saw her face. We can't keep a slave that looks like that. And I won't get near what we paid for her."

A woman's voice this time. Her mistress. "Just sell her as she is, Faustus."

Dacia moaned and opened her eyes. She understood at once that the man beside her was a doctor. He saw that she was awake. Taking one of her hands, he held it gently. "Courage, child. You're going to be all right."

The master and mistress shouted at one another for a while, he blaming her for sending a ten-year-old to serve at table for a fifteen-year-old and his randy friends; she blaming him for letting them ruin the looks of the girl she'd been training to be her ancilla. In the end, the doctor—Benjamin—offered to take her in payment for his services. When he brought her home, the mistress herself assumed her care, sitting with her, changing her dressings, and soothing her pain with cups of tea infused with thornapple. That night, Benjamin and Shifra had become the most important people in Dacia's life.

Shifra stirred. Dacia leaned in and brushed her hair back on her forehead. Her skin felt clammy. Dipping a cloth in the nearby basin, Dacia wrung it out and placed it on Shifra's forehead. Her mistress murmured. "Benjamin." Then, more loudly, "Benjamin?" She opened her eyes and raised herself on her elbows. "Where is he? I must go to him."

Dacia pushed her back gently. "The ladies from the synagogue are here. There's nothing for you to do."

Shifra pushed back, ridding herself of the coverlet and swinging her feet to the floor.

"Where is he? Where have they taken him?"

"To the triclinium, Domina."

Shifra stood and moved determinedly to the door.

Dacia moved swiftly. "Please, Domina. Your sandals, at least."

***

Dacia managed to stop her mistress long enough to help her put on her sandals and stola, but the distraught woman eluded her attempt to neaten her hair. Dacia hurried after her as she rushed from the room.

From the dining room floated the dark, fruity scent of myrrh and the droning sound of someone reading. Dacia and Shifra stepped past the huddled form of Haluk holding vigil in the passageway.

Benjamin's body, partially covered with a sheet, lay on one of the tables. A wooden pallet that would serve as the bier lay beneath the body. Two women were wiping the floor around the couch. Varda moved swiftly to Shifra and embraced her. "Shifra, dear child, we have completed the bathing with warm water and the purification. We're ready to begin the wrapping. We will need Benjamin's tallit."

Shifra turned. "Dacia, go fetch your master's prayer shawl."

"I'll send Haluk, Domina. He'll be quicker than I." Dacia stepped outside the dining room and told Haluk where he could find the shawl. She doubted that Haluk could outpace her, but she was curious about the preparations and didn't want to miss anything. She was especially curious about the lone man who had accompanied the women. He'd set up in a far corner and was reading from a scroll.

Shifra seemed to be arguing with Varda, but the older woman guided her away from the bier to one of the dining couches. "Rest here until we have finished with the wrapping, dear. Your part comes later." Shifra sat and Dacia took a seat nearby.

The man with the scroll was reading monotonously in Greek. Although her native tongue and Latin were the only languages Dacia spoke fluently, she understood enough of the Greek words to recognize that the words came from the Book of Psalms. How strange, that Jews and Christians took comfort from the same scriptures. And yet, she reminded herself, Christians quarreled among themselves about what it meant to be a Christian. She was a professed Christian, taught and baptized in her own country before being sold into slavery. Yet, according to the Bishop of Milan, Christians like her were heretics, while Christians like Ulpius Faustus and his wife were "true" Christians. Dacia made a scoffing sound. She was far better off in a family of Jews than with those brutal hypocrites.

Dacia turned her attention to the women who were preparing Master Benjamin for burial. They had begun wrapping at the feet, placing myrrh and aloes between the strips of linen and moving the body as necessary to enclose it. The corpse took on the tapered shape of a cocoon enclosing a metamorphizing creature about to be born into a new life.

Finally, only the head remained visible.

Haluk returned with his master's white woolen prayer shawl. With a strangled cry, Shifra jumped to her feet and took it in her arms. Tears streaming, she held it to her heart. "His parents gave him this on our wedding day." She buried her face in its folds.

Varda permitted her to hold it for a minute or so, then gently pried it away. "The sun will not wait. We must finish our work quickly." She shook out the tallit and grasped one of the tasseled corners. Then, with a small pair of scissors, she severed the tassel from the garment and handed it to Dacia. "Keep this for your mistress."

Shifra helped the women wrap the shawl around the shrouded shoulders. Now, all that remained was to cover the head. Shifra gazed down at the uncovered face. Bending low, she kissed it all over. Then, she smoothed his hair. Varda handed her a large square of linen. With a sigh drawn from deep within her, Shifra wrapped Benjamin's head with the linen cloth. The body of her husband was ready for burial.

A heavy gray December sky lowered over the procession as it made its way through the streets on the way to the Jewish cemetery outside the walls. Six men of the congregation carried the bier, followed by Shifra, Dacia, Varda and Rabbi Shemuel. Behind them rose the sounds of ululation and the shrill notes of flutes. A much-repaired wooden fence enclosed the Jewish cemetery, which resembled a deserted field more than a cemetery. No family mausoleums or large tombstones declared the place for what it was. The grave markers were small and flat, offering no temptation to those who might wish to topple them. A cold wind sprang up as Benjamin's wrapped body slid from the pallet into the open grave. Shifra, who had been stoically silent during the walk, now burst into heart-breaking sobs.

Dacia put her arms around her mistress, both to comfort her and to offer some protection from the cutting wind. The rabbi said the final graveside prayers and each mourner threw a handful of soil into the grave. When the crowd of mourners dispersed to their own homes, Varda and the women who had prepared the body returned with Shifra and Dacia.

"We will clear the workplace," she told Dacia. "In the morning, we'll return to sit shiva."

Dacia nodded. She knew the word *shiva*. After a death, for seven days, friends and acquaintances come to offer their respects, praying, mourning, and reminiscing about the departed. And eating! As if

Varda had read her mind, she patted her on the arm. "Don't worry. We will not come empty-handed. Food and drink will not be lacking."

Chapter Three

Inheritance Matters

Shifra had no recollection of the walk back from the cemetery. Finding herself again in her cubiculum being fussed over by Dacia, she tried vainly to remember entering the house. She couldn't remember mounting the three steps from the street, traversing the vestibule or passing through the atrium to her room. But there she was, and there stood Dacia, urging her again to take to her bed.

"Do lie down, Domina. I'll bring you a hot brick to warm the bed. Sleep is what you need, sleep to soften the sorrow." Gently, Dacia helped her mistress sit on the edge of the bed. "There, keep your cloak wrapped around you until I can warm the bed. I'll bring you something hot to drink as well."

Like a little girl placed on a stool by her nurse and told to wait, Shifra sat. *Benjamin.* What did life hold for her without him? She longed for his presence, his arms around her.

Dacia returned, followed by the little kitchen girl. Dacia placed a steaming cup on the low table by the bed. "We'll have you warm and cozy in no time." She gestured to the girl, who carried the heated brick for the bed.

"No." Shifra stood and moved purposefully to the door. "Bring a bed to the tablinum. I shall sleep in there."

In the tablinum, the servants placed the head of the bed near Benjamin's desk. Dacia went on for so long warming the sheets that Shifra finally lost patience. "That's quite enough, Dacia. You can go now."

Dacia turned a stricken face toward her. "But Domina, what if you wake and need me?"

"Go!"

As slowly as if she'd been summoned to a beating, the maidservant left, and Shifra had the room to herself. Benjamin's room, the last space they'd shared before he walked away to his death. Sliding into the warmth of the sheets, she sighed deeply, feeling his presence. From time to time in the night, she woke and imagined she could hear his breathing.

***

In the morning, sounds of footsteps and the murmur of voices told her that people were arriving to sit shiva, but when Dacia came to fetch her, Shifra refused to go. She wanted to be alone in her grief. She wanted to be enclosed in the comfort of Benjamin's room. The dreadful words of Job's wife strove for utterance. *Curse God and die.* No! Don't. Don't let the words in.

For two days, she refused to join the mourners. Dacia, silent as a wraith, came and went to attend her basic needs. Receiving nothing but angry words in exchange for her efforts to help, her ancilla had stopped speaking and did only what was necessary. For a moment, a pang of guilt distracted Shifra from her grief. Dacia, the poor little damaged slave girl deserved better. She promised herself that she would make it up to the girl, only, not now.

On the third day, Shifra sat at Benjamin's desk, staring at the papers he had been working on that night. He had just told her of the new appointment, medical officer for the prefect. How happy she'd been at the news that he would no longer have to risk unaccompanied night-time visits to dangerous neighborhoods. She laid her head on her arms. No tears came. She'd wept so much, she felt hollow inside, hollow and all dried out.

"It's time, my dear."

The voice, close behind her, startled her. She whirled to see Varda, the rabbi's wife. Until this moment, the women of the synagogue had respected her desire to be alone. She drew herself up, every muscle in her body tensed and hostile.

"How dare you enter without my leave?"

Varda came nearer. "It's time," she repeated. "Grief is lonely. You will always mourn that lovely man, my dear, but you must learn to live in the world again. Come."

The softly spoken words, rich in kindness, touched Shifra like a caress, releasing the tension of her muscles, replacing hostility with humility. Sighing, she rose from Benjamin's chair and went with Varda to join the mourners.

For the remaining days of shiva, she joined in the prayers and listened with appreciation to stories told about Benjamin by men and women she'd never met, stories of his kindness, his integrity, his generosity, his humanity in an often inhumane world. By the time the ritual week of mourning ended, she had found the strength to reject the words of Job's wife. Instead, she drew comfort from those of Job. *The Lord gave and the Lord has taken away. Blessed is the name of the Lord.*

Shifra resumed her duties and took on those of Benjamin. She informed the anxious servants that, although she had not yet read her husband's will—it was in the keeping of their lawyer, Atellus Vibius—she did not expect anything in it to affect their status. Confident that her inheritance would be sufficient for her needs, she expected things to continue much the same, only lonely. With Benjamin gone, she would occupy herself with additional charity work with the congregation. Her only family now were her son—somewhere in Palestine—and her brother, Akiva, with his wife and daughter in Egypt. She could count the letters they'd exchanged during the thirty years they'd been apart. Notices of births and deaths. She would write to him about Benjamin. And then, perhaps the next letter would be to Akiva from Vibius, announcing her death.

"A visitor, Domina." Dacia entered the tablinum where Shifra was working on the household accounts. "Atellus Vibius," Dacia announced. Then, in a whisper, "It must be important. He's wearing a toga."

Shifra smiled. "Don't you know by now? Atellus Vibius always wears a toga. Show him in."

She smelled the expensive bath oil before he made his way past the curtained doorway to the office. Togate and clean-shaven, Vibius wore his hair combed forward, the way folks said Julius Caesar had worn his, to disguise his baldness. Thick bushy eyebrows like a long black caterpillar met above intense dark eyes. He held out his hands. "My deepest condolences, Shifra. I would have come during shiva to express them, but you know how it is. One of Bishop Marolus's informers might have reported me for heresy."

Shifra rose from her chair and clasped both his extended hands. "Thank you, Vibius. I know you loved Benjamin. Like me, he valued those early days when we were young and our lives less complicated."

Their first friends in Milan, Vibius and his wife, Iris, had never regarded their Jewishness as a barrier to friendship, not even later, when Vibius and Iris converted to Christianity. Benjamin had believed that their motives had been more practical than spiritual. After all, their own son, Alexander, frustrated in his efforts to advance in his own legal career, decided to leave Milan rather than convert. Vibius had chosen to accept the terms that Alexander could not.

Dacia, remaining in the room, placed a stool for the visitor. Vibius waved her away and remained standing.

"Benjamin was a good man. Milan and its people are better off because of him." He paused, then resumed in a more intimate tone. "Iris sends her regards. She wants you to come to dinner as soon as you feel up to it."

Iris. How long it had been since they'd dined together. In those early days, when the children were small, Shifra and Iris spent much of every day together. Then, when Augustine, the rhetoric teacher from North Africa, and his wife, Mira, came to live in Milan, the three women formed a mutually supportive bond. Shifra and Iris especially benefited because Mira's son, in his teens, never minded helping with the little ones. Shifra smiled as she remembered the good-natured youngster with the long name. His father, much interested in theology, had bestowed on him the name *Adeodatus*—"a gift from god." The little ones, who adored him, called him *Datus*.

"I would like very much to come to dinner and reminisce about happier times."

The lawyer nodded, but did not respond. Frown lines deepened across his forehead and he walked past her desk to the opposite wall and back. Shifra recognized the energy that made sitting still impossible for Vibius when he had things to say. She rose from her chair. "Let's go out into the atrium, where you'll have more room to pace."

Dacia followed at a discreet distance. Sitting at the edge of the pool was a little boy in a rumpled brown tunic. Beside him, a satchel. At the sight of his master, he jumped up. Vibius waved him away, as he had Dacia. "You, Fabian, go wait in the kitchen. I'll send for you when I'm finished here." The boy knew the way and scampered off through the peristyle. Shifra seated herself in his place.

The boy had left behind the leather satchel. Vibius nodded at it. "I've brought a copy of Benjamin's will, but no need to read it to tell you what's in it. No surprises. Small bequests to the slaves. Everything else to you."

Dacia, had also taken a seat on the edge of the pool. She sat looking fixedly at the tile, almost certainly listening to the lawyer's words. For the first time since Benjamin's body had been brought to the house, Shifra wondered what someone else was thinking. Vibius spoke again. Dacia's gaze shifted to the lawyer.

"Benjamin did include one manumission." He nodded toward Dacia.

The girl's hands flew to her veiled face. A moan escaped her and she flung herself to her knees before her mistress.

"Please, Domina, I don't want to be freed. Where would I go? How would I live?"

A flurry of thoughts collided in Shifra's mind. Every other slave in the house was probably praying that the master's will would free them, but here, Dacia was begging to remain in bondage. For an unworthy instant, Shifra was glad of her ancilla's reaction. Quiet, uncomplaining, devoted Dacia, who anticipated her every need. Would a freed Dacia leave her? It shouldn't matter. She was only a slave.

Vibius lifted the weeping woman to her feet. "Stop your wailing, girl. Save your worrying until the will is settled."

Shifra stood and put her arms around her. "Don't fret. We'll talk about this later. Go see how Fabian is doing in the kitchen. Make sure Cook hasn't put him to work. He's not our house servant."

When Dacia was out of earshot, Shifra frowned at the lawyer.

"*Until the will is settled?* What did you mean, Vibius? Is there a problem with the will? Didn't Benjamin include an adequate amount of income for Dacia to be manumitted?" Vibius turned abruptly and circuited the pool. Shifra sat and waited as he made another turn around the pool. When he finally stopped and faced her, his rubicund face was set in solemn lines.

Shifra laughed nervously.

Vibius remained silent, staring at the water in the pool.

Shifra began to be afraid. "What aren't you telling me, Vibius?"

He met her eyes. "I've known you for a long time, Shifra. I believe you have cause to trust my counsel."

"Of course, I trust you. I'll never forget how you defended Benjamin against the blasphemy charge that cost our daughter's life."

Still, Vibius remained silent. Shifra's voice rose.

"Tell me, Vibius! Tell me why you told Dacia to wait 'until the will is settled.' Did Benjamin fail to provide a large enough stipend for her support as a freed woman? I can make up whatever difference may be necessary."

Vibius looked away but did not resume pacing.

"There's a tax."

Shifra pursed her lips. "I thought the spouse wasn't subject to the inheritance tax. By law, as a widow, I shouldn't be expected to pay any tax. But you needn't look so worried, Vibius. I know that, with your help, Benjamin invested wisely. How much of a tax? Five percent? That's not so bad. That's what non-relatives pay."

Vibius shifted his toga and sat beside her. "This is not the usual five percent tax for non-family beneficiaries. This is a special tax, recently granted to Bishop Marolus by the bishop of Rome to levy in certain circumstances."

Shifra frowned. "I thought taxes were the business of the emperor."

Vibius laughed humorlessly. "Ordinarily, that is true. This, however, is a special circumstance that lies in the bishop's jurisdiction and not that of the emperor."

Shifra shuddered. Only one thing would make her situation "special" to the bishop. Her religion. Marolus was the third bishop to succeed Ambrose. She'd always hoped things would get better for the Jews, the further the bishopric progressed beyond that fanatical man.

If anything, Marolus's attitude toward Judaism was even worse than Ambrose's had been. "How much of a percentage? Ten percent? Twenty?"

Vibius took her hand. "He can demand as much as ninety percent."

Shifra's throat closed. She could barely utter the question. "How will I live?"

The lawyer's black eyes bored into hers. "We won't give up hope just yet. I have dealt with similar situations. It is possible to...negotiate."

A flicker of hope pierced the dread. "Go to him, then, Vibius. Tell him I'm willing to pay the five percent or even ten percent. Remind him of the good Benjamin has done for the poor of the city. How he helped with the victims of the Visigoth siege ten years ago, when the emperor and his mother abandoned their palace here and fled to Ravenna."

Vibius opened the door to the peristylum. "You tell him, Shifra. He'll be here tomorrow at the fifth hour to discuss the matter with you."

Her mouth dropped open, but before she could protest, Vibius shouted for his boy.

"Fabian! Time to go! *Velox!*

The boy came flying from the kitchen, crossed the peristyle, and snatched up the leather satchel, which had not been required after all.

Vibius took his leave. "Try not to worry, Shifra. I'll be here too. Be ready at the fifth hour." Turning abruptly, he made a rapid exit.

Shifra stared after him.

The bishop of Milan.

Here.

Tomorrow.

Chapter Four
The Widow and the Bishop

Shifra did not wish to receive the bishop in the intimacy of the tablinum. Neither did she want him in the atrium. She decided to use Benjamin's examining room.

Like many city residences, Shifra's house had been designed with two partially enclosed rooms fronting the street, to be used as shops. The ones in her house had been totally enclosed. One, they used for storage. The other, Benjamin had fitted up as an examining room with an outside door for walk-in patients. It contained a raised pallet, a few chairs and a small table.

Well in advance of the fifth hour, Shifra settled herself in the examining room. She'd left instructions with the porter not to admit the expected visitors to the house, but send them round to the outside door to the examining room. Because of the cold weather, she told Haluk to take the visitors' slave to wait in the vestibule with the porter.

When the knock finally came, she herself opened the door.

Expecting an overfed prelate dressed in rich robes, she was surprised to see a tall man, slightly stooped and thin to gauntness, wearing a rather shabby brown cloak. Only the length of his tunic distinguished him in status from the elderly slave who helped him step out of muddy clogs and change into clean indoor shoes.

Vibius, impeccable in his toga, and redolent of bath oil, made the introductions. To Shifra, he said, "His Excellency, Marolus, Bishop of Milan." To the bishop, "Your Excellency, may I present Shifra bat Elad, widow of Benjamin ben Gershon."

Shifra studied his face, looking for an expression of distaste or disdain, but what she saw was an expression of sympathy.

"I regret the occasion of our meeting, my child. Your husband's death has deprived Milan of a very fine physician."

The gentle tone, the admiring words for Benjamin, surprised Shifra as much as his humble clothing. Was this the formidable money-grubbing, Jew-hating bishop of Milan? She gestured toward the chair she'd had placed beside one of the two braziers she'd had set up earlier to take the chill off the room.

"Please sit down."

Marolus sat as directed and glanced around the room. Vibius moved discreetly to one side of the room, as if to indicate that he was to be an observer only.

Unexpectedly, Shifra felt a need to be more hospitable than she'd felt when placing the meeting outside of her living space, in the least comfortable room available.

"Would you care for refreshments? I've not had anything laid out because I do not know what food or drink might be forbidden by your religion." She felt her face grow warm from the hypocrisy. "Do you partake of wine?"

Marolus smiled. "Of course, my dear. And of anything else the good Lord has given us." He held up a finger and recited, "*Do not call anything impure that God has made clean.*" Shifra didn't recognize the words as coming from scripture. She guessed the quotation must be from one of the Christian writings. He continued to smile.

"But, do not trouble yourself with refreshments. Our business should not take long. I believe that Atellus Vibius has explained the purpose of my visit." He nodded toward the lawyer.

"Not at any length. Just that it has to do with my husband's will."

"Yes, your late husband." He looked past Shifra, as if traveling to a different time in his mind. "Benjamin was a great help to us during the plague the Visigoths brought ten years ago. I tried then to persuade him to embrace the true religion."

He shook his head and met Shifra's eyes. His own eyes, close-set and intense, bored into hers. The smile had been replaced by an expression of sadness.

"It is a sorrow to me that such a fine man should die outside a state of grace."

Shifra recoiled. Red anger flooded her body. How dare he?

"My husband died carrying out his mitzvot, the responsibilities laid on every Jew by the Torah. He was coming home from saving the life of a woman who was not a Jew, but who needed his healing hands. Of course, he was in a state of grace when he died." Her whole body trembled. She felt a hand touch her shoulder. Vibius had moved to stand beside her. The bishop held up both his hands in a placating gesture.

"My dear woman, please. Please do not misunderstand me. I'm sure that your husband was a very good Jew indeed. I know that he was an excellent physician."

Heart still pounding with indignation, Shifra chose her words.

"Atellus Vibius said you would come here to discuss my husband's will. He said nothing about a religious visit. It was my understanding that you would tell me how much tax I must pay as Benjamin's widow."

Marolus leaned forward. No longer smiling, his face had taken on an earnest look of concern. "Your husband's will and religion are

34

intertwined, my dear." He frowned at Vibius. "Did you not tell the lady…"

Vibius shook his head. "I thought it best to come from you, Your Excellency. And that you meet the woman concerned before making any decision."

Shifra struggled to keep her voice out of screaming range. "How much will I be taxed?"

"That, my dear, will depend on you. Five percent if…"

Relief plugged Shifra's ears. *Five percent!* All would be well. She turned her attention back on Marolus. He was looking at her with a quizzical expression. She must have missed something he'd said.

"I'm sorry. I didn't hear what you after 'five percent.'"

"I said five percent if you do what your husband failed to do."

Shifra stared. "I don't understand."

The bishop stood. "You must embrace the true religion, my child. Accept Christ. Be baptized in His name, and not only will you inherit your husband's worldly goods, but you will escape perdition and inherit the wealth of life eternal."

The old man paused before adding, "If you refuse, you may retain five percent of his wealth."

Shifra's heart pounded in her ears. Her breath came in deep inhalations, pumping her head with dizziness. The bishop's features dissolved in the blur of her unfocused eyes. Before she could hurl the venomous words she felt rising, Vibius stepped between her and Marolus.

"If you please, Your Excellency, I did not prepare my client for these conditions. It would be gracious of you to allow us some time to speak further."

Marolus looked at Shifra. His harsh expression softened slightly. "Very well. Let us say, one week." He turned to Vibius. "Either way, the bequest must be valued. The inventory cannot wait." Without more words, he left by way of the street door.

Vibius took her by the arm and guided her to the interior door.

"Come along, Shifra. You'll be more comfortable in the house."

She permitted herself to be led to the atrium and sat on the edge of the pool.

"Why didn't you tell me, Vibius? Why didn't you tell me that he was going to demand that I become a Christian?"

The lawyer shrugged. "I thought it would be best coming from the bishop. He's not a bad sort, Marolus. Spends whatever he gets on the poor. He genuinely believes everyone should be a Christian for their own good."

"He said that Benjamin didn't die in a state of grace."

Vibius barked a laugh. "That's the biggest flaw with the Christians. Always claiming to know what's in the mind of God. Forget what he said. The gods know their own."

Instead of pacing, he seated himself companionably on the edge of the pool beside her. He spoke softly, cajolingly.

"No one would blame you if you went through the motions of conversion. Many good people do it and continue to practice their true beliefs in the privacy of their homes."

The muscles of Shifra's abdomen twisted like serpents and the skin of her face burned with a rush of blood. Faces flashed through her mind, Benjamin, Varda, her father.

"Never! I will never pretend to be what I am not. I am the daughter of Elad of Alexandria. My ancestors have lived openly as Jews for generations. I will not be the first of my line to hide my Jewishness for the sake of gain."

The lawyer said nothing. After several minutes of silence, Shifra spoke again, this time, in less passioned tones.

"What will I be allowed to keep?" She held her breath. "Will he let me keep the house?"

Vibius did not answer. Until that moment, Shifra believed that Benjamin's death had been the worst that could happen.

"What must I do, Vibius? What advice have you for me now?"

"You don't have to decide anything just yet. The bishop has given you a week to make up your mind."

Shifra groaned. Even if she sequestered herself in her bedroom, how could she bear knowing strangers were fingering their possessions, things that Benjamin had used, things they'd bought together. Vibius laid a hand gently on hers.

"Iris knows about the inventory. She knows how you would feel about having the bishop's people in the house. She wants you to come stay with us while it's going on."

A guarded sense of relief tempered Shifra's despair. "Can we do that? You and Iris stayed away from shiva to avoid repercussions. Won't it damage your reputations to have a Jewish houseguest?"

Vibius smiled. "This is different. Paying our respects at a Jewish ritual could be viewed as heresy. Having you in our house gives us the opportunity to convert you."

Shifra squeezed Vibius's hand. "I'll get ready at once."

Chapter Five

Loyalties in Flux

Iris greeted Shifra with a long embrace. "I am so sorry about what happened to Benjamin. He did not deserve such a brutal end."

The words exploded in Shifra's mind with a picture of the dreadful morning. Her husband's pale face as the soldiers brought him into the house, refuse from a midden in his hair. A sob escaped her and Iris held her closer. "That was stupid of me. It's too soon to talk about it, perhaps."

"No, not at all. I want to talk about him. But not about the way he died."

Iris stepped back and smiled. "Then, we will talk about him and the happy times we shared. We can all reminisce at dinner, when Vibius is here. But first, let's get you settled." She beckoned to a servant and, in a low voice, gave her instructions. Then, slipping her arm through Shifra's, she led the way into the house.

Once daily companions, the two women no longer had interests or activities to draw them together. Shifra had never been in the house Iris lived in now. For years, their meetings had been rare, yet, as happens with interrupted friendships, time fell away and Shifra felt the old companionable ease. As they entered the atrium, she made no attempt to conceal her amazement at its size and lush decoration.

"Good heavens, Iris! This is absolutely magnificent." Dolphins and other aquatic creatures frolicked in the mosaic floor, and the walls were bright with frescos. Because of the commandment against idols, Shifra always felt a childish guilt when looking at images of living beings or celestial objects. Before she understood that the commandment forbade the *making* or *worshipping* of such things, she'd believed she mustn't even look them. Even now, the old feelings of guilt lingered as she looked more closely.

Rural scenes with shepherds, fruit, and animals decorated three walls. The fourth featured two figures framed by a painted temple with columns and a triangular pediment above them. The figure on the left was a muscular man clothed in a short tunic and carrying a sheep across his shoulders. Surrounding him was a circle of plants, birds, and small animals.

The figure on the right was a woman in blue and white robes, holding a child in her arms. Above her head sailed a small ship on blue waves, and near her feet, a horn of plenty spilled its bounty onto painted flagstones. She'd seen such images during her childhood in Alexandria.

A cabinet with an arrangement of candles and basins stood against the wall, beneath the figures. A household shrine? She sensed Iris behind her.

"What do you think, Shifra. Aren't they exquisite? We paid for an artist to come from Rome to do them. I believe they are the finest frescos in all of Milan."

Shifra hesitated, but then decided that she owed the truth to her friend.

"They are beautifully painted, Iris. But I have to admit I'm surprised to see images of Hermes and Isis in a Christian house. Aren't you afraid that a pious visitor might report you to the bishop?"

Iris frowned. "That's not Hermes, Shifra. That's Jesus as the Good Shepherd. That's a lamb on his shoulders, not a ram. And the woman and child aren't Isis and Horus. It's the Holy Mother holding the infant Jesus."

It was Shifra's turn to frown. She'd spent her childhood in Alexandria. Not confined to temple interiors, paintings and sculptures of the old gods decorated walls and occupied niches everywhere in the city. She looked again. These exquisite paintings on her friend's atrium wall certainly looked like Isis and Hermes.

A table had been set up in a corner of the atrium. Iris, again smiling, drew her toward it. "Come. I thought you might like some refreshments before settling in."

Shifra took her seat and looked around for Dacia. "My ancilla. What has become of her?"

"I've sent her with one of the servants to the room where you will be sleeping. Is that the girl Benjamin took in payment from Faustus and Balbina? The one their son raped and spilled lamp oil on?"

"Yes."

Iris raised an eyebrow. "I'm surprised you've kept her all these years. At least you have her cover her face. That's a mercy."

"It's her choice to wear the covering. I don't think the scarring is nearly as bad as she does."

Iris shrugged. "I suppose you've gotten used to it. As for me, I wouldn't want to look at it every day." The little table held cups, two ewers, and a covered dish. She lifted a cloth, revealing a plate of baked goods. "Have a honey cake. Or several. I can never stop with one." She filled two silver cups from a silver ewer.

For the first time in days, something tasted good to Shifra.

***

The room that Marcella brought Dacia to was large for a cubiculum and, unlike most sleeping rooms, had a window. Her guide offered to take her to the kitchen for something to eat, but Dacia declined, preferring to be left alone for a time. She sat on the bed her mistress would use. The pallet she would sleep on lay rolled near the door. Slaves did not expect beds and rooms to themselves. But Dacia was no longer a slave. The master had freed her in his will. Did that mean she could refuse to sleep on a pallet laid across the threshold of her mistress's room?

Tears burned Dacia's eyes. Did she want to be free? What would she do? Where would she go?

She had no family to go to. Her parents were certainly dead by now. Her sister a slave somewhere. Her brother had been a baby when their parents sold her and her older sister into slavery to have the means to feed him and themselves. Even if she could find him, he would have no recollection of her and she no claim on his kindness.

Life with Benjamin and Shifra was the only life she'd known since she was ten years old. They'd been good to her, cared for her hurts, taught her to read, dressed her like a girl of their own class, and kept her safe from the dangers of being a woman in bondage. Only after she'd grown to love them had she learned that they were Jewish.

She'd been raised as an Arian Christian. Until she was brought to Rome as a slave, she hadn't known there was more than one kind of Christian. But she *had* known about Jews. According to her priest, Jews were enemies of Christ, perfidious, impious enemies of the one true faith, to be avoided at all costs. And yet, in their dealings with her, the Jewish doctor and his wife had shown her nothing but Christian virtues. Surely, what the Bible said about false prophets must also apply to ordinary people. *By their fruits you shall know them.*

Dacia slipped off the bed onto her knees beside it. "Help me, Jesus, help me know what to do." If Shifra was not her family, Dacia had no one.

***

Over honey cakes and spiced wine, Shifra and Iris renewed the friendship that had bound them during those early years as she and Benjamin, newly wed, settled into life in Milan.

Iris refilled their cups. "It must be thirty years since you and Benjamin came here. What a lot has happened since then!"

"That's true. And not just in our private lives. When Benjamin and I left Alexandria, the first Theodosius had just taken the throne in Constantinople as sole emperor. Now, his young grandson and namesake occupies his former throne, and his son, Honorius, rules the Western empire here in Italy."

Iris shook her head. "Our second Theodosius is only—what—eleven years old? *Woe to thee, O land, when thy king is a child.*"

It always startled Shifra when Christians quoted from the Hebrew writings. She nodded, but avoided saying anything that might be construed as treason. "We can hope the boy has good advisors."

"One can hope. Our Western emperor, his uncle Honorius, doesn't seem to have been too well advised since he had Stilicho killed four years ago. Not only was Stilicho an effective military leader, he was the emperor's son-in-law. Vibius says the reason Alaric and his Goths assaulted Rome last year is because Honorius and his new advisors do nothing to hold back the hordes of barbarians crowded along the borders. He says that if they're not stopped, they'll bring in not just disease, but barbaric ways that will destroy our Roman values and culture."

Shifra turned the conversation away from politics. "You know Vibius, Iris. If he had his way, we'd still be living in the old Republic, when heroes like Lucius Junius Brutus drove out the evil Tarquins. He thinks anything new is an insult to the old ways. Benjamin used to tease him about his devotion to wearing a toga. He'd say, 'You're a lawyer. Tell me why, as long as they're taking away the privileges of the Jews, why can't they forbid us to wear the toga?'"

Iris laughed. "He still loves togas. I started shopping for one more than a year ago because the one he has now is showing its wear. They've become so unfashionable, all you can find in the market are second-hand ones." She smiled. "Vibius doesn't know, but I'm weaving him a new one."

"You're joking! That would be a tremendous undertaking."

"Believe me, it is. First, I searched out the finest wool. The Canossan sheep are supposed to have the whitest wool in all Italy. I bought some in the spring and had it delivered to my sister's house so Vibius wouldn't know. I've been bringing it here in batches to spin. I'm on the last batch. When it's all spun, I'll begin the weaving."

"Spinning?! I do a little, just to occupy my hands in the evening, but a major project like a toga? We have factories now to card and spin and weave. Poor women still have to do it, but not women in our class. You could buy a toga already made."

Iris scoffed. "Hardly anyone wears a toga anymore. I can't remember the last time I saw a child in the toga praetexta. The fashions of Constantinople have caught on at Ravenna and are spreading here. They say Emperor Honorius never wears anything but embroidered tunics and capes." She paused at a thought. "He doesn't like trousers, though. He passed a law against wearing them."

"You could have your women make the toga."

"No. Making it myself is the most important part of the gift. You know how much Vibius loves Roman history. Look what he named our children: Lucretia and Junius! As soon as Lucretia was old enough to learn to spin, he told her that the ability to work with wool was the mark of a virtuous Roman woman. And then he told her that dreadful story about Lucretia and Tarquin's son and the founding of the Republic."

Shifra didn't remember the details, but she did recall that the story involved rape and suicide. "Poor child!"

Iris laughed. "Never fear. He managed to tell it in a very general way. His main point was to instill in her the concept of the ideal Roman matron. When I give him a toga I've made with my own hands, he'll be able to brag about his wife's antique qualities. He will love that as much as having a new toga."

Memories crowded in. Shifra's fingers tingled, recalling the motions with the distaff.

"My goodness, talking about spinning takes me back!" In those early days, in her scrupulous efforts to save money, spinning had been a daily task. The warm banks of Lake Como in summer rose in her mind. "Remember how we used to take the children to the lake and take our spinning with us?"

"Yes. We used to compete, to see which of us could spin the largest quantity in a day."

"You always won."

Iris laughed. "Yes—until Mira joined us. She could spin like two women."

Mira. Shifra's pleasant memories darkened. Mira and Augustine. When the couple came to Milan, she could see that Mira's love for Augustine was as deep as that of Iris for Vibius and hers for Benjamin. As a *concubina*, Mira did not have the protections of marriage, but it was clear that Augustine returned her affection. After fifteen years, he still brought her flowers and unexpected treats.

Shifra's change of mood did not go unnoticed by Iris. "I've always wondered if things might have worked out differently if Augustine's mother hadn't followed them to Milan."

Monika. The intense Berber woman from North Africa. She'd never approved of Mira.

"I'm sure of it," Shifra said. "Monika had been trying to persuade Augustine to become a Christian from the time he was a boy. As soon as he converted, she told him that as a Christian, he must have a 'proper wife,' one of his own class."

"I remember. She arranged a marriage with a ten-year-old and insisted that he send Mira away at once, even though it would be at least two years before the chosen bride would be old enough to marry."

"Anyone could see that Augustine didn't want to send Mira away."

They sat in silence for a while. Shifra always wondered what had become of Mira. Had she a family to go to? Augustine had kept the boy with him. Monika robbed Mira not only of her husband, but of her child as well. Hot tears coursed down Shifra's cheeks. A sob escaped.

In an instant, Iris was beside her patting her shoulders. "Shifra, dear, I'm so sorry. I wanted to take your mind off your troubles a little, remind you of happier times. I'm afraid I've only made things worse."

"No, the memories of our youth are good memories. They make me happy, but when I come back to the present, I see only uncertainty. If anything were to happen to Vibius, you could go live with your daughter or son. My daughter is dead. My son might as well be." She paused, fighting against the wave of self-pity, but could not withhold one more complaint. "What is anyone without family? I may as well be dead myself."

"Have you forgotten that you have a brother?"

A shiver went through Shifra. Akiva! Her little brother Akiva. He'd been fourteen years old when she and Benjamin left Alexandria. In the

45

years since, they'd exchanged a handful of letters. On his side, one when their father died. Another when Mother followed. There had been a letter announcing his marriage and one for the birth of a daughter. On her side, letters on the birth of her children and—then—the death of daughter and unborn grandchild. She hadn't written to him about Benjamin. She had thought of it, but why burden him with more of her sorrows?

"Yes, Iris, I have a brother, but he's in Alexandria and has another life. He was a boy when we parted. Now he is a man with a wife. No matter how agreeable his wife may be, two women in a household are always one too many."

Iris returned to her chair and fixed her with a serious expression. "Nothing has been decided yet. You can still inherit Benjamin's estate."

Shifra stared at her, uncomprehendingly. "Hasn't Vibius told you the bishop's terms? The only thing undecided is how much, if anything, will be left to me to live on."

"No. What has not been decided is whether you will permit Marolus to take the estate or act to secure it for yourself." She waved in the direction of the mural of the good shepherd and his mother. "Conversion does not have to mean giving up your beliefs. You simply have to learn how to live in the times."

***

At dinner, Vibius held forth in his usual style about the decline of old Roman virtues, thanks to weak emperors, unscrupulous traders, and, above all, the barbarian incursions into the Empire.

"Rome itself! Can you credit it? Just last year. Alaric and his barbarian Goths spilling into the most sacred precincts. Violating the very tombs of the emperors, snatching up treasure and abducting the emperor's own sister."

Shifra had known Vibius long enough to know that neither the old pagan religion nor the new Christianity he now professed commanded his soul. His spiritual center had always been *Roma*, not simply the city of Rome, but *Roma*, the imperial concept of world power and order. Even as most Roman men abandoned the toga for more comfortable business apparel, he clung to it as a symbol of the old, superior ways. She tried to say something comforting.

"The Goths spent only three days in the city. Perhaps they didn't do too much damage."

Vibius sighed deeply. "Physical damage can be repaired. But heathen savages striking at the very heart of the Empire—that sort of damage can never be repaired."

After an uncomfortable silence, Iris steered the conversation to a less stressful topic—old times. "Shifra and I have been recalling her early days in Milan. What do you remember about them, dear?"

His angry expression cleared. "Struggling to find clients who could pay in cash and not homegrown produce. Arguing philosophy with Benjamin and Augustine. Seeing Lucretia and Junius growing up and wondering how I was going to pay for her wedding and his education." He cast a mischievous look at Shifra. "And envying Benjamin and you your roomy apartment in a better section of the city."

Shifra glanced around the dining room, almost as beautifully decorated as the atrium. "I think that Benjamin would agree that any house envy would be on our side now."

Vibius smiled complacently. "Paying clients made all the difference."

What had made the difference, Shifra knew, was his conversion to Christianity. She smiled back, choosing her words. In these sensitive times, topics of religion, nationality, and politics were best approached carefully, even among friends.

"Might your changed relationship with the Church have had anything to do with your change of fortune?" She braced for a possibly angry response, but Vibius smiled more broadly.

"Even a lion knows to get out of the way of an elephant. Bishop Ambrose refused to permit the emperor and his mother to use churches for Arian Christian worship in Milan. Refused the emperor! And got away with it. I knew then that I had no chance to succeed in this city as a pagan lawyer."

"I don't understand, Vibius. As much as you love the old ways, how could you betray the old gods by consenting to conversion?"

"That's where you misunderstand me. I don't see it as betrayal. As I see it, there's the High God that created the world and everything that is in it. The High God manifests power in various ways. According to the old ways, the manifestations were seen as Hermes, Jupiter, Vesta, and that lot. In the new religion, the manifestations are Jesus, the Holy Spirit, and Mary. I can't see what I did as betrayal because I feel I'm still honoring the High God, just by way of different manifestations."

The significance of the paintings in the atrium became clear. Transferring their religious loyalty from the old gods to the new had not required betrayal for Vibius and Iris. They still worshipped the gods of their ancestors, simply under different names. It worked for them. It could never work for a Jew. *I am the Lord thy God. Thou shalt have no other gods before me.*

***

The remaining days of the visit passed pleasantly as the friends relived the happier moments of their friendship.

On the second day, while Vibius was away at work, Iris introduced Shifra to what she called "her tablinum," a room that belonged entirely to herself. "I'd always complained that it wasn't fair that Vibius had a room all to himself for his books and papers and important things, but I didn't. I said the wife should have a tablinum too. I was only half joking."

She led the way out of the atrium, through the "real" tablinum and into the walled garden behind. "When we bought the house, the kitchen was where it is now. The wall opposite the kitchen was blank, with nothing behind it but the grounds."

The previously blank wall now harbored a door and a wide window into the peristylum, shuttered against the winter weather. Iris stopped.

"Last year, while I was visiting Lucretia and her family in Ostia, Vibius added this room just for me." She opened the door with a flourish. "Here's *my* tablinum."

Expecting the door to open on the usual unlighted interior of a peripheral room, Shifra gasped at the light. At least a dozen lamps, all lighted, hung at intervals from the ceilings. Three lamps on stands added to the illumination. In addition, three large braziers added a red hue from their burning coals. A loom stood at the farthest end. Shelves containing book sleeves and small vessels covered much of the back wall. A large table took pride of place in front of them.

Shifra turned in a circle. "I've never seen so many lamps in one room in a private house!"

Iris stepped to the window and patted the wooden shutters. "When the weather permits and I can open the shutters, it's almost like being in the garden."

"It's lovely, Iris. Vibius is a most thoughtful husband."

"He is. And that is why I'm planning this surprise for him." She indicated the loom. "I'm almost ready to begin the weaving." Stacks of clean carded wool lay near the loom, waiting to be spun. Iris picked up a piece of wool and smoothed it against her thigh. "Look how fine and how white."

Shifra recalled their talk over refreshments on the day she'd arrived. "From the Canossan sheep."

"Yes." Two chairs flanked the loom. A distaff lay on each.

"I had my woman load a distaff for you."

"Let's see." Shifra sat in the chair, tucked the bottom of the distaff under her right arm, pulled the spindle from the mass of wool attached to it, and began to twist the wool into a strand of yarn. "This certainly takes me back!"

As Shifra manipulated the soft wool with her fingers, the warm days on the banks of Lake Como with Iris, Mira, and the children rose in her mind. Precious days.

In the days that followed, Shifra brought Dacia with her and the three women spun the remaining wool into thread. The weaving could begin.

***

All through the week, Vibius and Iris had been dropping not-so-subtle hints that, if she were sensible, Shifra would go through the motions of conversion. On that last night, Vibius shifted to a more direct approach. His friendly dinner tone of voice disappeared. Tonight, the lawyer's voice prevailed.

"The bishop's clerks finished their inventory today. They have labeled every item and made a list. If there is a price written on the label, the item belongs to the Church. If there is no price, the item has been deemed your personal property and you may take it when you move out of the house."

Shifra felt her stomach and throat tense. *Move out of the house.* Her home. She fought the tears and lost. Vibius pretended not to see.

"When we meet with the bishop in the morning, you must give your answer. Convert and keep your inheritance, or refuse and lose it."

The words fell on her ears like hailstones.

"As your lawyer, my advice to you is to agree to conversion. What you do afterwards, in the privacy of your home, will be up to you."

Shifra tried to imagine what it would be like to be to have to give up her home. As she lay sleepless that night, she wondered if it would be possible to retain her self-respect if she did as Vibius advised. For him and Iris, the choice had improved their lives without any real sacrifice. For Augustine and Mira, conversion led to the destruction of their marital happiness. Shifra had already lost her marital happiness. With Benjamin dead, should she, perhaps, seize comfort over appearances? Could she not retain her religion in the privacy of her home? What of the servants? Did she not have a responsibility toward them. Forcing them to change owners struck at their security.

Questions unresolved, Shifra fell into an uneasy sleep.

Chapter Six

Difficult Choices

Shifra and Vibius arrived at the house well in advance of the bishop. This time, they awaited Bishop Marolus in the atrium. Previously, Shifra hadn't wanted him to invade the sanctity of her home. Now, after a clutch of strangers had been swarming room to room for a week, the intimacy of the house was no longer a consideration. The chief violator might as well be admitted to the atrium. She would not offer refreshments.

Bishop Marolus arrived on the hour, as humbly dressed as the first time.

"Greetings, my child. I've come to hear your decision."

Three chairs had been brought, but no one chose to sit. Shifra took a deep breath. She fought to keep her voice steady. "You now know to the denarius what my husband's estate is worth. I would like to know the cost of my decision."

"In what terms, my dear? Worldly or spiritual?"

She wanted to scream at him, but held steady. "What part of my *worldly* inheritance will be left to me if I refuse to deny the religion of my fathers? Will I still have a roof over my head?"

"If you choose Christ, you will remain in this house and pay an inheritance tax of ten percent, five percent to the emperor and five percent to the Church.

"And if I do not?"

"Your portion will be five percent of the sale of the estate."

Shifra's heart pounded in her ears. Her breath came in deep inhalations, pumping her head with dizziness. Her stomach writhed. Vibius stepped forward and helped her to sit. Five percent. Hardly anything. How would she live?

The bishop came close, his face a study in compassion. "It should be an easy choice, my child. Embrace the true religion. Accept Christ, be baptized in His name, and not only will you inherit your husband's worldly goods, you will escape perdition and inherit the wealth of life eternal."

Shifra leaned forward, spewing her breakfast over the prelate's sandaled feet. Dacia hurried forward to her assistance. Marolus, as if unaware of the state of his feet, renewed his efforts to persuade.

"You ask the cost of your decision. Your very soul is at stake. Your poor husband died a Jew, forever lost, doomed to eternity in Hell. Choose salvation, my child. Avoid your husband's dreadful fate."

Benjamin in Hell? That good, kind, useful man in Hell for eternity? Shifra looked up at the elderly, earnest countenance hovering above her. All uncertainty gone, she spoke in steady tones. "Where my husband goes, I shall also go. I want no part of a religion so blind to a good man's worth as yours."

***

While Vibius showed the bishop out, Dacia took her mistress to wash and change her garments. Then, they rejoined the lawyer in the tablinum. Now that the mistress had refused to convert and would lose the house, Dacia's future was more uncertain than before.

Her mistress sat behind the desk and Dacia behind her, on a stool. Vibius's boy Lucius squatted in a corner, next to his perpetual burden, the satchel of legal papers. The mistress played absently with a stylus.

"So, Vibius, how much time do I have? When must I quit the premises?"

"Until I have found a buyer for the house, the bishop says you may remain, although he did urge me not to dawdle." He glanced briefly over her shoulder at Dacia. "I told Marolus that whatever penalty he decided to levy on you, it should not apply to your serving woman. After all, I told him, she's not a Jew."

Again he glanced at Dacia and spoke directly to her. "The archbishop knows that you are an Arian, Dacia. He offers you the same conditions he offered your mistress. If you convert to Nicene Christianity, you may receive the money your master left for you."

"If I refuse, will I remain a slave?"

"No. The manumission papers have been prepared." He gestured toward Lucius and the satchel.

Shifra had turned in her chair. Dacia wondered what if her mistress was passing judgement on her. Whatever Master Benjamin intended her to have, it would be far less than what her mistress was giving up by refusing to betray her religion. Dacia knew that the lawyer was waiting for her to speak, but she didn't know what to ask.

"It's a substantial amount, Dacia. Enough to set you up in a business. A small taverna for example, or a bakery." He paused, but still she said nothing. "If you don't take it, you will be free, but without a way to make a living."

She couldn't imagine another life. She looked at her mistress. "Can't I stay with you?"

"Of course, you can. But wouldn't you rather be free and in charge of your own life? Your case is not at all like mine. You are already a Christian. Why not accept the conditions and let Marolus baptize you? Without the inheritance, you can't set yourself up in business, and I won't have the money to help you."

"She could marry," Vibius said.

Dacia put her hand to her face, touching the cloth that covered her disfigurement. What man would want to marry her? "I wish to stay with my mistress."

The lawyer slapped his forehead. "*Cucurbita*, girl! You can do both, get the money and stay with your mistress." He turned and impatiently paced the narrow width of the office. "I've never understood the problem between Nicenes and Arians anyway. In the old days, before Ambrose stirred things up, the two had their own churches and rubbed along well enough. Then Ambrose comes along and tells the emperor and his mother they can't have even one church in Milan for Arian worship. The *emperor*, mind you!"

He came to a stop. "Tell me, Dacia, what would be so different for you? You worship on Sunday, read the same scriptures, sing the same psalms, and break bread in the name of Jesus. What, then, will you lose by converting?"

Dacia tried to think of how to answer Vibius. She had only a vague notion of why Arians were despised by Nicenes. It had to do with the *begottens*. Both sects taught that Jesus is God's "only begotten Son," but they disagreed on what it meant. It made sense to her that, as God's son, Jesus hadn't existed until he was *begotten*. And that, as a son, he would be subject to his father. But if Jesus the Son was exactly *like* God the Father, then that would mean there were two gods, but all the priests say there's only one God. She squeezed her hands against her temples and cried out. "I don't know, Avocatus. I just know that I can't give up my religion. I cannot."

Torn from her home country before the age of ten, shorn of family, language, and even her name, the name she'd been baptized with. The trader had found it too hard to remember the names of the slaves he bought. He called them by the name of the country in which he'd bought them. He had called her sister "Dacia Prima" and her, as the younger, "Dacia Secunda. No. All that remained of her former identity was her Arian religion. She would not give it up and be left with nothing to sustain her inner existence.

"Very well," Vibius said. "We can complete the manumission papers now." He motioned for Lucius to bring the bag.

"Shifra, you'll need to sign and Dacia can make her mark."

The words shook Dacia out of her inarticulate misery. She stood and spoke through tightened lips. "If you don't mind, Avocatus, I'd like to read it first. And then I'll sign."

The lawyer's face was a study in incredulity as he handed her the manumission papers. She was tempted to uncover her face, so he could see her smile.

**

At the end of January, Vibius had a buyer for the house, a newly married minor officer back from the frontier. His inexperienced wife was pleased to take the servants along with the house. Shifra knew from her own experience what a difficult undertaking it was to staff a house from scratch, especially on a meager budget. She guessed that the young wife was congratulating herself for being spared shopping the slave market. Everyone knew that most reliable slaves came from private owners.

As she made final preparations to move out, the task she most dreaded was parting from the servants, especially Haluk. The boy had been especially devastated by Benjamin's death. She called him to the triclinium, intending to comfort him with her regrets.

"If it were in my power," she told him, "I would take you with me."

His face broke into a grin of undisguised relief. "That's all right, Domina. Cook says you're going to live with your brother in Alexandria. I don't think I could bear going so far from home. And besides, those Alexandrians are always rioting over one thing or another. I'd be afraid to go to market by myself. I'll pray to the Lady Isis that you'll be safe there."

Vibius passed the boy as he came in. "Don't let him worry you, Shifra. Alexandria's not nearly as bad as folks make out. I still say that you'll be better off going to your brother than remaining in Milan."

"I wonder where Cook could have gotten his information."

Vibius bent to adjust his sandal. Shifra expelled a breath of annoyance. "I've told you. I've no intention of disrupting my brother's life as a figure of charity in his house. As I told Iris, two women in a household are always one too many. And besides, Milan has been my home for the past thirty years. I have friends here. I can manage."

She looked around the room in which she had passed so many pleasant evenings with Benjamin. Suddenly, it was no longer familiar. Like the desk that was labeled and priced, it belonged to its new owners, strangers who had nothing to do with her. The home in which she had brought up two children had become a shell. Another thought occurred to her. Her daughter and grandchild were forever lost, but her son, as far as she knew, lived yet.

"What of Alexander? What if my son were to come back and I wasn't in Milan?"

"He'd come to me and I would tell him where to find you."

"I must stay here for him."

Vibius held her eyes with his. "How long has it been since he left?"

"Three years and three months."

"How often has he written in that time?"

She looked away. Vibius knew there'd been no letters. Not one. She didn't meet his eyes. "I keep hoping he'll come back." Even as she spoke, Shifra knew she was lying. She'd given up that hope long ago. She knew that she was not being rational. Akiva's home in Alexandria was the obvious refuge.

"No." More loudly this time. "You've invested the five percent I was allowed to keep. You say that it will provide me with a monthly income."

"Not nearly enough, Shifra." He gestured at their surroundings. "Not enough to match what you're used to."

"I know how to live frugally. I'll be fine. Have you found me a place to live?"

Vibius nodded glumly. "A small apartment in the Jewish quarter. Not far from the synagogue."

"Good. Whenever you are ready to fetch us, Dacia and I have packed what I've been allowed to keep."

"I'll have a wagon here at the third hour."

Chapter Seven
The Price of Principle

Their new home was an apartment in a six-story insula two blocks from the synagogue. No heated floors here. Shifra suspected it may have been the rabbi's influence that got them on the lowest possible floor, directly above the shops. She was glad. She'd hate to have to use the dark narrow stairways every day to climb to a higher floor.

The rabbi's wife, Varda, had offered constant support in the way of food, such basics as towels and storage baskets, and, most precious of all, the assurance that she and Dacia were not without a friend in the new neighborhood.

On their first day in the new lodgings, Dacia demonstrated her delight by running up and down the stairs to the street four times in a row. "What good fortune, Domina, to live so near the street, and the public fountain just a few steps away."

Shifra was pleased for Dacia, whose duties now included fetching water several times a day, but she couldn't help wishing the apartment could be on the ground floor. She thought longingly of the private comforts of the domus they'd left behind. Here, running water could be had only on the ground floor. They'd have to go downstairs to use the toilets. Mercifully, latrine use was confined to the residents on the first two floors. People higher up had to rely on chamber pots.

Apart from some inconveniences, life for the two women settled into a routine more comfortable than not. Dacia made friends with other women at the fountain and regaled her mistress with news and gossip.

"There's an Arian house church, Domina, with an Arian priest. Not far from here. I'd like to attend services there next Lord's Day."

"I worry you'll be arrested, Dacia. Why can't you go to the Nicene church? You said you can't tell much of a difference in the services."

"It's the words, Domina. Sometimes an Arian priest says the mass in Gothic instead of Latin. I love hearing my own language."

"What if a Nicene neighbor reports you?"

Dacia laughed. "Ordinary Christians don't care. It's just the bishop and such-like. Most folk don't see what the fuss is about."

After the first month, it was clear that the allowance from the banker would cover rent and food, but little else. Dacia tried to be frugal with the shopping, but their only means of cooking was on a brazier. Anything requiring the use of an oven had to be bought from a bakery or a cook shop.

The shops on the ground floor of their insula included a bakery, a caupona—a little shop that sold wine and cooked meat—a cobbler, and a laundry. The early morning aroma of baking bread was pleasing, but as the day wore on, it had to compete with the smell of cooking from the caupona and urine from the laundry.

In her old life, Shifra could leave work involving physical exertion to a houseful of servants. For that matter, even Dacia's duties had involved nothing more onerous than making tea or caring for her mistress's clothing. Now, Shifra helped with the shopping and, sometimes, even the water-carrying. One bitter-cold late January day, as they filled their jugs at the public fountain, a new source of income presented itself.

Three or four small boys playing about the fountain, wearing only long-sleeved tunics and cork-soled sandals with socks, walked the raised edges, pretending to be acrobats. When one of the boys jostled Dacia's elbow, causing her to slam her pitcher against the stone, she shouted in exasperation. "You almost made me break my best pitcher. Go home. It's too cold for you to be out here anyway."

Patches of ice glistened in a few places along the fountain ledge, and the inevitable happened. The smallest of the boys slipped on an icy patch and fell backward onto the paving stones. His screams of pain split the frigid air and brought women running from the shops.

"Rufus! What have you done to yourself?" The injured boy belonged to Lavinia, the baker. She knelt beside him and pulled him into a floury embrace that caused him to scream louder.

Shifra joined the boy's mother on the ground. "Here, let me. I may be able to help." Calling on the experience gained by assisting Benjamin in the old days, she palpated the boy's extremities. Touching his right wrist caused him to scream anew. "Dacia, fetch me your master's bag." She hadn't been able to discard Benjamin's medical kit, not because she thought she'd ever use it, but because it represented him more than anything else he'd left behind. She helped carry Rufus into the back room of the bakery and instructed Dacia to fill a basin with water and to put a few pieces of ice in it. "Hold his wrist under the water," Shifra instructed.

When Dacia brought the medical bag, Shifra unwrapped a length of linen from a roll that had been stiffened with starch. "Now, take his hand from the basin and dry it."

The boy's mother, Lavinia, did as directed, and Shifra carefully and firmly bound his wrist. "There, now. Does it feel better?" Rufus nodded, his tear-streaked face pale, but no longer contorted with pain. "Good. Take care not to dislodge the bandage. I'll look in every day to be sure it doesn't come loose." She turned to Lavinia. "Best to keep him indoors for the next few weeks."

"Thank you, Domina. It's that grateful we are. You'll not go empty-handed from my shop."

Shifra and Dacia left the bakery laden with rolls and honey-cakes, followed by loud expressions of gratitude from Lavinia that filled the immediate neighborhood. "She's as good as a doctor, I can tell you. Set my boy's bone as well as any field surgeon."

Feelings of elation accompanied Shifra as they headed back to their apartment. At the caupona, two workmen stood at the counter, choosing their food. One of the men moved suddenly, forcing her off the footpath into the street.

Loud enough to be heard by everyone within half a league, he showed that he'd heard Lavinia's praise. "Good as a doctor! What a load of mule dung! Midwifery is one thing. That's women's work. But I've never heard of a female bonesetter."

A broad-shouldered man wearing a stonemason's apron, he didn't make eye contact, but it was clear that Shifra was the target of his contempt. More words followed as she went into the insula entrance. "God never intended for women to do men's work. And her a Jewess into the bargain."

Shifra tried not to let the words bother her. She'd never seen the man before in the neighborhood. She supposed he was there temporarily for employment. She comforted herself with the thought that he was an outsider and didn't speak for her neighbors.

In the weeks that followed, more and more of the people in the quarter called on her for help with medical matters. Careful not to intrude on the work of the local midwife, she responded to cuts, broken or dislocated bones, muscular aches, and fevers. Sometimes, patients rewarded her assistance with money, but more often, remuneration came in the form of produce or merchandise. She was especially pleased when the cobbler's wife contracted a fever that required five nights of bedside care that resulted in new outdoor shoes for both her and Dacia.

As her skills supplemented her income, providing not only necessities, but items of comfort as well, Shifra began to lose the feelings of fear and uncertainty that had clouded her decision to remain in Milan and reject the family support her brother could provide. Not only was she surviving, she saw her newfound work—ministering to her neighbors—as a link to Benjamin, his legacy through her. As her life again began to have meaning, she started to look past mere survival. When, in mid-March a morning dawned with neither rain nor cold, she had the urge to do something different from the daily round of chores. Something away from the shelter of the Jewish quarter.

"Put on your new shoes, Dacia. Let's go to the Tuesday market by the new church."

***

The "new" church wasn't really very new. Called the Basilica of the Virgins, it had been begun back when Ambrose was bishop. His successor, Simplicianus, completed enough of it to be buried there, but, ten years after his death, scaffolding remained in place on the south side.

As Shifra and Dacia picked their way past the tarps and piles of straw beneath the scaffold, the chink of hammer and chisel sounded above them. Rounding the side of the basilica, Dacia stopped and stared at the great west door. Shifra touched her arm. "Would you like to go inside before we begin the shopping?"

Dacia jerked away. "No. Never." I'd be afraid to cross the threshold of this church, Domina."

"Why? Is it because Bishop Ambrose said he only built it because he wanted a church in Milan that had never been used for Arian worship?"

"Not that." With her thumb, Dacia made the sign of a cross on her forehead and backed away a few steps. "It's because of where he built it, Domina. He laid the foundations on a pagan cemetery. The place must be filled with demons." She turned and hurried toward the market stalls. Shifra followed, uncertain whether to be concerned or amused.

The Tuesday market in the center of Milan boasted far more merchandise than anything to be found in their quarter. And the prices were considerably higher.

Shifra had not come with any expectation of making a lot of purchases; she just fancied a change of routine. They strolled among the stalls, calling each other's attention to especially fine fabrics and jewelry. Two officers of the city watch patrolling the market stopped to let them pass in front of them. Shifra recognized them as the men who'd brought Benjamin's body home. She nodded at them. They met her eyes, but neither acknowledged the greeting.

At the end of about four hours, all they'd bought were some wax candles and a few pieces of fruit.

"I'm ready to go home, Dacia. How about you?"

"I've been ready, Domina. These new shoes are making my feet hurt."

They returned the way they'd come, by way of the basilica.

Men were still at work on the scaffolding on the south side. The steady clinking above them changed suddenly to a clatter followed by a curse and a cry. Shifra looked up to see one of the men fall from the platform. His companion arrested his fall by grabbing his hand. He dangled, all his weight pulling on one arm as workers below scurried to snatch up one of the large cloths from the pile of materials and stretched it between them to form a soft landing. The man dropped to the cloth and the men lowered it to the ground. When they helped him to his feet, he screamed. He'd been saved from crashing to the ground, but he'd not escaped unscathed.

Shifra ran toward the knot of men, ignoring Dacia's cries for her to come back. She was certain that the man's arm had been pulled from its socket and she knew how to put it back. She pushed her way to where he swayed and moaned, his eyes squeezed shut in pain while his rescuers looked on helplessly.

"If you can get him to lie down, I know what to do." They lowered him onto his back. Feeling his upper arm and shoulder with her fingers, Shifra verified that the bone had slipped from its socket. Seizing his hand with both of hers and setting her right foot against his side, she pulled slowly, steadily, and firmly until she felt the bone slip back into place.

Carefully, she placed his forearm upon his stomach. Someone knelt beside her. Shifra turned to see a woman in a shabby cloak. "He's my husband. Will he be all right?"

Shifra touched her hand reassuringly. "Nothing seems to be broken, but you need something to tie his arm in place. He must keep it close to his side until it heals. It could slip out of place again, otherwise."

The muscles in the man's face relaxed and he opened his eyes, smiling when he saw the woman. Moving his head slightly, he looked at Shifra. His relaxed expression changed from relief to consternation to rage. "You!"

Shifra scrambled to her feet. It was the stonemason from the caupona, the stranger who had pushed her from the sidewalk, hurling insults. She and Dacia attempted to leave, but the crowd of onlookers pressed around them.

"She's the one I told you about," the man shouted. "The Jewess who seems to think she's a doctor." He moved the injured arm and cried out in pain. "What's she done to me?"

The woman stood. "How dare you put your unbeliever's hands on my husband!" She followed her words with a volley of slaps and blows to Shifra's face and head, forcing her backward as the crowd gave way. Dacia's cries for help mingled with shouts of encouragement from the onlookers. "Help. Someone! Help my mistress."

"You go, Vena. Give it to her. Teach her to come practicing her black arts among good Christian folk."

"Help. Please, for the love of Jesus!"

Dacia's screams for help attracted the attention of the two officers of the watch who had ignored Shifra's greeting at the market. "Coming through. Stand back there."

The crowd quickly thinned. The officers restrained the woman called Vena. "Enough there, woman. You've made your point."

An elderly woman came forward, and put an arm around Vena and moved to go.

Dacia protested. "This woman has beaten my mistress. Look at her bloody face. The prefect should hear of this. You can't let her go as if she'd done nothing."

The officer shrugged. "Nothing to bother the prefect with as I can see." He turned to Vena and the other woman. "Go along, the two of you. Next time, you just stay at home during your menses." He turned to Shifra, who held Dacia's bloodstained napkin to her nose. "The same advice goes for you two. Come along. We'll escort you back to your quarter. In the future, you might want to make do with the local markets and leave this part of the city to the folk who live here."

Chapter Eight

In Search of a Home

The day after the incident by the basilica, Shifra had a visitor. Vibius, replete in toga.

"Greetings, Shifra. You look awful."

Gingerly, Shifra touched her lips, verifying that they were still twice their normal size. That morning she'd been unable to eat anything solid for breakfast because she couldn't open her mouth wide enough.

"We'll have to sit at the table." She led him to the tiny table that served for dining, sewing, and any other activity requiring a work surface. "No atrium here."

Vibius was a large man and his shoulders, naturally wide, seemed even wider under the folds of his toga. He looked almost comical perched on a stool by the little table. He kept his face expressionless as he looked around. "Are you comfortable here?"

"We were."

"Until that business yesterday, I take it."

"I was only trying to help."

Dacia placed a honey cake in front of him. He picked at it. "For help to be helpful, it must be wanted."

The remark stung. She knew he was thinking of his own efforts to help her three months earlier, when he suggested she leave Milan.

They sat in silence, but her mind churned, knowing he'd come to see if she had reconsidered writing to her brother in Alexandria.

Vibius was first to break the silence. "Do you want me to press charges?"

For a moment, Shifra didn't know what he was talking about.

"The woman who assaulted you yesterday."

"Oh. No. What would be the point? It would be Dacia's and my word against everyone else's, including the officers who pulled her off me."

"I'm not without influence. I can make her regret her unprovoked attack on you."

Shifra shook her head emphatically. "No! I don't want her to pay. No one suffered for the attack on Benjamin. And he died."

The attorney's broad face, usually unreadable, expressed total incomprehension.

She smiled and wiped the tears with the backs of her hands. "I don't expect you to understand, Vibius. I see it as something I can share with Benjamin, a glimpse of what he was feeling during those last moments, being beaten for nothing more than being a Jew. And not only that, but being beaten after having done his best to help a Christian."

"You're right. I can't see it that way. I do think it should, if nothing else—it should cause you to consider the possibility that you'd be safer living with your brother in Alexandria than continuing where you are."

As much as she hated to admit it, after the events by the basilica, Shifra was ready to agree.

She stood, keeping her back to Vibius. How could she change her mind when she'd been so certain that her best course was to remain in Milan? Why was it so hard to admit that she'd been wrong?

"There's still Alexander, my son. He might come back."

"I'll tell him you've gone home."

Home. "Alexandria is so far away."

"No further away than when you and Benjamin made the trip from there to here." He stood too and turned her to face him. "As for Alexander, anyone who can travel from Milan to Palestine can manage to get from Milan to Alexandria."

Shifra sighed, releasing her last misgivings with the exhaled breath.

"I'll write to Akiva as soon as you leave."

"Good. I'll send my boy to fetch the letter first thing in the morning and see that it goes out with the public post at once. We might hear back within the month."

***

As the days approached the first of April, Shifra distracted herself from waiting for Akiva's letter by keeping busy. Twice a week, she went with Varda among the Jewish poor, distributing food, binding up cuts, and sometimes helping the midwife. Then, seven days past the kalends, Vibius came to the apartment in the early hours.

Dacia had gone for water and Shifra still sat at breakfast. She admitted the lawyer and invited him to sit. She looked behind him for Lucius, but apparently, he'd come alone. As he sat, his cloak slipped off behind him, revealing not the customary toga, but a slightly rumpled red tunic.

"What, no toga? I don't think I've ever seen you in a tunic on a workday, Vibius. And a red one at that."

"You know how long it takes to put on a toga," he said, his voice still gruff from sleep. "I know for a fact that Benjamin grumbled every time he had to wear one."

Shifra laughed, recalling her conversation with Iris.

He handed her something he'd been carrying. A letter.

"The messenger came while I was still in bed. As soon as I saw it was from your brother, I brought it straightaway."

Breathlessly, Shifra looked at the image stamped in the blob of green wax, recognizing the signet that had belonged to her father when she and Akiva were children—a fruiting grape vine, symbol of the Promised Land. A surge of sadness squeezed her heart. Her son should have Benjamin's seal, but there was no way to pass it on to him. She unrolled the papyrus and read.

Dearest Sister,

The news of my brother Benjamin's death shook me to my soul. I weep that Roman order has so far declined in these troubled times that such a thing could happen in one of the most important cities in Italy. Benjamin was a good man and I share your sorrow.

Your letter reached me even as I was struggling to write my own sad news to you. My dear wife Dinah has gone to our fathers. Not long after the Feast of Passover, she was stricken with a fever. For a time, we had hope that she would overcome it, but the Lord had other plans for her.

Our house is still a house of mourning, Shifra, but I pray that you will come to us and make it your home. My daughter Aella had her twelfth birthday two weeks ago. Your presence here would be a great help to me now that she has lost the mother who could guide her through these next years.

I have given instructions to Vibius regarding your travel arrangements, should you decide to come.

Signed and sealed by your loving brother, Akiva ben Elad

Shifra raised a fold of her stola to wipe away the hot tears, heart swelling with gratitude and relief. She had a home to go to. She read the message a second time before rolling it back up and raising her eyes to Vibius. "I think he really wants me."

"Of course he does." He waved a waxed packet. "These are my instructions from him." For the first time in months, Shifra saw the possibility of renewal. With his wife gone and a daughter approaching marriageable age, Akiva truly needed a woman in the house.

"How soon can I leave?"

"The sea lanes open in another week, but he says he doesn't want you on the water any earlier than the first of May. Too dangerous." He waved the packet at her. "It's all in here. Travel plans and a draft to cover your expenses from here to Alexandria. I'm to put the money out at interest until time for your departure. He says he'll send me a final list of your overnights closer to your departure time. Where possible, you'll stay at one of the imperial stations. Otherwise, in a private home. He doesn't want you stopping the night at any public hostels."

Vibius inhaled deeply and fixed Shifra with an admiring look. "You never told Iris or me what an important man your brother is."

Shifra frowned. "What do you mean? He's just a secretary. Something in the civil service."

"He's a secretary all right—to Orestes, the Roman Governor of upper Egypt." Vibius shook his head in a gesture of wonder. "Your brother is a man of considerable influence."

"What do you mean?"

He laughed wryly. "When I want to use the *cursus publicus,* all I can send is mail. Your brother has arranged for you to travel to Rome in an official vehicle."

Shifra did not know what he was driving at. He shook his head. "I'm astounded that a Jew could rise so high in the Imperial Service as to secure passage for a family member—even in Alexandria."

Shifra felt a glow of pride in her brother's achievements. Perhaps, unlike Milan, Alexandria had managed to hold onto its traditions of respect for the Jewish community. She felt an eagerness to get on her way. "How long do you think the journey will take?"

"If you leave mid-May, the land journey from here to Rome should take about ten days, weather permitting. From Rome to the port at Ostia is hardly a day's journey." He tapped Akiva's package of instructions. "Your sea journey will depend on private arrangements. It's especially good luck that Lucretia and her husband live in Ostia now. You'll be able to stay with them and Quintus, her husband, will search out a ship for you."

Milan. Rome. Ostia. The names took Shifra back to the journey in reverse, to the bride who had passed along the same route with her new husband. Hot tears blurred her vision. Memories of her wedding trip flooded her mind. She and Benjamin had landed at Ostia thirty-two years ago. She was sixteen; he was twenty. They had hired an open two-wheel cisium to drive the twenty miles from Ostia to Rome, where they stayed in the home of one of Father's business connections. Seven days in the very heart of the Empire. Rome in spring with Benjamin had been glorious. What would it be like without him?

"Shifra? Did you hear anything I said?" Impatience tinged his voice.

"What?" Shifra came back to the present. "I'm sorry, Vibius. I was just remembering when Benjamin and I first came to Italy. We spent a week in Rome before traveling on to Milan. It was glorious. I hope I have time to visit some of the places we saw together." They had stayed with Albina Flaviana and her husband Caleb. "Do you suppose I could stay with my hosts from last time?"

Vibius expelled a noisy breath and his face flushed bright red. "You are remembering a different Rome, a Rome unravished. A Rome before Alaric and his barbarians."

"It has been nearly two years, Vibius. They were only there for three days. Surely the damage has been repaired by now."

Vibius sighed deeply. "Physical damage, perhaps." He slammed a fist on the table. "Barbarians! Heathen savages striking at the very heart of the Empire. That sort of damage can never be repaired."

Shifra bit back a response. When it came to the unthinkable occupation of Rome by the Visigoths, mere words could have no effect on his sense of outrage. This man's spiritual center was *Roma*, the imperial concept of world power and order. The fact that no emperor since Diocletian had made Rome his capital, the fact that the emperors of both East and West had abandoned the toga for more comfortable dress on formal occasions, no matter that the Altar of Victory installed by Augustus no longer graced the Senate chambers. For Vibius, the City of Rome held the beating heart of the Roman Empire. She waited until his complexion had resumed its normal, less crimson, hue of ruddiness.

"If I'm to be ready to travel by the middle of May, I'd best get busy. When you write to Akiva about my accommodations, please tell him that I'd like to stay with Albina and Caleb while I'm in Rome."

"How can you be sure they are still living?"

"Our rabbi stayed with them last spring."

"Of course," Vibius said. "I'll be sure to tell your brother when I respond."

***

The weeks passed quickly as Shifra packed and saw to the various details of leaving the city that had been her home for three decades.

Almost sooner than she'd thought possible, she found herself sitting on a trunk outside the insula on a fine May morning, surrounded by the boxes, bags, and trunks that would travel with her and Dacia on the long journey to Alexandria.

Vibius had not yet arrived with the vehicles that would take them to the imperial cursus station. Dacia was making a last walk through the apartment to be sure they hadn't left anything.

Gazing idly about, she saw Rabbi Shemuel and Varda turn a corner into her street, followed by two boys pushing a handcart loaded with an enormous picnic hamper. Having already made her farewells the previous day, Shifra was surprised to see them.

She stood.

"Dear Varda, Rabbi, I never expected to see you again this morning!"

Varda squeezed Shifra to her matronly bosom. "I couldn't let you go on your way without something to fortify you, child. Hashem only knows when you'll be able to eat real Jewish meat rolls again. No one in Alexandria knows how to bake a real meat roll."

Shifra, face buried in the other woman's shoulder, smiled at the memory of her old nurse uttering almost the same words some thirty years previously: *I've packed all your favorite foods, my darling girl. Enjoy them along the way. You certainly won't find proper Jewish fig bread or date honey in the godforsaken Italian hole where you're going.*

The sound of wheels on gravel signaled the arrival of Vibius and two vehicles, one a little open *capsum* for the passengers, and the other a farm cart for boxes and trunks. A porter reached for the picnic hamper.

"Watch how you carry this," Varda snapped, releasing Shifra and following the hamper.

Next to Shifra, Vibius stared after the rabbi's wife and her precious cargo. "Your hosting families are in luck. Judging by the size of that hamper, they'll be spared the expense of feeding you altogether."

Luggage loaded, the rabbi pronounced a blessing and then, with some difficulty, led his weeping wife away. Dacia emerged empty-handed from the house and joined Shifra in the smaller vehicle. As it pulled away from the insula, Dacia glanced back briefly. "I won't miss the smells."

***

The imperial cursus station stood just inside the southern gate, an enormous facility with stables for forty to fifty animals, covered porticoes for hay, and a spacious central courtyard for hitching and loading. A roofed *carpentum* stood in the center of the courtyard.

"That can't be our carriage, can it, Vibius?" She hadn't expected anything as elaborate. More comfortable than other types, the carpentum was a closed carriage with four wheels. Six mules were hitched to this one. Benjamin and she had ridden in one part of the way to Milan. That one had cushioned seats.

Vibius descended. "I'll go see. If it is, you ought to make good time with six mules."

Shifra and Dacia remained seated in the capsum. When Vibius returned, he verified that the four-wheeled carpentum was indeed the carriage that Shifra and Dacia would be traveling in. Four imperial slaves made short work of transferring the luggage. Because the carpentum could seat four, the food basket and a few other items could travel in it. The larger trunks went to one of the cargo wagons.

A man in the short tunic of a slave stood beside the lead mules, talking to them. Shifra noticed something odd about him. "Vibius, what is that man wearing on his shoulders? It looks like a piece of wood."

"It's called a *furca*. It's a form of punishment. Maybe he tried to run away."

Dacia shook her head vehemently. "That's not a proper furca. I saw one once. This one is too short. It comes only to the end of his shoulders. The one I saw was longer, as long as both arms like this." She held her arms straight out, forcing Shifra to lean back out of the way. "It's like walking around crucified."

Vibius spoke. "Here comes the *manceps* in charge of the station." Another man, in military garb but helmetless, accompanied him.

The administrator bowed slightly. "Greetings, Domina. I am Dentatus, manceps here. This is Gaius Marius. You will be traveling with his convoy to Rome."

Vibius helped the women descend. Tall and broad shouldered, the centurion towered over Vibius. The livid scars on his jaw and above his left eye spoke of survival against terrible odds. He struck his fist against his chest in a military salute.

"Domina."

Shifra nodded graciously. Even minus the scars, Shifra could judge his battle experience by the numerous disk awards attached to the harness that crisscrossed his chainmail shirt. "Thank you, Marius," she said. "I am honored to be placed in the care of one of your distinction."

The centurion's face remained expressionless. Shifra suspected that he was far from honored to be burdened with two women. The excitement she'd felt earlier at the prospect of beginning the journey cooled as she was brought face to face with the fact that she and Dacia would be the only women in a military convoy made up of soldiers and slaves.

Part Two

From Milan to Alexandria

June – August 413 AD

Chapter Nine
A World of Differences

To the delight of both women, the carpentum did have cushions. The vehicle pulled out of the station, exited Milan by the south gate and drove onto the Via Aemilia, which would take them to Ariminum. A pleasant breeze rustled the leaves on the avenue of birch that lined their departure route. Shifra looked at the map that Vibius had sketched for them. The squeal of the carpentum's metal-shod wheels made it necessary for her to shout to be heard.

"Vibius said we'd probably spend the first night at Placentia. From there, it's a straight line to Ariminum, which is just about halfway to Rome." She handed the map to Dacia to roll up. "We couldn't ask for better weather for a journey."

About an hour into the journey, the centurion Marius rode up alongside. "I trust you ladies are comfortable."

There was no mistaking the sarcastic note in his voice. Shifra chose to ignore it.

"How long to our first stopping place?"

"Ordinarily, we'd ride for three or four hours before stopping," he said, "but I've been given instructions. On this trip, we must stop every two hours for the comfort of the women." He glanced at Dacia and back to Shifra. "Mind you, when we do stop, you'd better be quick about it if we're to make it to Rome in ten days." Kicking his horse, he vanished from view.

The first halt offered only a thick cover of bushes for the women's needs. They relieved themselves as quickly as possible and returned to the carriage, but did not resume their seats. As much as she appreciated the amenities of cushions and leather strap suspension, Shifra welcomed the chance to stretch her legs. She relished the absence of the sound of iron striking stone. She walked back and forth with Dacia until the horn should sound for the convoy to move.

"Ten days to Rome, Dacia," Shifra explained. "Even with good weather, that's a long time with a grumpy centurion."

An explosive laugh erupted from the driver's bench. Shifra hadn't noticed that the tattooed slave had resumed his seat and had been listening. Shifra looked up at him, frowning. "You have something to say, driver?"

The driver looked down at her, smiling. "Old Marius is not a bad sort, Domina. If not for him, I'd have a brand on my forehead instead of this piece of wood on my shoulders for trying to run away. He's no way near as severe as some I've served."

Shifra shuddered to contemplate a life in which locking a piece of timber around a man's neck could be seen as kindness. And she didn't understand why her own well-being hung on the whim of a centurion. She gestured at a mounted soldier moving past.

"I didn't expect to travel in a military convoy," she said. "I thought the cursus publica was run by civilians."

The driver shook his head. "It's whoever's got the animals and the vehicles. Sometimes they're requisitioned from farmers along the way. Sometimes everything's state-owned. Sometimes, a mix. Ask me, you hit it lucky landing with our outfit. Marius keeps a sharp eye out. You won't be cheated at the stops and none of the men will dare treat you with anything but respect."

"I can't say that I've found him to be especially respectful to me."

"It's nothing against you ladies. He's just concerned about losing time. He doesn't like being away from his command any longer than can be helped. It hasn't been that many years since the Visigoths—same lot that invaded Rome two or three years back—tried to take Verona. Stilicho stopped them that time."

The strident call of the horn split the air, signaling the end of the rest stop. The women scrambled back into the carriage. Shifra still had questions. She hoped that their lunch break would give more opportunity for answers.

The lunch stop was at a private villa where the servants' toilets were made available to them. They were well kept and hardly smelled, but Dacia crossed herself going in and going out. When Shifra rejoined her on the outside, she asked her what was troubling her.

"Demons, Domina. Latrines like these are dangerous places. You never know what might come up and snatch at you while you're doing your business."

The midday stop offered more time to get acquainted with their driver. Dacia spread a cloth on a level place and brought out some of the food Varda had provided. Shifra invited the driver to share their lunch of boiled eggs, apples, and cheese.

Everything about the slave repelled Shifra. A rougher kind of slave than she was used to, he spoke Latin with a barbarous accent and was sometimes difficult to understand. His face was spotted with small round blue marks, and a tattooed eagle embraced his right shoulder. A smell embraced his person, a combination of leather and mule.

His name was Goar. He identified himself as an Alan, a member of the Alani tribe. "I'm from Persia," he explained. "My people joined with the Germans—the Vandals and Visigoths—to fight the Romans at Adrianople."

"I've heard of Adrianople," Shifra said. "The battle there took place about three years before my husband and I married. Even though it happened as far away as Turkey, it was all that people talked about in Alexandria for months. Nobody could believe that barbarians could defeat a Roman army."

Goar and Dacia exclaimed at the same time. "*Barbarians!*"

Shifra frowned, stung by the reaction. She looked at them, silently demanding an explanation. Dacia looked away. Her flushed complexion showed she was upset, but, in familiar fashion, she kept her anger to herself. Goar, on the other hand, responded.

"Romans are quick to apply the word *barbarian* to people who are no more savage than themselves. Why shouldn't an army of Germans, Goths, Vandals, and Alans defeat a Roman army? They've been learning their techniques for half a century—as enemies and as allies."

Shifra remembered the shock and dismay that shook the city when the news of the Roman defeat at the hands of a barbarian army reached Alexandria. Her sympathy had been with the Romans.

"If you were on the winning side at Adrianople, how is it you're here now as a slave of the Romans?"

Goar laughed. "Sheer bad luck. The battle was winding down when I got tangled in a pack of fleeing Romans. They had a horse with them. One of the men picked me up and slung me onto its back. As soon as he reached safety, he sold me into the Imperial slave pool."

Shifra guessed him to be about the same age as Marius the centurion. "You must have been quite young at Adrianople," she said.

"Twelve years. My parents put me inside the wagon circle for safety, but I was insulted to be grouped with a bunch of sniveling children. I sneaked out, grabbed a spear from a fallen soldier, and hurled myself against the enemy." He laughed again and tugged at the collar that marked him as a runaway. "Reckon I still don't know when to stay put."

The horn had not yet sounded when they'd finished lunch, so Shifra and Dacia walked among the wagons. They saw Marius come out from behind the carpentum. He nodded, but did not speak.

In addition to their carriage, the convoy included a supply wagon and a covered cart drawn by four large mules. The cart was ventilated by two small windows, one on each side, set high and barred. When they returned to the carriage, Shifra asked Goar about the cart. He answered curtly.

"None of my concern, Domina." Adding, as he climbed back up onto the driver's seat, "And none of yours, I'm thinking."

The women resumed their places in the carriage. The signal sounded and the convoy moved on. Shifra turned her attention to the passing countryside, long stretches of cultivated land punctuated by large villas with outbuildings. She inhaled deeply. The May afternoon was redolent with the scent of new leaves, Alpine lilies, and freshly turned earth. An unfamiliar feeling of freedom grew within her the further she traveled from the place of her recent grief.

"It's like a summer outing," she said to Dacia. "Like last year, when we went to Bellagio on Lake Como. Oh, Dacia, I feel I'm doing the right thing. Do you?"

Dacia didn't answer at once. When she did, it was with her usual lack of expectations. "Time will tell, Domina."

Chapter Ten
Pagans and Others

At Parma, the party lodged at the home of a high official. The master did not welcome them personally, but a well-trained, attentive staff provided all they needed. Baths were followed by a copious meal that included meat dishes and plenty of wine. The centurion especially enjoyed the latter. Marius took his wine unwatered, and, as the meal continued, his daytime taciturnity devolved into professional reminiscence. A soldier from the age of fifteen, he'd spent his days fighting along the frontiers.

"Fought with Alaric once. Back in the days before he changed sides. Fine leader, Alaric."

"Alaric?"

Shifra and Dacia exclaimed the name in unison. Dacia crossed herself and Shifra stared. Her knowledge of the Visigoths and their leader came from Vibius. When news of Alaric's sack of Rome reached Milan, the lawyer had reacted with such rage Shifra thought he might have a stroke. *Barbarians, skin-clad savages* were the least offensive epithets he'd heaped on them. she could not believe that a centurion would have anything positive to say about the man who had defiled Rome.

Marius returned their stares and scoffed. "You pagans have no idea of how the empire has treated these people."

Shifra and Dacia gasped.

"Pagans!" Shifra croaked. "I am a Jew. I worship the one true God of Israel!"

"And I'm a Christian," Dacia exclaimed, her eyes reflecting the horror Shifra was sure showed in her own.

Marius stared at them uncomprehendingly for a moment, as if they were speaking neither Latin nor Greek. Then he slapped the table and hooted with laughter.

"I keep forgetting the way the Christians have taken over army slang."

Shifra frowned. "A *pagan* is an idol-worshipper."

Marius laughed. "A pagan just means a country dweller. Soldiers often refer to civilians as *pagans* because country folk are usually ignorant of anything beyond their home fields. To soldiers, civilians haven't a clue of what it's like in the field.

"How can a word have two such different meanings?" Shifra asked.

"Easy enough—when folks take over words that already mean one thing and force their own meanings onto them." He took a long draft of wine. "Christian preachers like to think of themselves as soldiers fighting against all the other religions in the world. They talk about their Christian cult as if it were a military organization. They've appropriated *pagan* to refer to anyone who doesn't belong to their imaginary army."

For a few minutes, Shifra pondered the vicissitudes of language. A word that meant one thing to her and Dacia, meant something entirely different to Marius. And a man she thought of as an enemy of the Empire, was someone whom Marius—a Roman centurion—could admire. Vibius despised the Visigoth Alaric with all his being. She broached the subject again.

"I want to understand how you can express admiration for Alaric. A lawyer friend in Milan says that Alaric received great honors from Emperor Honorius and repaid him with disloyalty."

Marius placed his wine cup on the table and stroked the sides of it with his fingers. His movements were slow and controlled, but she could see his face darken as blood rose. Several times it seemed as if he was going to speak. Finally, he did.

"No offense intended, Domina, but your friend doesn't know what he's talking about. I met Alaric eighteen years ago at the Battle of the Frigidus." He paused, as if expecting a reaction. When neither Shifra nor Dacia registered recognition, he made a derisive sound and addressed Shifra.

"Back on the road, I heard you say that you remember hearing about the Battle of Adrianople when you were a girl living in Alexandria."

"Yes."

"You remember a battle that happened over thirty years ago nearly a thousand miles from where you were living at the time, but you've never heard of Frigidus."

He took another deep draft of wine. "For your edification, Domina, Frigidus was fought eighteen years ago—within a week's ride of Milan." The muscles of his face writhed in anger. Shifra suspected that he was repressing more choice soldier language. When he had his emotions under control, he went on.

"I'll tell you why you remember the one and not the other, Domina. Because a disaster is horrific only when Romans are killed by non-Romans. You remember Adrianople because forty thousand Romans were killed there fighting an army of Germans and Persians. Frigidus, on the other hand, was a battle between two Roman emperors with armies made up mostly of immigrants." Marius took several deep breaths, as if preparing for a plunge. His voice deepened and

Shifra could see a vein throbbing at his temple. "Ten thousand Goths died at Frigidus, Domina, but no matter. They weren't Romans."

Shifra could think of nothing to say. Eighteen years ago, she'd been living in Milan, but she'd been occupied with the day-to-day concerns of a wife and mother, only vaguely aware of the happenings of the world at large.

Marius drained his cup and slammed it down. "The Visigoths did not enter the Empire as pillagers," he said. "Emperor Valens gave them permission to cross the Danube in order to escape the Huns who were pushing them out of their own lands. They came looking for a safe place where they could settle their wives and little ones." He raised his head and stared accusingly at Shifra. "They expected protection from their new rulers. But instead, they were abused and exploited by officials who should have acted in their interests. Worst of all, they were denied food until they were reduced to sell some of their children for money to feed the ones remaining. How can you blame them for turning on their betrayers?"

He stood abruptly. A new emotion flickered in his eyes, not anger and not fear, but concern. "Forgive me, Domina. We've an early start tomorrow. Sleep well." He turned and left the women to stare at his retreating back.

Shifra sighed, at a loss to reconcile Marius's view of Alaric with that of Vibius. According to the lawyer, Alaric was a monster, an ungrateful immigrant assaulting the timeless values of *Roma*. Or was Vibius mistaken? Were Alaric and his people no more than uprooted human beings seeking only a safe place to raise their families?

The women followed a servant to the guest room assigned to them. Soon they would leave the Via Aemilia and join the Via Flaminia, which led directly to Rome.

***

Shifra was not surprised when Marius avoided her and Dacia. He had uttered some opinions unbefitting a Roman military officer. Perhaps he feared his words might get back to his superiors.

The weather continued fine. The jouncing of the conveyance was a minor discomfort compared to the delight of seeing the temples, villas, and grand tombs unrolling along the roadsides like a moving art gallery, their architectural beauty offering glimpses of the luxurious grandeur enjoyed both in life and in death by the wealthy.

The turn-off to the Via Flaminia lay a few miles beyond Ariminum. The convoy stopped for the midday break only a few miles after making the turn. Finished with lunch, the women took a short stroll. Glancing around her, Shifra noticed a temple situated on a hill a short distance from the parked convoy. The white columns and triangular roof façade gleamed against a rich blue sky strewn with wispy clouds. She caught her breath at the beauty of it.

Beside her, Dacia muttered something in her own language, made a gesture toward the temple, and spat on the ground. "Too many of those old pagan temples are still standing. I don't know why they haven't all been torn down."

In Alexandria, pagan temples had been a part of daily life, even for a Jew. One of the most famous, the Serapeum, dedicated to the god Serapis, drew visitors from around the world. Unknown to their father, Shifra and Akiva had been inside. Their pedagogue, Atlas, could always be worn down. On one of their outings to the central city, he succumbed to their pleading, and the three of them had mounted the one hundred steps to the entrance.

Inside, the statue of the god was so big that its right hand touched one wall and its left, the opposite wall. The basket on its head almost touched the ceiling. Walls plated in shining bronze reflected the light from the candles and sunlight that penetrated a slit in the ceiling. The statue itself was a shimmering blue. Atlas told them that the color was the result of a mixture of ground gold and silver and precious stones like sapphire, emerald, and topaz. What a treasure the old Bishop of Alexandria acquired when he looted that temple.

Gazing at the lovely edifice, Shifra thought of Benjamin. On their way to Milan all those years ago, he too had been taken with the beauty of the rural temples. Emperor Theodosius had already passed his laws to close the temples and forbid pagan worship, but new laws take time to become acknowledged. At the time of their honeymoon journey to Milan, many of the temples remained open and crowded with worshippers.

Suddenly, Shifra felt an urge to go close. To go inside. Seeing Marius talking to one of the mule drivers, she hurried over.

"I would like to walk over to that temple and look inside. Is there time?"

Marius turned from the muleteer. "As it happens, yes. One of the animals has a damaged shoe. The time it takes to fix the straps should allow a quick visit."

"Good!" She turned. "Come, Dacia."

Dacia stepped back. "No, Domina. I'll not go near that cursed place."

A surge of anger sent the blood to Shifra's face. How dare she tell her no? Before she could speak, the centurion stepped to her side. "You're in my care, Domina. I'm the one to go with you."

They picked their way across the rough terrain and up the rise on which the temple stood. Shifra stumbled and Marius grasped her elbow to steady her. She breathed his scent, a mix of leather and sweat. She tried to shake off his hand, but he held firm. "Not until we're at the top, Domina. I don't need a casualty to worry with."

The climb proved steeper than it had seemed from the road. As soon as they reached the flat area that surrounded the temple, Marius released her. "Now what?"

"Before we go inside, I'd like to walk around the outside. It's not a very big building."

Close up, signs of neglect and decay became evident: gaps in the façade where scavengers had been mining marble from the walls; graffiti scrawled on the plinth. She stared at them, unable to make sense of the words.

"Your woman would approve of those," Marius said. "They're binding spells. Supposed to confine the demons to the temple."

Shifra found the Christian terror of demons difficult to take seriously. They should understand that demons—like all the rest of God's creatures—can do nothing without His permission. People who live according to God's law—whether or not they're Jews—have nothing to fear from demons.

Their circuit brought them back to the front, where they discovered they were no longer alone.

An ancient couple sat on a bottom step, determinedly shaking their heads *no* while a woman younger than they, perhaps a grown daughter, stood over them, apparently trying to persuade them of something. Their clothing marked them as poor country folk. Again, Shifra's mind returned to the honeymoon journey. She and Benjamin had noticed people like them gathered on temple steps, bringing offerings, asking for prayers, partaking of sacrificial meats. The temples had been central to their lives and now, the vibrant places that had been so important to them were derelict. She tried to understand what she was feeling.

Secure in her belief in the true God of the universe, Shifra could feel no regret about the decline of pagan worship. But if a Christian emperor could outlaw pagan belief, what might be in store for her own religion? Synagogues remained open in the Empire, but building new ones was forbidden. How long before Judaism itself was declared as illegal as the worship of Isis?

She followed Marius up the broad steps. As they crossed the threshold, something skittered across her foot, forcing a cry.

"Not to worry, Domina. Nothing but a field mouse. Places like these are alive with them."

The interior of the temple felt several degrees cooler than the air outside. Narrow shafts of sunlight pierced the shadows, creating a mysterious play of light and shade. The plinth that would have held the god's image rose several feet above their heads. Shifra leaned her head back until her neck hurt. The base was empty of its deity. "It must have been difficult to get that image down. I suppose religious fervor gave them strength."

Marius laughed harshly, "More like fervor to get their hands on the gold overlay. There's plenty of money to be made when religion changes hands."

A few minutes sufficed to tour the interior. Anything moveable had been removed. Even the brightly painted murals peeled in strips from the walls, baring the white plaster beneath. This time, Shifra led the way out.

Outside, the old couple still sat where they'd been, but the younger woman approached them.

"Can you tell me, please, do any of the priests remain here?"

Perhaps of an age, the woman was taller than Shifra by a head. Her skin sun-darkened, her clothing poor, but clean.

"No. It looks as if the place has been abandoned for some time."

The woman sighed. "I tried to tell them. But my mother begged until I could no longer refuse. If nothing else, I thought it might make her feel better. It's her arm. She cut it accidentally on a spade. I tended it as well as I knew how, but it's getting worse. She hoped to find a priest who would pray over it."

"No priests of any kind around here," Marius said. "Just a convoy of sinners on our way to Rome." He looked at Shifra. "That shoe will be ready by now." He stepped off the bottom step and headed back, clearly expecting her to follow. She moved to do so, but the woman put her hand out.

"Please, Domina, can you help us?"

Shifra hesitated, looking from Marius to the old couple. Then, to the centurion, she said, "Please, just a few minutes more. Maybe there is something I can do. I've some experience." She went with the woman.

The old woman's arm was swathed in a cloth. Shifra knelt beside her. "Let me have a look." As the cloth came away, a foul odor arose. The flesh from wrist, halfway to the elbow was red and swollen and oozing with pus. The old woman groaned. A startled sound escaped Marius. Shifra looked up at him.

"I think I can help her. But I need some things from the carriage."

Marius worked the muscles in his jaw. Shifra could tell that he regretted every minute lost. At the same time, she had seen how appalled he had been at the sight of the infected wound on the woman's arm. "Very well," he said. "I can move faster than you can, so I'll go. What is it you need?"

"Tell Dacia to bring her master's bag and a cup of unwatered wine."

"Her master's bag?"

"My husband was a doctor. I kept his medical bag."

"And you know what to do with it?"

Shifra felt her face redden. "I managed to learn a few things in the thirty years we were married."

Marius strode rapidly away. When he returned, not Dacia, but Goar followed, carrying the requested items. In addition, he brought a basket, but set only the bag and the flask down on the step beside Shifra. She un-stoppered the flask.

92

"What I'm going to do is going to hurt. I want you to drink this first. It may help you endure the pain."

When the woman had drunk as much as she could, Shifra went to work on the wound. First, she cleansed the area with vinegar, shutting her ears to the woman's cries. When the wound was clean, she applied a generous amount of honey. Next, she wrapped the wrist with a strip of linen. Finally, she slathered the bandage over the wound with olive oil. She turned then to the daughter.

"It's important to keep the area moist. That's the reason for the olive oil. Do you have any at home?"

"Yes, Domina. And plenty of honey. But nothing like that soft cloth you wrapped it with."

Shifra cut several lengths of the linen for her and gave instructions for dressing the wound. At last, extracting herself with difficulty from the family's expressions of gratitude, she joined Marius and Goar and returned to the convoy.

They found the vehicles drawn up in order, ready to pull out. Her curiosity renewed, she opened her mouth to ask Marius about the cart with the barred windows, but he spoke first.

"Best hurry. You have about ten seconds to get to the carpentum before I give the signal to move out."

She hurried, but she still wanted to know what or who was in the cart.

Chapter Eleven

The Barred Cart

Three days later, the party reached Ariminum, the final overnight stop before they turned southward to Rome.

Dawn had not yet broken when a gentle but steady shaking woke Shifra. She opened her eyes to see a shape kneeling by her bed. Dacia.

"What is it, Woman? It can't be time to rise yet. Go away!" Shifra attempted to roll away, but the handmaid gripped her shoulder, preventing her.

"Domina, *please!*"

Shifra's efforts to hold onto sleep failed. Her senses awoke. "Well? What is it? Why are you dragging me from my rest?"

Dacia sat on the edge of the bed.

"So many temples along the way, Domina. I couldn't sleep. I could feel the presence of the demons."

Shifra made a sound of annoyance.

"Sorry Domina. I know I promised not to speak any more of demons. Truly, Domina, I would rather die and go to the eternal flames than quarrel with you."

"You couldn't sleep. What, then?"

"I got up and went outside. The moonlight was near as bright as day, and I walked as far as the place where the mules and horses are picketed. I didn't notice any guards, but then I wasn't paying attention to anything but my own troubled thoughts.

"Looking for a quiet corner, a little grassy place where I could pray. I found a spot not far from the back of the cart with the barred windows. As I usually do, when I'm alone, I prayed in the language of my birth. Oh, Domina, I nearly died of fright!"

Shifra sat up. "Why? What happened?"

"I heard a voice."

A shaft of early light penetrated the guest room, revealing Dacia's wide-eyed wonderment. Her face was bare. The irregular scar on the disfigured side of her face gleamed dimly.

"As I prayed, a voice, a deep male voice, joined me in my prayer. In my own language! *Glory be to the Father through the Son in the Holy Spirit...*

"Please don't laugh at me, Domina, but I thought I was hearing an angel."

Totally awake now, Shifra freed her legs from the bedcovers and sat up. "Why would I laugh? I've never heard an angel speak, but I know they move among us on God's business every day. Go on."

"My own voice dried up, I was that frightened, but the voice finished the prayer. And then, the voice said, 'Who's there?' I could tell then that the voice came from inside the barred cart. I tried to speak, but I was that frightened. And then, before I could say anything, a guard came round the back of the cart and I ran."

"So you don't know who's in there?"

"No. Just that it must be a Visigoth."

"Did the guard see you?"

"I don't know."

Shifra expelled a deep sigh. "I suppose we'll know soon enough. The sun is up. Marius will be up with it."

When Shifra and Dacia emerged from the guest quarters Marius and one of his men were waiting. The centurion cast a long harsh look at Dacia. "I ought to put this woman in irons." He thrust his head toward Dacia.

"You, Woman! What were you doing by the wagons in the middle of the night? Why were you talking to my prisoner?"

Dacia looked beseechingly at her mistress. Shifra stepped forward. "What are you accusing her of?"

"Spying. Attempting to assist a prisoner to escape." Marius nodded at the soldier beside him. "Tell her what you saw."

The soldier looked uncertainly from Dacia to Shifra. "It was a woman. I'm sure of that. I saw her long white dress as she ran."

Marius whirled on the soldier. "You told me it was the serving woman."

The soldier recoiled. "I figured it must be her because a fine lady wouldn't be skulking round the wagons in the middle of the night. Sir." He backed away and again looked from Dacia to Shifra. "But now I can't be sure. I only saw her back."

Marius looked disgustedly at the man. "Say what you heard."

"I heard two voices, Sir. One was male, the other female."

"And?"

"And they were speaking the Goth tongue, not Latin."

Marius turned to Shifra. "To my knowledge, we've only one Goth in this party, and that is your Visigoth maid. How long has she been in your service?"

Shifra placed herself in front of Dacia. "Since she was a child of ten years. She is no spy I picked up in Milan at the last minute before joining this travel party. We had no idea what you were carrying in that closed cart until..." She broke off. Too late.

"Until when?" Marius shot back.

"Very well, not until last night when the man in the cart spoke to her."

"So!" Marius exclaimed, "Why would he speak to her and in her own tongue if she hadn't signaled him of her presence?"

"He heard her praying." Shifra said. "She was reciting prayers in her own language and he joined with her."

Marius scoffed. "You expect me to believe that? One of Alaric's men more concerned with Christian prayers than escape?" He moved menacingly toward Dacia. "Out with it. What did you talk about?"

Above the veil that now covered her scars, Dacia's blue eyes flooded with tears. She moved closer to Shifra and clung to her arm.

"She's telling the truth," Shifra said. "She thought she was alone. She was frightened almost out of her wits when the man joined in on her prayers."

"He must have uttered something besides prayers," Marius insisted. "He's had no contact with anyone but me or one of the guards who bring his food and take away his waste. You can't make me believe that he wouldn't have asked her for help."

Trembling, Dacia spoke. "He said, 'Who are you?' Before I could say anything, the guard saw me and I ran. I swear, that's all he said other than the words of my prayer."

Marius cast both the women a skeptical look and shrugged. "Very well. I'll have to accept your story. For now. But see that you stay well away from the cart if you don't want to travel the rest of the way to Rome in shackles." He looked at Shifra. "I have more than one pair, Domina."

With that, he pivoted and stalked away. The soldier shambled after.

***

Now that the women knew the secret of the prison cart, Marius permitted the Visigoth to be exercised openly. They had their first view of him at the noon break. Wearing only a simple unbelted tunic and no shoes, the man stood half a head taller than any of his captors.

"How sad he looks," Dacia said.

"Yes," Shifra agreed. "And thin. They can't be feeding him."

"They feed him well enough, but he leaves most of it in the panier," Goar interjected, squatting on the ground within earshot. Now that the secret was out, he apparently had no qualms about discussing the cart's occupant. He even seemed eager to tell them what he knew.

"His name's Roderick. Came into Italy as a boy, back when the eastern emperor Valens permitted a group of Visigoths to cross the Danube. It was Alaric's bunch, but before Alaric became chief."

Shifra frowned. "Was he captured in that battle Marius told us about?"

"Frigidus? No. He survived that one. But he was with Alaric at Rome two years ago. Only he didn't move south with Alaric after. He went back north, to your neighborhood."

The horn sounded the end of the midday break. Goar stood and stretched. Dacia stepped between him and the carriage. "Why is he a prisoner?"

Goar shrugged. "Bad luck. He tried to sell some of the booty he picked up in Rome. It had identifying marks they traced to some senator who wants to punish him personally. Says he has something really special in mind." He moved to remount the driver's seat, but Dacia persisted.

"What will happen to him?"

Goar shrugged again. "Could be anything. Nothing easy, I'll be bound." He grinned. "Some of those senators would make a barbarian look tame."

***

A few miles past Ariminum, the convoy left the Via Aemilia and the Adriatic coast behind and headed south towards Rome along the Via Flaminia.

Shifra's heart raced. Alexandria loomed in her mind as a place of new freedom and security. Thanks to Marius and Goar, she'd learned how ignorant she'd been of what had been happening in Italy in the years since her marriage. The all-powerful and single-minded Roman army she'd believed in hadn't existed for decades. As for the mighty emperors—a child of ten sat on the throne in Constantinople, and a spoiled man-child held court in Ravenna.

She laughed bitterly as she recalled the story that went round after Alaric's occupation of Rome. She'd heard it from Vibius. When aides told Emperor Honorius about it, his first thought was of a pet chicken he'd named *Roma*. When the aides explained that they were talking about the city, Roma, Honorius expressed relief that it wasn't the chicken.

Tears of grief and anger moistened Shifra's eyes. In the thirty-two years since she left Alexandria, Milan had gone from the culturally thriving seat of the Western emperor to a parochial bishop's domain. Her people had gone from citizens with protected rights to a barely tolerated class of outsiders. She dreamed of the Alexandria of her childhood, an exciting city in which Jews could achieve high office. She clung to what Vibius had said about Akiva's ability to obtain imperial transport for her. Being a Jew had not held back her brother. After the sorrows of Milan, Alexandria shone in her imagination like the famous lighthouse that stood in its harbor, a comforting beacon to the weary traveler.

The next morning's rest stop found them far from any farm or settlement, so Shifra and Dacia did their business in the bushes.

The weather was lovely, the heat mitigated by a refreshing breeze. Reluctant to reseat themselves in the carriage sooner than absolutely necessary, they strolled back and forth without straying too far.

Stopping near a milestone, Shifra pushed one foot against the base to relieve the tightness in her leg muscles. Dacia came to stand beside her. She nodded toward the cart with the barred windows.

"I so wish the centurion would let me speak to him. What harm could it do?"

Shifra changed feet and stretched the other leg. "None that I can think of."

"Look," Dacia said. "Someone is going in."

As they watched, one of the soldiers unlocked the door and went inside.

"He's not carrying anything," Dacia said. "I suppose he's going to take away the pee bucket."

Before Shifra had time to chide her maid for indelicacy, the sound of cursing came from inside the cart. The soldier re-emerged, shouting for the centurion. Marius ran to the cart, went inside, then stuck his head out for a moment to give an order before going back. The soldier he'd spoken to came running toward them.

"Your bag, Domina," he said, "Marius says for you to come quickly and bring your bag." Shifra stared at him uncomprehendingly for several seconds before she realized he was talking about Benjamin's medical bag.

Dacia, however, made the connection at once and had the bag in her hands and was heading for the cart by the time Shifra reacted.

Light from the high windows illuminated the interior of the cart, but the air was thick with the odors of several weeks of human habitation in close quarters. The prisoner lay back on a heap of straw and blankets, his arms extended, palms upward. His wrists glistened bright with blood.

"Bring water," Shifra said and knelt beside the wounded man.

"Here, Domina." Someone had already gone to fetch water and towels. Within moments, Dacia placed a brimming basin beside her, and Shifra washed away the blood before applying an astringent from the bag. The cuts were ragged, but not deep. Shifra had Dacia apply pressure to the left wrist while she did the same to the right. Soon the bleeding stopped. Shifra spread honey on the cuts to guard against infection, then wrapped both wrists tightly with gauze and strips of linen. Throughout the process, no sound came from the prisoner. Shifra leaned back against her heels and looked at his face for the first time. He was looking back at her from half-shut eyes.

"Many thanks, Domina," he said in Latin. "If I'd known this would bring me women, I would have tried it a long time ago."

Chapter Twelve

Amalia

Marius rode to the side of the carpentum next morning, before the command to move out was given. His manner differed from his usual authoritative and ironic manner. He seemed barely able to look Shifra in the eye.

He glanced briefly at Dacia before addressing Shifra.

"The prisoner will survive," he said. "The cuts were superficial."

"How did he get a weapon?" Shifra asked.

Marius shrugged. "A nail had worked itself out in the flooring. He scraped his wrists against it."

Shifra studied his face. He seemed to be in the grip of a strong emotion. His lips tensed as he spoke and his skin seemed pale under his tan. The scars on his jaw and above his left eye stood out more than usual.

He spoke directly to Dacia.

"I am satisfied you were telling the truth about your exchange with the prisoner." He paused, as if reluctant to continue, then spoke in a rush. "Today, at the noon stop, you can talk to him, if you like." He wheeled his horse and rode away.

The women exchanged puzzled looks.

"I wonder what happened to change his mind," Shifra said.

"Prayer, Domina. I have been praying ever so hard."

More likely guilt. The centurion's respect for Alaric must extend to his Visigoth prisoner. Permission to talk with a woman from his own people could only be a gesture of compassion.

***

Dacia could hardly believe it. Her prayers had been answered. She was to be allowed to speak with the captive, the man who spoke her language. She longed to talk to him about their people, their shared experience, but, because he was a man, her lack of confidence in speaking to anyone threatened to intensify. When the convoy stopped for the lunch break, she kept dropping things as she set up the folding table and stools and laid out the food.

When Varna's bounteous hamper of food ran empty on the fourth day out—hurried along by Goar's bottomless appetite—Dacia started collecting food from their evening meal to serve as lunch for the following day. Today, the spoils included cheese, boiled eggs, apricots, and honey for the bread.

"You've done well for us today, Dacia. The apricots are especially fine."

Dacia flicked away a fly with her napkin and glanced at Shifra's plate, willing her to hurry.

Shifra took a maddeningly slow sip of water. She looked at Dacia's plate and raised her eyebrows. "You haven't eaten anything. Are you feeling ill?"

"No, Domina. I'm just not hungry." Her stomach writhed with anxiety and excitement. Introducing food into it was unthinkable.

"Oh!" Shifra's eyes widened. "You are to speak to the Goth!" She stood. "Go, Dacia. I will put away the lunch things. The table can wait until you get back. You might want to take a stool with you."

Dacia grabbed a folding stool and made her way to the barred cart. She ignored the shouts and whistles of the soldiers she passed, thinking only of how she would introduce herself to her countryman.

The sole entrance to the cart was open and the prisoner was seated in the opening, an empty plate on his knees, a pewter cup in his hand. Dacia stopped uncertainly, about six feet away from him. He smiled at her and her heart raced. He was handsome in the way of her people, blond and broad-shouldered. She couldn't tell from this distance, but she supposed his eyes were blue.

"Nay, don't be afraid to come closer, lady."

Lady! Who would call a serving woman *lady?*

"Come closer. The centurion says we have the freedom to talk, but at this divide, we'll have to shout."

She halved the distance between them and set down her stool.

"Much better, lady. My name is Roderick. What's yours?"

"Dacia." The word came out strangled. She cleared her throat and tried again. "Dacia."

The smile turned to an angry frown.

"Dacia! What kind of name is that? Dacia is a country, not a woman."

A guard stationed several feet away moved closer, perhaps alerted by the angry tone. Roderick waved him back, saying in Latin, "Not to worry, officer. No danger. Just a cultural thing." The soldier stepped back.

"Keep it civil, then, Goth. And be quick with your conversation. They'll be sounding the buccina soon to signal the end of the lunch break."

Roderick looked back at Dacia. "Apologies, lady." He brandished the pewter cup. "Too much posca, I suspect."

"Posca?"

"The soldiers' drink. Diluted wine vinegar with plenty of herbs for flavoring. What I wouldn't give for a swallow of good Gothic beer."

Studying his face, Dacia began to feel more at ease. It was a kind face, marred by lines of suffering, but one she felt could be trusted. And the eyes were blue as the waters of Lake Como.

"You seem thin," she said. "Do they not feed you well?"

Roderick laughed. "They feed me like one of their own, lady, and that is well. No common man eats better than a Roman legionnaire. Plenty of bacon, cheese, mash, and cabbage. If I look thin, it's because I don't often feel like eating."

Dacia's next question was going to be why her name had seemed to anger him, but just then, blasts from the buccina sounded, signaling the end of the break and their conversation.

The guard strode to Roderick and took the plate and cup from him.

"Inside, you. And don't be making any more messes for me to clean up."

***

Dacia returned to the carriage and, when they were on their way, she opened Vibius's map and handed it to Shifra.

"Can you tell how many more days until we reach Rome, Domina?"

Shifra smiled and handed it back. "I don't need to study the map. I asked Marius while we were at Ariminum. He said from there, it was another five days of travel."

"Oh!" Dacia's stomach sank. Five and this already the second day. Tears sprang to her eyes. "Only four days left! Today, we barely had time to introduce ourselves." She fell back against the back of her seat and looked across at her mistress. For the first time since the master rescued her from the cruel family in which she'd received her disfigurement, Dacia felt resentment. For the first time, she discovered what it was to desire something for herself that was in conflict with her duty to her mistress. How much time tomorrow would she be forced to waste serving Shifra lunch before being free to visit Roderick?

**

Next morning, Dacia gave special thought to her face covering, fastening her scarf in such a way that she could lift food to her mouth behind it. She planned to serve her mistress as quickly as possible and take her own lunch with her to the barred cart. Smiling, she thought of the extra food she'd taken from the dinner table the night before, unaccustomed treats for Roderick.

When the horn sounded the midday stop, Dacia almost leaped off the seat. Shifra laughed.

"My goodness, Dacia! This isn't the first time you've heard the midday stopping signal."

Dacia did not respond. Tensing as the wheels rolled to a stop, she rehearsed in her mind the actions she must perform before being free for the meeting with Roderick. Help Shifra descend. Back into the cart for the folding stools, table, and food. Set up the table. Serve the food. Her stomach muscles felt as tight as leather straps holding up a mattress.

As soon as the wheels stopped, she jumped down, lowered the steps and reached up to help Shifra exit the carriage. Instantly, she jumped back in and pulled out the stools.

"Don't bother with the table," Shifra called. "Just give me my share of the food. I'll stay close to the carriage and use the steps for a table."

Dacia gasped in relief. "Oh, thank you Domina. Thank you!" She set up a stool, and placed a platter on the top step of the carriage and filled it with food for her mistress.

"Now, go," Shifra said. "Take the rest of the food and join your Visigoth for lunch."

Dacia bobbed her thanks and, with the other stool and the bag of food, hurried to the barred cart.

Roderick, already holding a plate heaped with mash and cabbage, smiled broadly at her approach.

"Greetings, Lady. I hope you brought your own refreshments, although I'll be happy to share."

Dacia set her stool down in talking distance and prepared to take food from the bag.

"Not so fast!" The guard strode over and snatched the napkin. One of the berries fell to the ground and Dacia uttered a cry.

The guard held the napkin toward her. "Eat one," he ordered.

"But I brought them for Roderick."

"How do I know you're not trying to help him finish what he started with that nail?"

Dacia frowned. She didn't understand what he meant. Roderick laughed.

"He thinks you've come to poison me, Lady."

Dacia's hand flew to her mouth. "I would never…"

"All the same," the guard insisted. "I want to see you eat one. And if you've anything else you plan to give him, you'll take a bite of it as well."

Dacia had brought two boiled eggs and four honey cakes. The guard required her to take a bite of both eggs and each cake. When she'd finished, the guard grunted.

"Strawberries! For the likes of him?!" Muttering, he returned to his post.

Fighting tears, Dacia looked at Roderick. "I'm so sorry," she said. "It's all ruined now. You won't want to eat after me."

Roderick rose from the steps and came to stand beside her. She looked up and saw the kindness in his eyes. He smiled and held out his platter.

"Please," he said. "I can think of nothing I would like better. It was very kind of you to bring these things for me."

Dacia shared out the food and he resumed his seat on the cart steps. They ate awhile in silence. He finished first. "Excellent strawberries," he said. "You eat well for a slave."

Not knowing how to respond to such a comment, Dacia simply stared.

He frowned. "You *are* a slave, aren't you? I assumed, because of your name…"

"Yes. Or no, or, not exactly." Dacia struggled to find words to describe her situation. "My late master freed me in his will. Only, the bishop in Milan would not permit me to have the money left to provide for me. Without the money, my emancipation cannot be completed. So I stay with my mistress."

Roderick frowned. "Is that what she told you? Your mistress?"

"No. That's just the way it is."

"I know how Roman emancipation law works. Even without the money, you can complete the process by marrying a freedman."

Dacia felt her face grow hot. She touched the damaged side of her face through her veil. "Marriage for me is out of the question." Fearing he was about to probe her reasons for rejecting marriage, she asked him the question she'd wanted to ask the day before.

"Why did you become so angry when I told you my name?"

He threw back his head and laughed humorlessly. "Ah, the name. *Dacia.*" He leaned forward. "Because it's a slave's name. You can't tell me it's the name your mother and father gave you when you were born."

The words struck Dacia like projectiles. Her mother and father. She couldn't remember the last time she'd thought of them or her sister, or anything to do with her life before the years in Milan.

"What was it?"

Roderick was speaking.

"What? What did you say?"

"What was the name you received at birth?"

She thought. Her mother's face swam before her mind's eye. Long forgotten memories of home, family gathered round the hearth fire. "Amalia," she said. "They called me Amalia."

The raucous call of the buccina split the air. The guard strode over and snatched the panier from the step beside Roderick. "Time's up. Back in the cart."

Dacia folded her stool and draped the empty bag over her shoulder.

Roderick, on the top step, looked over the head of the guard and smiled at her. "Until tomorrow, Amalia."

Dacia returned slowly to the carriage.

Amalia. The sound of the syllables uttered in Roderick's deep voice nestled in her ears like some precious little rescued animal, warm, breathing with grateful life.

"Come along Dacia!"

Her mistress, already seated in the carriage, called. "If you walk any slower, you'll root!"

Dacia quickened her steps. Goar snapped his whip. She ran, thrust the stool into the moving carriage and clambered in after it.

Shifra smiled at her. "Well? How was today's visit?"

Dacia didn't bother to remove the empty bag from her shoulder. "Pleasant." She leaned back and shut her eyes. *Amalia.* She heard his voice, saw again his smile as he said, "Until tomorrow, *Amalia.*"

"Is that all you have to say?" Her mistress clearly wanted an account of her visit, but her time with Roderick was private. The visit belonged to her, to Amalia. She opened her eyes. One thing she would share.

"The guard thought I'd come to poison his prisoner."

Chapter Thirteen
Lunch with the Visigoth

Shifra sensed something different in Dacia since she had been lunching with the prisoner. The past two mornings, she had taken more pains over her clothing than usual. During the two days she'd been allowed to speak to the prisoner at the midday stop, she'd spoken less to Shifra. When spoken *to*, she often seemed to be lost in thoughts of her own.

This morning marked the fourth day since their departure from Ariminum and the third day since Marius had given permission for the midday visit.

At the mid-morning break, Dacia spent most of the time simply staring at the barred cart, parked with its door facing away. Back in the carriage, as the morning wore on toward noon, she moved restlessly on her seat. Shifra noticed tears in her eyes.

"Dacia! You are crying, child. What is the matter?"

The young woman looked back at her with anguished eyes. "Oh, Domina. The centurion said we would reach Rome in five days from Ariminum. Today is the fourth day. I have only one more day to speak with Roderick."

Shifra understood. She reached out and placed a hand on Dacia's knee. "I know the words will seem harsh, but what cannot be changed is not to be mourned. Before you knew of his existence, Roderick was bound to Rome and whatever fate awaits him there. Take pleasure in the visits that remain to you. And think of the mitzvah—the good deed—that you are providing him. Before he heard you at your prayers, he had no one to show him kindness, only captors to remind him of his condition. Go to him today as soon as the carriage stops. Leave me my share of the food and go straight to him."

***

Dacia took her mistress at her word. She placed Shifra's share of the food on the top step of the carriage and hurried to the barred cart. The night before, she had divided the food and packed it in separate napkins so as not to lose time. This time, she also took a paring knife. If the guard forced her to taste everything before giving it to Roderick, she would slice off pieces, not bite them.

Roderick stood beside the cart, stretching. Lack of exercise showed in loose arm skin and an enlarged belly, but even so, he seemed more fit than the soldier guarding him.

"Greetings, Amalia. You are here before my cabbage and mash. And much more welcome, I will say."

Grateful for the face-covering that hid her blush, Dacia set up her folding stool and drew three packages from her bag.

The guard brought a panier heaped with cabbage and cast a disapproving look at her and her packages. "More delicacies for the barbarian, I see."

Dacia held out one of them. "This one is for you, Sir."

The guard's face transformed from disdain to confusion. His mouth opened, but no words came out.

"I'll eat one first if you like," Dacia said. "But I assure you they're wholesome."

The guard took the napkin and let the folds fall away, revealing glistening red strawberries. His eyes widened in speechless delight. Dacia opened the napkin of food she had brought for Roderick and drew the little knife from the pouch at her belt.

"Today I've come prepared to cut off pieces rather than bite them."

The guard reddened. "No need. Yesterday your mistress complained to Marius and he came at me. Says for one thing, you'd be the last person to want to poison a Goth, and, for another, if you *did* slip him his last meal, the poor sod would be better off than with what's waiting for him in Rome."

Dacia slipped the knife back into her pouch and turned her attention to Roderick. The guard withdrew to a distance and set to work eating his strawberries.

Roderick sat on the cart's lowest step. "It's a wise woman who knows how to tame a lion."

Dacia sat on the folding stool, her face hot with pleasure under her scarf at the praise. "No one likes to be left out."

They ate in companionable silence for a time. Roderick finished first and leaned back against the top step. "So, tell me, Amalia, how long have you been a Dacia?"

She laughed at the oddness of the question.

"I was eight when my family sold me. We were all starving. Our parents tried several times to cross the Danube to join the Goths who had gone over a few years earlier, but by then, the Romans were limiting immigration." She paused, unused to speaking at such length to anyone. Roderick nodded encouragingly for her to go on. "It had been a terrible winter and food was so scarce people were eating their dogs." A sudden rush of tears choked her words.

Roderick stood and took a few steps toward her, but the guard shouted for him to halt. The Goth remained standing. "I'm sorry to have stirred such painful memories, Amalia. I would like to hear more, but stop, if it is too hard."

She looked up through her tears. "No, Roderick. I want to tell you. You will understand."

Roderick resumed his seat on the steps. Dacia dabbed her tears with the end of her scarf and continued.

"My father struggled to feed us for as long as he could. In the end, he sold me and my sister Clotilde to a Roman slave trader. We had a younger brother and sister. He had to choose. I suppose he reasoned that because we were older, we could bear it better."

"And so, *Amalia* was no more."

Dacia nodded. "Father told him our names, but the trader called his merchandise by their country of origin, plus a number. He called my sister *Dacia Prima* and me, *Dacia Secunda*. Father set a condition that we were to be sold together, but in Rome, we went to different households. I went to Milan. I never saw Clotilde again."

They sat awhile without speaking. Having shared her story with him filled Dacia with an unfamiliar and welcome sense of satisfaction. Now, she wanted to hear his story.

"What of you? When did you come into the Empire?"

"My family came with the Goths you mentioned, those who entered with permission." His features clouded. "The Romans liked the Goths well enough when 10,000 of us died fighting the usurper Eugenius for them at Frigidus. Even Alaric was there, fighting on the side of the emperor Theodosius."

Dacia thought back. Her earliest memories of life in Milan were shrouded in pain, but once she went to live with Benjamin and Shifra, they became clearer. "I remember when Alaric came to Milan with his soldiers. Were you with him then?"

He smiled. "I was at Milan, Amalia, but not with Alaric. At Frigidus, I served under Stilicho, the old emperor's finest general. When

Theodosius died, leaving his ten-year-old son Honorius on the throne of the Western empire, Stilicho became the boy's guardian. I accompanied him to Milan to settle Honorius into the palace there." He paused. His eyes looked past her, as if seeing something. "Actually, Amalia, we may have passed one another in the street at some time. Milan is where I married and made my home."

Dacia caught her breath. Married. She forced her voice to remain indifferent. "Where is your wife now? Have you children?"

A muscle in his jaw pulsed. His eyes glistened. He opened his mouth to speak, but the blast of the buccina split the air. If he'd said anything, Dacia did not hear it. The noon stop was at an end. The guard hurried him into the cart and fastened the door shut.

With slow steps, Dacia returned to the carriage. Tomorrow would be their last meeting. At least, she might hear his story before he moved out of her life as abruptly as he had entered it.

***

Shifra watched Dacia approach, as slow and bent as an old woman. The girl's normally attractive light-skinned complexion had taken on the gray pallor of death. Suppressing the desire to question her about the day's conversation, Shifra showed her concern by taking the folding stool from her and stowing it behind the seat. No tears today, she noted. Sometimes sorrow is too deep for tears.

That evening, Marius called the halt for the night well before sunset. Shifra could tell from the arrangement of buildings—one large structure and three smaller ones—that they'd arrived at a public changing station and not a private residence. When she and Dacia had descended from the carriage, she looked around for Marius.

Still mounted, the centurion was speaking to a stranger, also on horseback. Unlike the travel-stained soldiers and slaves going about the business of setting up for the night, this person looked fresh in a bright blue summer cloak and unmuddied red leather boots. Even his white horse showed little road grime. He couldn't have ridden far.

Shifra turned to Goar. "Who's he?"

Goar spat, carefully missing her feet. "Joined us about an hour ago. Brought a riderless mule with him. I'm guessing he's a messenger from Rome, come for Roderick."

Dacia cried out, a sound like the sob of a child. Forgetting her usual disdain for the tattooed driver, she grabbed his arm. "When? Surely not yet. We have another day yet, and another night before we reach Rome."

Goar's tone shifted from insolence to conciliation. "I don't know for sure who he is. Could be he's here for something else." Cautiously, gently, he removed the hand gripping his arm. "I'll see what I can find out." He moved quickly toward the main building, where several other slaves stood awaiting orders.

Shifra watched as Marius and the stranger dismounted and handed their reins to a groom. The stranger walked toward the large building, but Marius came toward her.

"As you can probably tell, Domina, this is a public resting station, one of the bigger ones."

Shifra nodded, a spasm of fear contracting her stomach. The public waystations were notorious not only for filthy facilities, but also for robbery and rape. For that reason, Akiva had insisted on private homes for the nightly stops. She looked towards the large building thronged with travelers and staff. "It's not yet dark," she said. "Could we not continue to a better place before sunset?"

Marius offered neither explanation nor excuse. "This station has some small guest houses that provide more security and privacy than the rooms in the main building. You and your woman will be safe in one of them. Wait here while I make the arrangements. I'll send someone to conduct you to your accommodations." He left the women to wait by the carriage.

Dacia had ceased weeping, but she wore misery like a cloak. Shifra moved to her side and pressed against her in silent sympathy until their escort should arrive.

***

Two women came to the carriage to guide Shifra and Dacia to the small building where they would spend the night. The entrance opened on a windowless corridor. The women went first, one carrying a lantern. A soldier stood outside the first door on the right, and Shifra assumed that must be their room. However, their guides continued past him to the second door on the left.

The sparsely furnished room appeared clean. The servants, a middle-aged woman and a girl, had brought fresh bed coverings and a large pitcher of hot water. After nearly ten days on the road, Shifra longed for a proper bath. One more night on the road, and then Albina and Caleb's house in Rome. She could hardly wait.

Dacia, who had plodded like an old woman from the carriage to the building, suddenly commenced a nervous pacing, her attention fixed on the door.

"No need to be afraid, Dacia. Marius will make sure no one can harm us during the night. He's already posted a soldier out there in the hall."

The face Dacia turned to Shifra reflected not fear, but excitement.

"I don't think that soldier is there for us, Domina. Don't you recognize him? He's the one who reported me to Marius the night Roderick spoke to me from the cart. If he's here, that can mean only one thing."

Shifra laughed. "Surely you don't imagine that the Goth is behind the door the soldier is guarding now? What possible reason would prompt Marius to move Roderick from the barred cart to a room?"

The servants finished their work and left. Within minutes, a single loud knock announced the centurion's arrival. Dacia pulled open the door almost before the sound ceased.

Marius had found time to freshen up. He stood in the doorway, one hand on the hilt of the sword sheathed at his side, and made a slight bow. Shifra frowned, puzzled by his formality. Could it have something to do with the well-dressed stranger on the white horse?

"Greetings, Marius," she said, mirroring his manners. "As you can see, we are ready and will not keep you waiting."

He looked from Shifra to Dacia, his glance resting on the maid a moment before returning to the mistress. "Seen and appreciated, Domina." He paused, making no move to lead the way to dinner. Clearly, he had more to say. Shifra waited. He glanced briefly at Dacia. Then, to Shifra, he spoke quickly, as if to get it over. "I have an unusual request and you will certainly be within your rights to refuse. It concerns my prisoner, the Goth." A cry escaped from Dacia and Shifra turned. The young woman's gaze was fixed on the centurion, her clasped hands pressed to her chest.

Marius continued. "The senator whose goods he stole has sent a messenger to take him to Rome. Immediately."

Another cry from Dacia. "Why now? Why can't he wait until we all get there?"

Shifra prepared to chide the maid for interrupting a superior, but Marius turned and spoke kindly to her.

"The messenger says the senator is impatient to make an example of the criminal who helped Alaric desecrate the Eternal City. He has orders to take him back immediately, but I told him he must wait until morning."

A centurion overriding the orders of a senator? Shifra wondered why Marius would risk offending a senator. Then she recalled the dinner when Marius, having drunk to indiscretion, expressed admiration for Alaric the Visigoth. He must sympathize with Roderick. She waited for him to explain.

Marius reddened slightly. "I have taken the prisoner out of the cart for the night and put him in one of the guest rooms."

This time, the sound Dacia made indicated delight rather than distress. She had drawn the correct conclusion about the soldier in the hallway.

Shifra gasped. "He's in this building?"

"Well guarded, you can be sure. I've had a meal brought to him and he's asked that your maid might share it with him."

There. It was out. Shifra's impulse was to say, *Of course not!* But the pleading in Dacia's eyes stopped the words. Instead, she asked, "Will she be in the room alone with him?"

Marius spoke quickly. "The guard will be there."

Shifra sighed. As she often did when faced with a difficult decision, she tried to imagine what Benjamin would do. Dacia stood a-tiptoe, taut with silent begging. Shifra sighed again and nodded. "Very well. She may join him for the meal."

The guard opened the door for them, entered, and stood to one side. A table took up most of the space in the small room. The scent of roasted meat emanated from a covered dish surrounded by serving plates heaped with fruit and cheese. A sumptuous spread for a prisoner and a servant. Not even wine was lacking.

Roderick stood on the far side of the table. He was wearing a clean tunic and his hair looked different.

Marius turned to the guard. "You have your orders."

The guard saluted smartly and Marius and Shifra left the room. As the guard shut the door behind them, Shifra felt a sudden stab of regret. Leaving her alone with a man…But no. Not alone. The guard was there.

She followed Marius to the dining hall in the main building.

Chapter Fourteen

Roderick's Story

Dacia wondered if Roderick or the guard could hear her heart beating. She took three deep breaths in an attempt to calm herself.

Roderick smiled reassuringly. "Come, Amalia. We actually have chairs and a table for our meal. Please, sit. I will serve you."

Dacia sat as directed, her heart pounding and her stomach queasy with guilt. Not since she was a child, taken home by Benjamin to be tended for her injuries, had she received such attention. Roderick held the serving dishes for her and filled her cup with wine. His clothing and skin gave off the pleasant scent of lavender.

As her heartbeat slowed to normal, the food began to be appealing. She smiled shyly at Roderick, who sat down across from her. "Your hair looks nice," she said.

Roderick laughed. "Marius has laid it all on for me. Not just food, wine, and a comfortable bed. Before he brought me here, he sent me to the commandant's apartments for a bath."

A sound behind her caused Dacia to turn. The guard had opened the door to the hallway. A surge of dismay caused her stomach to clench. "She can't have finished her meal already!" She stared at the open doorway, expecting her mistress to appear and call her to their room.

"No," the guard said. "You two will have at least a couple of hours." He sent a leering look from them to the bed and closed the door behind him. Dacia looked questioningly at Roderick. He smiled.

"Another gift from the centurion for my last night. A bath. A real meal. And time alone with my beautiful countrywoman."

Dacia's heart speeded again. Alone in a room with a man. A thing she'd never allowed to happen since her rescue from the household of Faustus Ulpius. Gazing at Roderick's handsome face, she realized that it was not fear that sped her heart. Then his words penetrated.

"Your last night?" she repeated.

"Yes. A messenger has come from the senator whose goods I took from Rome. Seems His Honor has something special planned for me and is tired of waiting. The messenger wanted to take me tonight, but Marius put him off until morning with some excuse."

Marius's generosity could mean only one thing. Certain that Roderick was going to his death, the Roman was showing his respect by giving his prisoner one last night of creature comforts—herself included.

Roderick reached across the table and placed his hand over hers.

"Fear not, Amalia. I will not force myself on you." He stood, refilled her wine cup, and moved his chair around to her side of the table. "For now, let us continue our conversation. When the signal sounded today, I was going to tell you how I happened to join Alaric after serving Stilicho and the young emperor."

He leaned back in his chair. "Even after Alaric turned against him, I remained loyal to Stilicho. At Frigidus, he fought like one of the old gods. Emperor Theodosius rewarded his valor by giving him his own royal niece in marriage." He made a scoffing sound. "I've always thought that did him more harm than good."

Dacia laughed in surprise. "How could that be? That was a very great honor."

"Of course it was. Too much of an honor for a barbarian."

"Stilicho was a barbarian?"

Roderick grimaced. "I was being sarcastic, Amalia. Stilicho was as much a Roman and Christian as any of the men who called him a barbarian. Yes, his father came from a Germanic tribe like ours, but his mother was a Roman woman, born and bred. And for his entire military career, he served the Roman Empire. But as far as some Romans are concerned, one drop of barbarian blood disqualifies a man for the human race."

Roderick drained his wine cup. The muscle in his cheek pulsated angrily. Dacia tried to imagine him as one of Alaric's followers, spreading destruction in Rome. She'd heard the lawyer Vibius describe the attack in grisly detail often enough. But Roderick did not seem to her to be capable of wanton cruelty.

"What was it like, Roderick? When you fought with Alaric at Rome? My mistress's lawyer says the men who sacked Rome were savage barbarians."

He laughed humorlessly. "For the sycophants who surround the emperor, a barbarian is anyone whose parents weren't both from the senatorial class. Theodosius himself was Spanish-born and plenty of Stilicho's detractors insulted the emperor behind his back." Roderick sat up and took Dacia's hands in his.

"To me, a barbarian is someone who looks upon anyone not like himself as less than human. Yes, there were some barbarians with Alaric at Rome. But Alaric was not one of them. He gave strict commands before we entered. People were not to be injured. Looting was to be confined to public buildings and the most ostentatious private villas. He designated two of the city's largest basilicas as sanctuaries." A frown furrowed his forehead and he sighed deeply. He loosed Dacia's hands and turned to the table, reaching for the wine jug.

Dacia spoke to his back. "My priest said the Visigoths did terrible things to people during those three days."

Turning back around, Roderick nodded. "In any large group of people, some will be despicable creatures. Most of us followed Alaric's orders. Some did not.

"On the first day, as I headed toward a magnificent pillared dwelling certain to contain rich prizes, I passed a modest house and heard a woman's screams coming from it. I ran in and saw two of our men beating an old woman. A younger woman, source of the screams, stood pummeling the men's backs, beseeching them in God's name to stop. I pulled them off the old woman and asked them what they thought they were doing. They said they were making her tell them where her gold was buried. I told them to use their eyes. The house had nothing to loot. The place had hardly any furnishings, no murals, nothing to suggest affluent residents. As for the old lady, if I'd seen her on the street, I would have thought her a scullery slave, so coarse was her clothing."

He stood and peered down into the wine pitcher. "Still some left." He topped up Dacia's cup and refilled his own.

"What happened to the old woman?"

Roderick shrugged. "I took her and the other woman to one of the sanctuaries. The old one had been badly hurt, so what happened to her afterwards, I've no way of knowing. I went on to a much richer house where I stole the fine goods that put me where I am." He took a deep draft of wine and stared past Dacia, his mind clearly on painful memories. It pleased her to know that he'd performed a kindness in the midst of the sack of Rome. Still, she wondered what caused him to turn from defender of the Empire to a follower of Alaric.

Perhaps it was the wine, but she had the courage to ask. "What made you change, Roderick? After serving Rome with Stilicho, why did you go over to Alaric?"

He looked at her with eyes filled with pain. "When Emperor Theodosius died in Constantinople, he left two young sons. Stilicho's enemies gave them bad advice. They persuaded Honorius to execute Stilicho and his son and widow too."

Roderick stood, kicking back his chair and beginning to pace. Dacia saw tears in his eyes.

"If that had been all they'd accomplished with their poisonous lies, it might not have been so bad. But they went further. They spread the lie that every Goth in the empire threatened the safety of Rome. Honorius declared that it was the responsibility of every citizen to wipe out the enemy within. In towns everywhere in Italy, killing immigrants became a patriotic act.

"After Stilicho was killed, I made my way back to Milan to protect my family." He stopped pacing and stood beside Dacia's chair. A sob shook his body. She stood, aching to comfort him.

"What is it, Roderick? What terrible memory makes you suffer so?"

Breathing raggedly, he stood, head bent over hers. After what seemed a long time, he spoke, his voice clogged with grief. "I returned to our house and found it ransacked. My family, my beautiful wife and sons, lay hacked in a heap by the back door. On the wall, written in their blood, were the words, 'Death to barbarians.'"

Dacia sobbed and pressed her head against his chest. He put his arms around her. She felt as well as heard the words in her hair.

"I left Milan and joined with Alaric."

***

In the dining room in the main building, Shifra looked again at Marius. Seated several places down from her, he continued in an apparently endless tale about something that kept his listeners laughing and pounding the table. She had already gathered boiled eggs, some desiccated apricots, and two round loaves of bread for tomorrow's lunch. She was ready, had been ready, to return to her room and be helped to bed by Dacia. Her impatience came not only from fatigue, but also from worry that she'd been foolish to permit the girl to dine alone with the handsome Goth. Yes, the guard was on duty inside the room, but what difference would that make to a man starved for a woman? She looked again at Marius, trying to catch his attention, but still he narrated to his appreciative audience of sweaty merchants and couriers.

***

Dacia felt the sobbing subside in Roderick's body. Still they stood in an embrace. She wondered if the pleasure she felt in having his arms around her was something she should confess next time she had access to a priest. With a stab of dismay, she felt him pull back a little, but he did not remove his arms.

"So, my little Amalia. You understand perhaps why I renounced my allegiance to Rome?"

"I understand. And I do not judge."

He lifted his left hand and placed it against the side of her face. "Now I have a question for you. You told me that you were manumitted in your former master's will, but that you would not marry in order to obtain your freedom. Why is that?"

Dacia gasped. She felt that all air had left her lungs. His hand was on her scarf. She placed hers over his, to keep it from moving. He'd told her his deepest anguish. She could do no less.

"I…I am disfigured. No man would want me."

"Would you permit me be the judge of that?"

Dacia supposed he was looking at her, but she kept her eyes cast down. She did not speak. She could not. She took her hand away from his.

What seemed like several minutes passed. Then, his hand moved. The scarf slipped from her face. He ran his fingers across her scar, the hideous reminder of the night the master's son raped her and spilled hot lamp oil on her face. She opened her eyes and saw Roderick's returning her gaze. "And this is what you so fiercely hide from all eyes, Amalia?"

"Yes."

He lowered his head and brushed his lips across the scar where his fingers had touched. "Any man who could not see beyond this little blemish to the loving woman beneath would not be a man worth having."

He kissed her now on the lips and she returned the kiss with all her heart.

And then came an urgent scratching at the door.

Dacia pulled away and covered her face. They stood facing the door as it opened, revealing the guard. He stepped inside, shut the door, and resumed the position he'd held when Marius and Shifra left them.

"Best sit down," he told them.

Quickly, Dacia and Roderick resumed their seats. The door opened again and Marius strode in, carrying something in his left hand. Dacia could see her mistress and servants behind him, in the hallway.

"So, Decius, any disturbances?" The guard stood at attention. "No, sir. All quiet here."

Marius cast an appraising look from Dacia to Roderick. "All good things must come to an end." He signaled to the servants in the hallway. They hurried in and set about clearing the table. Dacia and Roderick stood to get out of their way. Roderick retreated behind the table. Dacia moved to one side, struggling to stem the tears blinding her. The same painful sense of separation she had when her father left her with the slave-trader threatened to overwhelm her.

The servants made swift work of clearing the table and were about to leave when Marius called out. "Leave the cup," he said. He walked over to the table and set what he was carrying beside the cup. A small pitcher. "A little more wine for you, Roderick." He fixed his prisoner with a look that seemed to hold some meaning. "But drink it only if you have the thirst of a wolf."

To the guard, he said, "Go wait in the hall. And shut the door." The guard obeyed.

Marius looked from Roderick to Dacia and shrugged. "I prolonged dinner as long as possible. Whatever remains undone must stay that way."

When Dacia did not move, he took a step toward her. "What are you waiting for, woman? The visit has ended."

She took one last long look at Roderick. He stood proudly, handsome head erect, golden hair pulled back in the Suebian knot of their warrior ancestors. He returned her gaze. "Farewell, Amalia. Remember who you are."

Marius opened the door to the hall.

Lifting her feet as if pulling them from quicksand, Dacia turned away. In the hall, she turned back for a last glimpse, but the half-shut door obscured both men.

Feeling someone touch her arm, she whirled irritably. Shifra held something toward her, a bag, Dacia's bag, the one she used to gather food from the evening meal to serve as next day's lunch. Absently, Dacia slipped the strap over her head. Marius came out. Roderick, unseen, called after him. "Many thanks, Marius. You're not a bad sort, for a Roman."

The centurion called back. "Nor you for a Goth. *Vale.*" He turned to the women.

128

"Still here, ladies? Best sleep while you can. We must make an early start if we are to reach Mount Soracte and the house of Mordecai for our last night on the road."

Dacia followed Shifra to their room and helped her mistress prepare for bed.

"Well, Dacia? How was your visit? Tell me about it."

Dacia wanted to hug the evening with Roderick to herself, not share a moment of it with her mistress. Yet, one thing she did want Shifra to know—Roderick's rescue of the old woman in the midst of the sack of Rome. She wanted her mistress to know that Roderick was no barbarian. Nothing else would pass her lips.

Chapter Fifteen

Roderick's Escape

Shifra was wakened by a commotion in the hall. Dacia stood by the open doorway.

"What is it, Dacia? What is happening out there?" She sat up on the edge of the bed. Dacia was fully dressed. Possibly had never undressed.

"I can't tell, Domina. The door to Roderick's room is open and soldiers are milling about in the corridor. And now there's Marius coming in." She stepped back, just before the door slammed shut in her face. "Marius saw me and sent a man to shut the door." She went over to the washstand. "No one has brought hot water. Shall I go fetch some?"

Shifra moved purposefully toward the bench that held her outer clothing. "No. I can manage without it this once. If we hurry, you may have time to see Roderick one more time and bid him farewell."

Within minutes, the women stepped out into the hallway. A lantern had been left on the floor outside the prisoner's room, which now stood open and empty.

"They've already taken him away!" Dacia cried, and hurried out of the building. Reversing roles, Shifra picked up the lantern and followed the maid.

Outside, only faint glimmers of dawn were visible. The wake-up signal had not yet been sounded, but the area around the vehicles throbbed with activity. The mules had already been hitched to their carriage. Goar stood beside the lead mule, stroking its neck.

"The buccina is about to sound," he said. "Potiscus here doesn't like it a bit."

Just then, the harsh blast of the horn shattered the air and the mules shuddered, except for the one beside Goar, which kicked and brayed. "There, there, Potiscus, lad, it's all right, see, now, it has stopped." When the mule had settled under his stroking, he moved to mount the driver's bench. Dacia stopped him.

"Where is the prisoner's cart?" she asked. "I don't see it anywhere."

Goar took a step back. He raised his hand and rubbed his mouth and chin before answering. Finally, he spoke. "We won't be needing it the rest of the way, so it's being left here at the station. Marius says we can pick it up on our way back."

Dacia stood at tiptoe, no doubt hoping to catch a glimpse of the Visigoth. She walked away, looking between animals and vehicles. Goar spoke to Shifra. "I thought because you ladies and Roderick spent the night in the same building, you'd already know."

"Know what?"

Before Goar could reply, one of the outriders passed and sliced at him with a short whip. "Get moving, slave. Get this carriage on the road." Goar ducked a second blow and scrambled up to the driver's bench. Shifra hurried after Dacia and brought her back to the carpentum. "It's no use, Dacia. The senator's messenger must have already taken him to Rome."

Dacia sat back in the seat and covered her face with her hands. Shifra could hear her sobbing. Best to let her cry herself out. Nothing she could say would comfort her. She would have to wait until the first rest stop to find out what Goar had been about to tell her.

131

***

The morning's drive took them again into the mountains. At the early stop, Goar did not linger near the carriage. Not until the noon break did Shifra have an opportunity to question him about what he had been on the verge of saying before being interrupted. Not until Dacia went to refill their water jug, did he stop avoiding her.

He followed Dacia with his eyes. "I didn't want her to hear what I have to tell you," he said. "This morning, I thought you already knew. You being in the same building and all."

"Knew what, Goar?"

He shifted from foot to foot. "We all knew that the senator's messenger planned to take the Goth on to Rome this morning. The night guard told me what happened. He had orders to wake Roderick before dawn and escort him to the stables. Roderick was still in the bed, so Decius—the guard—went to wake him. That's when he saw that the Goth wasn't asleep. A wine cup lay on its side on the floor next to the bed. Stains by his head and on his mouth showed he'd thrown up." Goar shuddered. "He was stone-cold dead."

"Poison?"

Goar nodded. "Decius said he'd seen it before—wolfsbane. Only they usually throw up more with wolfsbane. Said it must have been a big dose to have acted so fast."

"But how? Who would give him poison?"

The driver looked around and moved a few steps nearer. He spoke softly. "Decius figures Marius did it. Says he saw Marius bring in a jug of wine last thing last night."

Shifra thought back to when she was in the hall, waiting for Dacia. And yes, Marius had gone into the room carrying a small wine pitcher. He'd said something to Roderick as he placed the pitcher on the table.

Something about a wolf. "The thirst of a wolf." The phrase struck her odd at the time. The usual idiom was "the *hunger* of a wolf."

The wail of the buccina sent Goar running back to his post. Shifra followed slowly. What reason would the centurion have for killing a man already under a death sentence? Poor Dacia! Better for her to think of Roderick riding away, seated on the mule brought for him, not strapped across its back like a bale of goods.

***

As it happened, Shifra did not need to be the one to break the news to Dacia. The news had been on everyone's lips. She returned with the water in silence, took her place inside the carriage without looking at her mistress, and sat in stony silence the rest of the day. During the midday stop, Dacia left the carriage briefly to use the latrine, and immediately resumed her place. Shifra sought out Marius. She found him leaning against a tree, talking to two men. He saw her coming and waved the men away, but did not move otherwise or greet her. Clearly, he intended for her to speak first.

"What happened to Roderick?"

"He died."

Shifra wanted to slap him.

"I know he died. I even know how he died. I want to know why he died. At least, why he died last night. I know that death awaited him in Rome."

"As you say, Domina. He would have died during the next few days anyway. What matter that he died here last night?"

Tears welled in Shifra's eyes. What she wouldn't have given for one or two more days with Benjamin. "A day matters. He would have had another day to see the sun." She wept.

133

Marius moved to stand closer to her. He spoke, quietly, earnestly. "Do you know what a lamprey is?"

Shifra stopped crying and stared. "A lamprey? What does a lamprey have to do with anything?"

"Have you ever seen one?"

She wiped her face with the edge of her mantle. "Only at a distance, in the market. It's something Gentiles eat, but is not permitted to Jews."

"It's a sea creature, something like an eel, but bigger, with a mouth full of teeth. They are blood-sucking parasites that can latch onto other animals and suck the life out of them."

"Don't avoid my question, Marius. I want to know about Roderick. I believe that you made it possible for him to drink poison and I want to know why. Dacia needs to know."

Marius did not attempt to equivocate. "I brought Roderick the poisoned wine, but I left it up to him as to whether to drink it."

"But why would he do it? He might still have had a chance to live. Perhaps he would be sent to the games as a gladiator. Perhaps, simply enslaved."

The centurion scoffed. "Nothing simple about being enslaved, Domina. But no matter. That fancy messenger couldn't resist telling everyone who would listen what the senator had in mind for the Goth. His Honor had read somewhere about a punishment used by a rich freedman in Augustus's day. He decided he'd set it up and charge people to come watch." Marius spat. "The messenger told us how the senator filled a pool with salt water and stocked it with sea lampreys. Not just one or two. A man could pull off one or two. This pool holds a colony of them and they haven't been fed. The plan was to throw Roderick in and let the lampreys finish him off while everyone watched. It could have taken hours or even days."

Shifra felt weak. Her anger at Marius drained away. He had given Roderick the chance to avoid a death more horrible than beheading or poisoning.

"Time to go, Domina."

She nodded and returned to the carriage. Marius remounted, and the horses, mules, and wheeled vehicles moved out.

Chapter Sixteen
Mount Soracte

Shifra might as well have been alone in the carriage, for all the life Dacia exhibited. The ancilla sat unmoving on the bench opposite, staring at nothing. Even her tears had stopped, but surrounding her was an invisible barrier that forbade communication. Shifra withdrew into her own thoughts. Only one more night and they would leave the carpentum for the next phase of their journey. Not quite two weeks since they had set out from Milan, but it might well have been two months.

Never, until traveling with this military convoy, had Shifra been in daily proximity with such disparate people. Goar, the tattooed driver, who, as far as she could tell, prayed to fire. Marius, the scarred centurion who worshipped Mithras, praying beside his horse each morning as the sun rose. Roderick, an Arian Christian like Dacia, but a Visigoth warrior who had pillaged Rome. To her mind, all of them barbarians, lesser creatures with coarser sensibilities, uneducated in the finer things and yet—Goar's gentle touch with his mules and his consideration of Dacia's feelings, despite the fact she openly reviled him for his paganism. Marius, who spared a slave from branding and a senator's prisoner from a horrible death. Roderick, the complicated Gothic immigrant whose wife and children had been murdered by Romans and yet who had made the effort to rescue a Roman woman from the cruelty of his own countrymen. She wished she could talk about these things with Benjamin.

The landscape outside the window stretched flat away, but when the angle was right, she could see Mount Soracte rising in the distance, a bluish hump with a jagged ridge, like the back of a dragon whose other parts were hidden in the earth. Several miles back, they'd crossed the Tiber, but now the river had disappeared away to the east.

Their last overnight stop would be with Mordecai, a Jew who had been an acquaintance of her father. He must be terribly old by now. She couldn't remember ever having met him, but she looked forward to the comfort of being in a Jewish household again.

The House of Mordecai hugged the slopes of Soracte like a small city. In the courtyard, an army of servants swarmed the arrivals, directing and escorting. A tall, elegant woman in a pale blue stola, followed by two boys in short tunics, approached as Shifra alighted from the carriage.

"Have I the honor to greet Shifra bat Elad?"

Shifra smiled and nodded. Not since she'd left Alexandria had she been so addressed anywhere but the synagogue.

Behind her, Dacia handed down a bag from the carriage. The woman looked up at her.

"Don't bother with anything else. Felix and Taurus here will bring your things. Just show them what you want." Two comely boys in clean tunics sprang to handle the needed luggage.

The woman, who introduced herself as Abigail, led them up the steps and into a wide entry hall that reminded Shifra of the temple she'd visited along the way. Marble floors, pillars, and walls declared immense wealth.

"I know you must be tired," Abigail said as they moved toward the interior, "but Reb Mordecai ordered that I bring you to him before taking you to your rooms."

She stopped before a door flanked by two large servants wearing red tunics gathered by belts of golden links. They were not armed, but imposing nevertheless. One of them opened the door to admit the women.

Mordecai sat in a padded chair set beside a firebox. Shifra had heard of the device, but until now had never seen one. Larger than a brazier, it was designed to carry a good-sized fire from room to room as needed. Behind him stood a beardless young man in a toga. Despite the summer heat, a fur mantle enclosed the old man's shoulders. The translucent skin of his face resembled the silvery membrane on some large cuts of meat. He held out his arms.

"Welcome to my home," he said. "The daughter of Elad is as mine own."

Shifra bowed deeply. "The friend of my father is as mine own."

The young man at Mordecai's side whispered into his ear. The old man smiled.

"Young Aaron here urges me to cut short our introductions. He is my secretary and nursemaid, always fussing and making me rest." He half-turned to speak to his companion. "I'll tell you when I'm ready, Aaron." Turning back to the women, he shifted his attention from Shifra to Dacia.

"Who is this young woman who stands silent with an expression as dead as that of Lot's wife on the plains of Sodom?"

"This is Dacia, my ancilla," Shifra said. "She mourns the death of a friend, a man we met on our journey."

"I see." He looked over at Dacia. "All that is mortal dies, my dear."

Dacia shifted her position, but remained silent.

"Was his death unexpected?"

"Not entirely," Shifra said. "But we had expected him to live a few more days." She did not want to add to Dacia's suffering by saying too much. She hoped that Mordecai would drop the subject and tried to think of some way to turn the conversation. Their host, however, persisted in his attempt to comfort.

"Death is not always the worst thing, my dear." He held up his withered arms. "Do not think that life is a joy in a body such as this. Death often comes as deliverance."

"It's not just his death," Dacia cried. "It's the *way* he died." Mordecai cast a questioning look at Shifra.

"Dacia is a Christian," she said. "The man drank poison and she believes that act condemns him to eternal damnation."

"Ah. Suicide. What were the circumstances?"

Dacia sobbed. "The circumstances do not matter. He took his own life and that means God will punish him with eternal hell fire."

"Where in the scriptures did you read that, my dear?"

Dacia stopped in the middle of a sob. "I don't know where it is in the scriptures. My priest told me."

Mordecai leaned forward in his chair. "I have had many years to study the scriptures, my dear. I have also perused the new writings of the Christians. I have not read any scripture, old or new, that condemns suicide."

"But, my priest…"

Mordecai interrupted her.

"Never mind your priest. All truth lies in scripture." He leaned back again. "You know the story of Samson?"

"Yes."

"Then you should know that the Lord has not forbidden suicide."

Dacia frowned. "I don't understand."

"The story of Samson proves it. When the Philistines chained Samson to the pillars of their temple, he was a broken man, blind and shorn of his strength."

"But," said Dacia, "his hair grew back, renewing his strength."

Mordecai shook his head. "No. He had long hair earlier because he was a dedicated Nazarite. Before Delilah cut it, the hair on his head symbolized his dedication to the Lord." He paused. "Once cut and regrown, the hair was only hair."

Like Dacia, Shifra had always believed that Samson's strength had come back with the second growth of hair. She couldn't restrain a question. "Then how was he able to do push down the pillars?"

"He prayed to the Lord to restore his strength. His hair was long, but he lacked strength to push down the pillars. He prayed to the Lord to restore his strength." Mordecai closed his eyes and recited the words from the book of Judges.

"Samson got a good hold on the two middle columns supporting the building and leaned on them, on one with his right hand and on the other with his left. Then, crying, "Let me die with the Philistines!" he pushed with all his might; and the building collapsed on the chiefs and on all the people inside."

Mordecai opened his eyes and looked at the women.

"Would the Lord help a man commit suicide and then punish him for it?" He smiled gently at Dacia. "I do not know why your friend chose to take his own life, but I do know you must not assume that he is in Hell. Death has many doors. Suicide is but one. Each door has its reasons. Despair, fear, courage, self-sacrifice." He held out his arms. "Come to me child." He held out his arms to Dacia.

She went and knelt before him. He placed his hands against her head and rubbed her temples with his thumbs, saying something in a low voice. Shifra thought he might be speaking Hebrew. Then he sat heavily back into the chair. Dacia rose and rejoined her mistress.

Shifra marveled at the change in the young woman's face, from pain to something ethereal, almost as if she'd had a vision.

"We will talk again at dinner, Shifra," Mordecai said. "Until then, go with Abigail. She will see to your comfort."

Abigail led her charges down a corridor lighted by high windows. "First, the baths, and then to your room where you can rest before dinner."

A ten-minute walk suggested the tremendous size of Mordecai's house. When they reached their destination. Shifra gasped at the magnificence of the baths—a complete array, not only the three compartments of warm room, hot room, and cold room of the public baths, but also a steamy *sudatorium* and dry hot *laconium*. The man's wealth must be immense.

Two bath attendants hurried forward.

"Olive and Melissa will see to your bathing and take you to your room when you are finished. I'll come for you when dinner is ready."

The guests were laved, scraped, perfumed, and massaged into a state of absolute flaccidity. Shifra noted, with a twinge of indignation, that the attendants made no distinction in their treatment of Dacia, but served her with the same care they did her mistress.

By the time they'd passed through all the stages, Shifra's muscles felt like the soft flat pasta cooks wrap around some meat dishes. When she and Dacia had sufficiently recovered the use of their legs, Olive led them to a bed chamber.

Instead of the usual arrangement of a bed for the mistress and a pallet on the floor for the ancilla, the room contained two beds.

Dacia looked at Shifra in some confusion.

"Do they know that I am your ancilla, Domina?"

"You heard me introduce you to Mordecai," Shifra said shortly. "In this house, the ancilla seems to be the Domina's equal."

As soon as she'd spoken, Shifra felt a stab of shame. How often had she told someone that she regarded Dacia as a daughter? And yet, here she was, feeling resentment that she should be treated as equal to herself. She laughed shortly, recalling the treatment she'd been subjected to when she'd tried to help the stonemason in Milan. What was life, but an ever-shifting turnabout between oppressor and oppressed, all depending upon circumstances?

Dacia stood uncertainly by the door. "Is there anything you wish me to do for you, Domina?"

Shifra lay down on one of the beds. "I'm going to sleep until dinner time, Dacia. You may as well do the same."

Chapter Seventeen

Dinner with Mordecai

Abigail came to announce dinner as promised and ushered the women to a small triclinium. Shifra's muscles still felt limp from the baths, so she was pleased to see they would be reclining for the meal. To her surprise, the table was flanked by only two couches. Past dinner arrangements had usually included Marius. Dacia, of course, would sit on the floor when not serving.

The two burly men she'd seen guarding the door to Mordecai's reception room entered, carrying the host in a kind of sedan chair, followed by Aaron, the secretary. The bearers deposited the chair at one side of the table, removed the litter poles so as to place the chair closer, then exited, taking the poles with them.

Aaron produced a folding stool and seated himself behind his master. "Please ignore me, ladies. I have already dined."

Mordecai grunted. "He's just here to keep his eyes on me. In case I topple over during the meal." He looked at Dacia and motioned toward the other couch. "That one's for you, missy. Make yourself comfortable. My people will serve your mistress."

Mouth ajar, Dacia looked to Shifra for confirmation, then awkwardly mounted the unfamiliar seating.

Mordecai beamed at them. "I hope you have been well tended to, ladies."

Shifra smiled back. "Never have I known such luxury, reverend sir. You are too generous."

"The Lord has blessed me with material things. It is my pleasure to share the blessings."

Servers streamed through the doorway, bringing plates heaped with fruits, vegetables, and roasted meat. Although he ate but little, Mordecai recommended the different dishes and urged the women to fill their plates. Shifra wondered at the absence of Marius, but felt it would be impolite to ask. As if reading her mind, the old man provided the answer.

"I asked the centurion in charge of your convoy to join us, but he declined."

"Did he say why?"

Mordecai smiled somewhat apologetically. "Something to do with the accommodations. He suggested that the facilities are rather more, ah, liberal, than his men are accustomed to. He said he'd best remain with them to see they mind their manners."

"I see."

And Shifra did see. If everyone from Goar on up received the treatment her own waiting woman had, proper discipline could suffer. Iris and Vibius had often teased her and Benjamin about being too lenient with their inferiors, but even they had never invited servants to share the privileges of their superiors.

Dinner ended. The servants cleared the table and brought nuts and Falernian, wine served only in the wealthiest households.

Mordecai seemed in no hurry to end the visit, so Shifra ventured to satisfy her growing curiosity about this man who lived in such isolated splendor.

"How long have you lived here?"

"You would not believe me if I told you how many years." Aaron said something into his ear. The old man shook his head irritably. "Yes, it's enough to say 'a long time.'"

"It is an extraordinary place, more like a city than a villa or a farm." Mordecai nodded. "We are self-sufficient."

"I think it's wonderful that a Jew has been able to build and hold on to something like this. My husband was killed, Reb Mordecai—murdered—for no other reason than that he was a Jew. And when it came time for me to receive my inheritance as his widow, the local bishop withheld it from me. It could be mine only if I abandoned my religion and agreed to become a Christian." She studied his face, looking to see an answering indignation in his eyes.

His expression did not change. "What choice did you make?"

She stared. "The only one possible, of course. I relinquished the inheritance and chose the religion of my fathers."

He sat silent for a time. At length, he spoke. "And how have you managed without your inheritance?"

Shifra felt her face grow hot. "At first, for several months, I tried to make my own way in Milan, but I could not cope with the prejudice. I am going to live with my brother in Alexandria." She felt it necessary to justify her decision. "It seems that in Alexandria, it's still possible for a Jew to thrive."

Mordecai raised his eyebrows. "You are certain of that, are you?"

"Yes. My brother holds an important position in the imperial civil service. He's secretary to the governor of Egypt." She gestured at the exquisitely painted walls and marble floors. "Here too, it seems, a Jew does not have to choose between status and religion."

"It pleases you to think so."

Shifra recalled the rooms she'd looked into on her way to the baths and her sleeping room. "I have seen very little of what is here, but I did see what looked to be a magnificent library."

145

"Ah, yes. The library. I must admit to great pride in my collection of scrolls and codices. It is, perhaps, not so grand as the fine libraries your native city is known for, but it contains many a scroll that has no duplicate in the world. I confess, the library is the treasure which would grieve me most to give up."

"You must not have any Christian slaves. In Milan, some years ago, our most successful Jewish baker converted for nothing more than business reasons. All of his workers, who had been pagan when he bought them, converted at the same time. His Gentile competitors immediately reported him for owning Christian slaves. If that baker hadn't agreed to convert, his workers would have been confiscated without payment."

Mordecai pursed his lips and nodded. "A practical business decision. To have done otherwise would have meant ruin for him, his wife, and anyone dependent upon them."

His calm remarks surprised her, provoking her to anger. "He betrayed his religion. Does that not offend you?"

"Why should another man's decision—when it does not affect me personally—offend me?"

"Because you are a Jew! How can you not be offended? What happened to him could happen to you."

"It did happen to me," Mordecai said, still expressionless.

Shifra stared, doubting her hearing.

Mordecai went on. "Five years ago. Not slaves in my case. Taxes. A fellow from the tax office came round to update his records. I had always paid the same percentage as any Roman landowner, but this fellow informed me that, as a Jew, I had to pay a higher rate. The new rate would have driven me into bankruptcy within two years. Like your friend with the bakery, the choice offered me was to convert or lose everything."

Shifra felt tears spring to her eyes as she glanced around the room with its costly furnishings. Clearly, Mordecai had not lost everything. How unfair. Perhaps because she was a woman. Perhaps because the bishop of Milan had a harder heart than Mordecai's tax man. Her next question came with an edge in her voice. "It's plain that you were permitted to keep the regular tax rate. How did you manage that?"

Mordecai laughed wryly. "I managed it the only way possible. I converted."

Shifra's mouth went dry. A weight seemed to press on her head. "But, how is that possible? You're a rabbi, a Jewish scholar."

He smiled. "The people here still call me 'Reb,' but now it is a term of respect only."

Hot anger replaced Shifra's feelings of admiration. "You're an apostate! A traitor to your heritage."

"And if I had refused and stood on principle? What would have happened to the men and women who depend on me? Anyone who bought me out would have sold off a third or more of my people. My library would have been broken up and sold, putting an end to my work."

"But you betrayed the Lord of Israel!"

"No, my dear, I did not. I found a way to go on caring for my dependents and continuing my work. I gave the men in authority what they wanted in order to keep what I needed, but I did not relinquish who I am. What, after all, is this ritual of 'converting'? An empty form of words and water. From the eighth day I drew breath, the Covenant has been written in my flesh. They can force words from my mouth, but they cannot force belief from my being."

Shifra struggled to understand. "Words without belief? How can that be?" Her breath came short and her heart pounded. To apostatize? To deny one's religion and take another? "The Word is belief and belief is the Word. If words do not matter, why does Proverbs tell us to value good words and shun false utterances? The Law is written in words." She snatched at her stola and held the end of it towards him. "Look at this closely woven fabric. Look at the sleeve of your own garment. Can you unravel the threads and still be covered? Words and belief. They are one."

Panting, Shifra fell back on the couch.

Mordecai responded mildly. "The strength of your belief does you honor. You are still young and have much to learn."

Despite her anger, Shifra laughed. Nearly fifty, she considered herself far from young.

Mordecai laughed too. "Yes, compared to me, you are quite young, my dear. It remains to be seen what things you have yet to learn that may build new opinions in your mind."

Shifra's previous indignation threatened to reassert itself. "Whatever I learn in Alexandria won't make me believe that it is possible to pay lip service to Christian ritual and remain a Jew. The unchanging religion of Abraham is inseparable from the words that express it."

Laughing again, Mordecai fell into a coughing fit. When he could speak again, he explained.

"Judaism is indeed very old, but not unchanging. No religion exists unchanging across centuries of human interaction. Life in Babylon, life in Egypt—our every experience has imprinted the religion of Abraham with different customs for worship, different ways of interpreting the ways of the Lord." He smiled. "What is Christianity, but a borrowing of Jewish scripture and belief? In borrowing, they have altered and misinterpreted. They interpret Jewish scriptures according to their own lights and religious background. They write new scriptures based on them. They've mistaken the promised Messiah for a god. And yet, their stated creed begins with a line that no Jew could object to."

He looked over at Dacia. "Nor any Arian, is that not so?" Dacia blushed. Mordecai smiled encouragingly. "Is not the first line of the orthodox creed the same as yours?" he asked.

Dacia nodded.

"Say it for your mistress, please."

To Shifra's surprise, Dacia did not hesitate, but responded promptly.

"I believe in one God, the Father Almighty, Maker of heaven and earth and of all things visible and invisible."

Mordecai nodded as if to say, "See?"

Shifra objected. "But what of the rest? I've heard Dacia recite the whole thing. Everything that follows describes their beliefs about Jesus."

Mordecai shrugged under his fur wrap. "When I must attend church services, I recite the first line with great fervor. That's always enough to satisfy anyone who may be watching me for signs of insincerity."

"So," Shifra said accusingly, "you see no harm in the way the Christians force Jews and others to convert or suffer persecution."

Mordecai's benign expression turned severe. "I didn't say that. In that there is great harm. The orthodox Christians insist upon universal conversion to their ideas. They imagine they will always be in a position to coerce religious conformity in the Empire. They are wrong." He broke off into another coughing fit. Aaron whispered something to him, but Mordecai waved him away with an impatient gesture. He took a long drink of water and then continued.

"The bishops imagine that they will go on having the support of the government, but the Roman Empire will not last forever. Dangers to its stability abound. The emperor in Constantinople is a child. His armies are made up mostly of Germans, not Romans. And more

Germanic peoples push past the borders daily." His breath was labored, but his eyes burned like a prophet's.

"The day will come when some new people, not Greek, not German, not Roman, will adopt both the Jewish and Christian scriptures. Taking their cue from the Christians, their religious leaders will pick and choose the texts that speak to them, and again a new religion will be born. When this new religion achieves political power, its leaders in their turn will do their utmost to wipe out all other religions. The trouble with persecution, my dear, is that it teaches the persecuted how to behave when their turn comes."

He broke off into another coughing fit. Aaron spoke, into his ear and this time, the old man nodded. His last words to Shifra before the bearers carried him away raised chills along her arms.

"Time is a grand tapestry made up of many panels, each stitched to the next. Along the seams, ideas and customs—old and new—mingle and clash until the new order is achieved. We exist along one of the seams, my dear. It is a dangerous time to be alive."

Chapter Eighteen
The Milvian Bridge

The convoy prepared to move out at dawn. Marius moved among the vehicles, everywhere at once, listening, inspecting harnesses, and shouting orders. Shifra and Dacia looked for their carriage.

"I see it, there," Dacia said. "But who is that harnessing the mules?"

As they drew closer, Shifra recognized Goar, resplendent in a new yellow tunic. His usually unruly hair had been trimmed and the scent of lavender had replaced his usual aroma of sweat. The modified furca was gone from his shoulders.

"My goodness, Goar," she exclaimed. "How fine you look this morning!"

The muleteer grinned. "This is no ordinary place, Domina. Everyone in the convoy, slaves as well as free, received the same welcome last night. Baths and all the food we could eat." He stroked his tunic. "The bath attendant told me my old tunic wasn't fit to wear and gave me this one. I think this place is blessed by Ahura."

Aaron joined them.

"Reb Mordecai sends his regrets. He is not used to much physical activity and was too tired to leave his bed so early in the morning."

Although Shifra knew that her visit had contributed to the old man's fatigue, she felt no compassion for his indisposition. What sympathy did an apostate deserve? "He is very old," she said. "What will happen to this establishment when he dies?"

Aaron's eyes narrowed and Shifra knew she'd overstepped the bounds of courtesy, but the expected reproof did not come. The secretary's benign expression returned. "The succession of ownership has been secured," he said mildly.

Beside the carpentum, under Abigail's supervision, Felix and Taurus were loading Shifra's overnight luggage, along with two unfamiliar baskets.

"We'd best hurry," Shifra said, and moved toward the carriage. Aaron walked with them and Abigail greeted them.

"The baskets contain something for your lunch," she said. "And I have something here from the Reb. He wants you and your woman to have a memento of your visit."

She held out two *pyxides*, little glass containers of the sort one used to hold earrings and other small pieces of jewelry. She handed one to Dacia and the other to Shifra.

Dacia lifted the lid on her *pyxis* and gasped. "It's a ring. And it's gold!"

She slipped the ring onto her finger and held it out for Shifra to see. The ring's head was a flat oval with an incised symbol.

Shifra looked from Abigail to Aaron. "What is that symbol?"

"It's called a *staurogram*," Aaron said. "It combines the Greek letters *tau* and *rho*."

Familiar with the Greek alphabet, Shifra recognized the *rho*, which looked like the Latin letter *P*. "I suppose the line under the top part represents the *tau*."

Aaron nodded. "Mordecai says the *staurogram* is used by Christians to represent Christ on the cross."

Shifra shuddered. She never could understand how Christians could make an icon of such a hateful instrument of torture. "I see. The top of the P represents his head and the T stroke under it, the cross-beam for the arms."

Dacia gazed at her new possession with awed delight. "It's the sign Constantine saw in the sky before the battle at the Milvian Bridge!"

"Perhaps," said Aaron. "Some say this was the sign. Others say it was the *chi rho*, similar to this, but with a *chi* over the *rho* instead of a *tau*."

Shifra nodded. She had seen the symbol on an old coin. The chi rho, also called the *labarum*, looked like a *P* with a Roman number ten over the stem. She turned her attention to her own pyxis, wondering if her gift would be a Jewish symbol. If so, she would have to be careful where she wore it, unlike Dacia, who could flaunt her Christian symbol anywhere. She lifted the glass lid. She stared. "It's a rock."

Although set in gold and attached to a gold chain, the object looked for all the world like an ordinary stone that could have been picked up anywhere along the road. She looked at Aaron for an explanation.

"It is no ordinary rock, I assure you, lady. It is a stone from the Holy Temple destroyed by Titus in the reign of his father, Vespasian. Mordecai has long treasured it. He says someone in his family picked it up from the ruins of the Court of the Women, just outside the Sanctuary."

Shifra looked at the object with new eyes. Where before she'd seen a worthless rock, she now saw a precious relic worth more than the gold that bound and suspended it. A physical tie with the holy city of Jerusalem. The spiritual home of every Jew. *If I forget thee, O Jerusalem, let my tongue cleave to the roof of my mouth.* She would treasure it always.

"You may wear it openly as a symbol of your faith." Aaron said. "Only *you* need know its origin and significance."

Shifra and Dacia drove away from Mordecai's luxurious aerie at Mount Soracte in very different states of mind than they arrived. The handmaid sat in the carriage, gazing at her new golden ring, not speaking, but no longer sunk in sorrow.

As for Shifra, Mordecai had shaken her certainty about the life that awaited her in Alexandria. Yes, her brother was a Jew, but his work required him to move among Gentiles, many of whom were Christians. Would she be expected to interact with them? Mordecai's apostasy in exchange for his estate shocked her. And yet he continued to treasure his Jewish heritage. How was it possible to deny and affirm at the same time? She grasped the precious stone that now hung round her neck. She would never submit to conversion. Not if it cost her life.

***

Soon after the midday break, road traffic increased. Two-wheeled and four-wheeled carriages, farmers' wagons, small flocks of sheep guided by dogs and men on foot streamed onto the thoroughfare, all bound for Rome.

The landscape too gave evidence of the city's nearness with gleaming white tombs and farm buildings visible on either side of the road. As they got closer, they could smell the Tiber again. She felt her heart race. Almost to Rome! Then, only twenty miles from Rome to the port of Ostia and the ship that would take her to Alexandria.

The sound of the buccina drowned the clatter of the wheels. The call to halt.

Dacia also recognized the signal. "We've already had the afternoon stop and sunset is hours away. Why would we be stopping?"

Shifra looked out. The other vehicles were wheeling into formation. "Perhaps one of the vehicles has broken down."

Goar stopped the carriage and, when all the vehicles stopped moving, he helped the women descend.

"Why have we stopped?" Shifra asked.

"Centurion's orders. Only I thought we were supposed to stop a few miles further back, to avoid the crowd."

Marius, on horseback, rode toward them and stopped. He dismounted and handed the reins to a groom, who took the horse away.

"Has something happened?" Shifra asked.

Showing no sign of concern, the centurion stretched his arms and rotated his neck. "No. Just stopping till time to enter the city."

"I don't understand! Why stop at all? We must be nearly there."

"That we are." He nodded at the bridge that stood only a few yards away. "All that's left is for us to cross that bridge."

The man who had taken away his horse now brought a camp chair. Marius sat, stretching out his legs.

"Then why don't we cross?"

Marius met Shifra's angry glare with an infuriating smile and leaned back comfortably. "City statute. No wheeled vehicles allowed inside the city any earlier than two hours before sunset. Been that way since Julius Caesar. Course, if you're important enough, you can bring horse-drawn wagons during the daytime, but that doesn't apply to ordinary folk." He looked at the sky. "We've got about an hour to go yet. You might as well make yourself comfortable."

On the road, a steady stream of wheeled vehicles slowed and pulled over, crowding the verge and edging close to the carpentum. Shifra thought back to the only time she'd been to Rome, thirty years ago, on her honeymoon. She couldn't remember anything about such a law, but Albina and Caleb's house had been set well back from the street. *Albina and Caleb!*

"The people I'll be staying with! How will they know when we arrive?"

"I've sent a runner ahead to your hosts. He'll direct them to the station where we'll be stopping."

Shifra regretted her earlier angry outburst. She should know by now that Marius would have everything well in hand.

Dacia brought over a folding stool for her mistress and set it up near the centurion's. She set her own stool up next to Shifra's. Marius watched her sit and look toward the bridge.

"You, serving woman. That's the Milvian Bridge you're looking at."

Dacia gasped. "Really? The Milvian Bridge?"

She turned excitedly to Shifra. "This is a holy place, Domina. This is where Christ gave Emperor Constantine a sign." She held out her hand excitedly. "This is the sign! This is the very place where he vanquished the evil pagan Maxentius." She jumped to her feet. "My priest told us how, the day before the battle, the emperor saw this symbol shining in the sky with words written under that said 'in this sign, conquer.' And then, that night, Christ visited the emperor in a dream, telling him that if his soldiers would paint the symbol on their shields, they would be victorious. So they did and they were and the emperor became a Christian!" She looked up at the sky, as if expecting the symbol to still be up there. Then she looked at Shifra. "If you please, Domina, I would like to go closer to the river."

Shifra nodded permission and Dacia ran toward the bridge. Within a few feet of it, she dropped to her knees in an attitude of prayer, oblivious to a wagon arriving within inches of her.

"I don't think I've ever seen my ancilla this excited. Do you know anything about the battle she says took place here?"

"She's right about the battle. Took place on this very spot on the Tiber just about a hundred years ago—not on the bridge, mind you. On the river bank. Maxentius destroyed every bridge into the city, so as to keep Constantine out." He laughed scoffingly. "If he'd had the sense to stay inside the walls, he might have hung onto his part of the Empire. But he couldn't leave well alone. A soothsayer made him think he was destined to win, so he built a pontoon bridge and took his army to meet the enemy in the field. When Constantine's army pushed him and his men back, they'd nowhere to go but the river. The pontoons couldn't hold the rush. Most of the army drowned, including Maxentius. It was quite a sight, all those bodies bobbing in the river."

Shifra laughed. "If the battle happened a hundred years ago, Marius, how can you know what it looked like?"

"My old grampy was in Constantine's army. Just a lad he was. Lived to be an old man and never tired of telling anyone who'd listen about the days he marched with the man who whipped all the competition to become sole emperor."

"What about the business with the sign in the sky? Did your grampy say anything about that?" Shifra asked her question jokingly, but the look Marius returned froze her smile.

"The emperor saw something before the battle, all right. And plenty of the men did too, including Grampy. Not the day before, but a few days earlier. Two little suns shining ghost-like, either side of the true sun. I'm not saying it wasn't an omen. I know the gods send them." He nodded in the direction of Dacia, who still seemed to be rapt in prayer. "What irritates me is the details the Christians have added in the telling." He scoffed. "Greek words written under it. And then, a dream the night before the battle, telling the emperor to have his soldiers paint the symbol on their shields." He laughed and slapped his thigh. "I've been in many a skirmish, Domina and believe me, we didn't have a whole lot of time for shield-decorating the morning of the battle—even if we'd had paint and brushes in our packs to do it with."

He stopped laughing and briefly crossed his arms in front of his chest. "Maybe the Christgod *did* send the sun sign. No mortal can know the ways of the gods. But I'm pretty sure that—at the time—

Constantine believed the sign was sent by Sol Invictus, the Unconquerable Sun."

"How can you know that?"

Marius stood, drew something from a small pouch on his belt, and handed it to Shifra. A soft expression flitted across his face. "Grampy carried this for luck and now I do."

It was a bronze coin. On the front—a bust of Constantine wearing a laurel wreath and armor. On the back, Sol Invictus, standing, a radiate crown on his head to represent the sun, his right hand raised in command, and in his left, a globe representing the world.

"To hear the Christians tell it," Marius said, "Constantine was converted to Christianity by the vision at this bridge and never looked back. Fact is, that coin—honoring Sol Invictus—was struck four years after Milvian."

Shifra handed the coin back to Marius, who returned it to its place at his belt.

"I don't understand," she said. "If Constantine credited Sol Invictus with his victory here, why did he credit Christ with it in his later years?"

"Grampy said it was because later on, Constantine figured that the new Christgod was the same as Sol Invictus."

Shifra thought back to her stay with Iris and Vibius during the inventory. She recalled the paintings in the atrium that she'd mistaken for images of Hermes and Isis holding the infant Horus. Iris had corrected her. *That's not Hermes, Shifra. That's Jesus as the Good Shepherd. That's a lamb on his shoulders, not a ram. And the woman and child aren't Isis and Horus. It's the Holy Mother holding the infant Jesus.*

"What do you think, Marius?"

"I think the High God is unknowable. Sol Invictus, Mithras, Isis, the Christgod—all are faces of the High God. I think our Christian rulers insult the High God by insisting that everyone abandon all the other faces to worship only the one they prefer."

As a Jew, Shifra found the idea of multiple gods barbaric and repugnant. Could it be possible that Gentiles unknowingly worshipped the one true God at the heart of her own religion?

Surely not.

Chapter Nineteen
Rome at Last

The transport station inside the gate churned with movement and noise as soldiers and slaves hurried in every direction, unhitching draft animals, unloading baggage, and cursing with astounding lung power. Shifra and Dacia descended from the carpentum that had been their home for the past ten days and stood uncertainly, as close beside it as possible. Goar stood at the head of the lead mules, comforting them. In the midst of the maelstrom, Marius gestured and delivered well aimed blows and kicks, bringing order wherever he went.

Dacia pulled at Shifra's arm and seemed to be saying something, but her words were lost in the din.

Shifra scanned the scene before her, hoping for a sign of her hosts. Marius had sent a runner in time for them to arrange transportation. They might very well be there in the surging crowd and she couldn't see them. The constant movement of men and animals blocked her view of the street and prevented any attempt to move toward it. She followed Marius with her eyes, willing him to come to her assistance. As she watched, a civilian slave approached the centurion and spoke to him. Marius nodded, gestured in Shifra's direction, and walked toward her, the slave following. Unlike Dacia, Marius was able to make his voice heard.

"Your host's slaves are here with a cart for your luggage. A chair's outside for you." He shouted at Goar to join him and, together, they cleared a way for Shifra and Dacia to the street, where a chair and bearers waited.

As Shifra turned to Marius, she was surprised to feel a pang at parting.

"I did not always understand your decisions," she said, "but I thank you for bringing us safely to Rome. You are a good man."

Marius gave her the formal salute with which he'd first greeted her in Milan.

"Gods go with you, Domina," he said. He turned smartly and strode back into the depot. Goar stepped away to follow, but Shifra called him back.

"Domina?"

Shifra withdrew a coin from her purse. "This is for you, Goar, in thanks for all your kind services to us on the journey." She placed it in his open palm.

He looked at the coin in his hand and gasped.

"A solidus! Oh, Domina!" He continued to hold out his open hand, as if expecting her to change her mind and snatch it back. The gold coin represented enough money for a pair of leather boots or a warm woolen cloak fine enough for a senator. It also represented a significant percentage of the money Shifra had brought from Milan.

She reached out and closed his fingers over it. "Use it in good health, Goar. Farewell."

Then she turned to the waiting conveyance. It was a large closed *sella*, a type of litter that permitted passengers to sit side by side, rather than recline. The curtain had been thrown back and a woman wearing a rich embroidered mantle leaned out. "Shifra bat Elad?" she asked.

The woman's face was framed by the folds of her mantle, giving her dark eyes prominence. Shifra struggled to recognize the lively

161

young hostess from her honeymoon journey. The full, laughing mouth that she remembered had shrunk to straight, narrow lips and the dark eyes had lost their luster. Shifra leaned closer.

"Albina? Is it you, Albina?"

"It is. And I've come to take you to my villa. Do get in." Albina moved further toward the opposite side of the seat. Shifra climbed in and moved close to her hostess to make room for Dacia. As Dacia made to follow, Albina spoke sharply.

"Your woman can come behind us, with the baggage."

The bearers moved off briskly and the women did not speak again until they arrived at their destination. The porter, a huge Nubian, handed his mistress out of the chair. Shifra got out on the other side without help. She looked back toward the direction from which they'd come, but saw no sign of the baggage conveyance or Dacia.

The house was a substantial urban dwelling, twice as large as Shifra's former home in Milan. Albina addressed herself to the porter. "When the luggage gets here, put everything in the storeroom." She turned to her guest. Again, the perfunctory smile, so different from the genuine expressiveness Shifra remembered. "When your woman gets here, she can bring in whatever you need while you're here." She led her to a cubiculum where a servant was pouring steaming water into a wash basin. "Drusa will help you with whatever you need. I know you must be fatigued after a long day on the road, so I'll leave you to get comfortable for the night."

Shifra stared. She had expected a different reception from an old friend. Warm embraces, shared memories, food and wine. And where was Caleb? Albina's husband was the son of Shifra's old nurse. Her father had treated him like a son, setting him up in the weaving business. Older than Shifra and Akiva, he had never been their playmate, but he'd been a presence in their childhood. Surely, he should be there to welcome her. Was she to be treated no differently than a traveler stopping at an inn? *Here's your room, sleep well.* Shifra glanced at the sour-faced servant. Surely, Dacia should be here by now. She put out her hand to stop Albina. "Shouldn't the men with the luggage be here by now? They left when we did."

Albina shrugged. "We weren't pushing a heavy cart. I'll send your girl to you when they get here." She paused on her way out. "Meanwhile, Drusa will bring you something to eat. Sleep well."

***

The luggage—and a bedraggled Dacia—arrived well after sunset. The sullen Drusa had brought and cleared away a meal and readied Shifra for bed. Now, she brought Dacia to the cubiculum.

Shifra's first instinct was to scold at the delay, but as she looked at Dacia's face in the lamplight, she recognized distress and fatigue. As she seated her on the bed and sat beside her, she heard the girl's stomach growl. She must not have eaten since midday. "You, Drusa. Go to the kitchen. Bring food for my woman. Bread. Fruit. Cheese."

"Mistress doesn't allow servants to have food between meals. You miss dinner, you don't eat. Besides, Cook's gone to bed."

Shifra stood and summoned her most commanding tones. "If you do not want a beating, you will go to the kitchen at once and bring the food as I have asked. You can tell your mistress that it is for me. Go!"

Drusa fled. Shifra sat back down beside Dacia.

"What took you so long? Why would men with a wheeled cart take so much longer to get here than the bearers who brought me?"

Dacia held her head between her hands. "Horrible creatures. Horrible, horrible. They stopped three times for wine and never for a minute did they stop saying disgusting things. I was afraid they…" The rest of her words were lost in tears. Shifra held her close and murmured comforting words until Drusa returned with bread, fruit, and even a small flask of wine.

"Will that be all, Domina?"

"I do not see where my ancilla will sleep. Bring bedding." By the time the girl returned with a pallet, sheets and pillows, Dacia had recovered sufficiently to eat and drink. When she'd had her fill, she lay down on the pallet and was asleep in minutes.

Lying in bed, Shifra sighed deeply. She had been looking forward to spending several days in Rome with her old friend, revisiting places she had seen with Benjamin all those years ago. Now all she wanted was to move on to Ostia and the ship that would take her to Alexandria and the sanctuary of her brother's house.

Part Three

From Ostia to Alexandria

Chapter Twenty

Old friends, New Impressions

Three days after the disappointing welcome in Rome, Shifra and Dacia were again on the road, this time, to the port of Ostia, where they would stay with the daughter of Vibius and Iris until before boarding a ship for Alexandria. The noise of iron wheels on stone made conversation impossible, so both women sat absorbed in their own thoughts. Shifra struggled to understand the cold treatment she'd received from Albina and Caleb in Rome.

From the time she decided to leave Milan, she'd imagined seeing them again—revisiting landmarks and enjoying long conversations as they shared happy memories of Benjamin. Instead, the days had transpired into a stiff round of uncomfortable meals, talking about the weather, the immigrant problem with the Goths, and the ever-increasing costs of supplies and shipping. Albina was courteous, if distant, but Caleb hardly put in an appearance.

Their sole outing during her stay in Rome was to the Salarian Gate to view the remaining evidence of Alaric's sack of Rome little more than two years previously. The parklands surrounding the magnificent tomb of Augustus had apparently served as a campground for the three days the Goths occupied the city. They'd stripped trees of low branches and churned the lawn into a muddy rutted expanse. Caleb's comments then had been his longest utterance to her for the entire visit.

"It could have been much worse. The main target of their looting was the homes of the wealthy. Alaric forbade his men to loot the churches or to harm anyone who sought sanctuary in them."

After that singular outing, Caleb left the house before breakfast and returned halfway through dinner. On Shifra's last evening, he missed dinner altogether. Stung by his absence, she broke her resolve not to ask personal questions.

"Talk to me, Albina. Tell me why Caleb is avoiding me. He spent so much time in our house when I was growing up that I thought he was part of our family. What can possibly have happened that he cannot bear to look at me?"

A sudden rush of red suffused Albina's face. "Oh, Shifra, I cannot tell you why. Only that it has something to do with what your father meant to him. Your father was his hero. Whenever he had a decision to make with the business, he asked himself, 'What would Elad do?' In his eyes, your father was the epitome of the competent, honest businessman. Always, it was 'What would Elad do?'" She scoffed. "Sometimes I would get so angry when he said that. 'Do what *Caleb* would do,' I'd say."

Shifra waited for her to continue, but she said no more. Shifra wanted to shake her. "What does any of that have to do with why Caleb has avoided me this whole time?"

Albina returned Shifra's angry glare with a look of infinite sadness. "Four years ago, he faced an enormous decision, one that would determine whether he could continue with the business or lose everything." Her tears glistened in the lamp light. "The decision he made saved the business, but, because of it, he could not face your father and therefore cannot face you."

Shifra shook her head in bewilderment. "My father loved Caleb. What kind of business decision could be so terrible as to change that?"

Albina sighed. "Caleb asked me to tell you that it is not lack of respect that keeps him from seeing you. Rather it is an excess of it." The words had released a torrent of tears. No amount of pleading could persuade Albina to reveal the nature of the business decision that tormented her husband.

A change in the sound of the wheels drew Shifra back to her surroundings. Ahead, she could see the walls of Ostia. The carriage slowed as they passed through the gates and rumbled to a halt at the rental depot.

Shifra and Dacia descended and watched as the luggage was unloaded and stacked beside them. Caleb had sent their trunks on ahead to their hosts' home.

Not as large as the transportation depot at Rome, the one at Ostia still managed to present a picture of chaos. Porters shifted luggage and passengers jostled their way to a line of vehicles waiting in the late afternoon sun. Unlike Rome, Ostia had no law against daytime wheeled-traffic.

The women stood beside their bags, scanning the faces in the crowd. The rest of their things would be at Lucretia's house by now.

Shifra frowned. "I'm not sure I'll recognize Lucretia after all these years. Last time I saw her, at her wedding, she was only sixteen." Someone touched Shifra's arm and she whirled to see a woman in a bright yellow tunic belted with an equally bright green sash.

"Aunt Shifra?"

"Lucretia?!"

"Please! *Lucretia* is such an old-fashioned name! Father and his 'tradition'. He's sooo old-fashioned. Everyone here calls me *Lucia*." She gave Shifra a hug that squeezed the breath from her and then leaned back, holding her at arms' length. "You look wonderful, Aunt Shifra."

Her smile suddenly altered to a frown of consternation. "Oh, but I was so sorry when mother wrote to me about Uncle Benjamin. He was so lovely to me growing up. Whoever did that to him should be sent to the Sicilian mines."

Talking nonstop, Lucia directed her driver with hand gestures, accomplishing the loading of luggage and helping the women mount to the passenger bench.

As the cart moved away from the depot, Lucia explained her husband's absence. "Quintus is at the warehouse, overseeing a huge shipment of wine and olive oil that must be kept safe until it can be loaded. He'll be home for dinner and is looking forward to meeting you."

Chapter Twenty-One
Local Landmarks

Shifra's welcome in Ostia was everything that Albina's had not been in Rome. The old feelings of affection she'd had for the girl who had been her own children's playmate in Milan rekindled.

Lucia's husband, Quintus, like his father-in-law, trained as a lawyer, but now held the position of *curator* for the largest warehouse in the port city. Every bit as charming and as lively as his wife, Quintus greeted Shifra with an embrace. "I have booked places for you and your woman on *The Queen of Heaven*. The cabins were already reserved, so I've arranged for a tent on the deck."

Shifra could not restrain a sound of disappointment. "Is that safe?"

Quintus laughed. "Perfectly safe. And, in my opinion, much more comfortable. Cabins below decks are stuffy and smelly. On deck, you'll have fresh air and be surrounded by plenty of people."

"When does it sail?"

"Depends upon how long it takes to load. Anywhere from three to five days. I'll be notified when it is time for you to board."

Three to five days. The three days she'd passed in Rome had felt like a month. Shifra's dismay must have shown on her face, because Lucia laughed and patted her hand.

"Never fear, Aunt Shifra. The wait will pass quickly. There's a lot to see in our little town. Quintus and I plan to show you everything we can in the time you have."

Shifra's hosts were as good as their word, even including Dacia in their plans.

On the first day after their arrival, they toured some of the *horrea*, the famous storage houses along the Tiber for goods on their way to and from Rome. Sizes varied. The Imperial *horreum* that Quintus managed was enormous, with ramps leading from the courtyard to different levels for wet and dry storage. Under a raised floor, enclosed by thick walls, grain waited for transport. Another level held huge amphorae containing wine and oil.

For lunch, they stopped at a riverside food vendor where they could watch cargos being loaded and off-loaded with the help of pulleys attached to wheels turned by men. "The devices are called 'kneeling storks,'" Quintus told them. "They save a lot of time."

That evening, at dinner, Lucia and Quintus laid out their plans for the following day.

"If it's not against your principles, Aunt Shifra, tomorrow, we'd like to show you the old temple of Hercules. The treasures have been removed, but the building is still there and the grounds are kept up."

"I'm surprised to hear that. In Milan, the temples have long served as stone quarries for other buildings." Bitterness clouded her memory. "The bishops of Milan were no friends to synagogues, either." She looked at her hosts. Like Vibius and Iris, Quintus and Lucia had converted from paganism to orthodox Christianity. She didn't know how strongly they felt about their new religion. They waited for her to explain, so she did.

"Eight years after Benjamin and I settled in Milan, a Christian mob destroyed the synagogue at Callinicum. Benjamin's brother Simon was living there at the time. The first Theodosius was emperor and

Simon's first letter to us about the outrage told how the emperor immediately ordered the Christian bishop to rebuild the synagogue and refurnish it."

Quintus nodded approval. "The only just act for the emperor of a diverse empire."

Lucia's husband wasn't much older than Lucia—who'd been a toddler at the time of Callinicum. Much had changed in those thirty years since they were children.

"Back then," Shifra explained, "the Empire had only one emperor. Whenever he was in Italy, he stayed in Milan and attended Bishop Ambrose's church. When Ambrose heard about the command to rebuild the synagogue, he urged the emperor to rescind the order. He said that the bishop of Callinicum should not be forced to rebuild the synagogue because Jews had burned churches when Julian was Emperor and no one made them build them back. He told the emperor that synagogues deserved to be destroyed because they were houses of unbelief and despised of God. He told Theodosius that if he forced Christians to rebuild the one at Callinicum, he would be risking his own salvation."

Quintus grinned wryly. "You've got to admit that bishops have an advantage even an emperor can't counter—the threat of eternal hellfire."

Shifra was not amused. Lucia left her seat and hugged her.

"What happened then wasn't fair, Aunt Shifra, but nothing's to be done about it now. The Jews of Ostia, as we will show you tomorrow, are still blessed with a magnificent synagogue that has been standing since the reign of Claudius. We'll show you the synagogue and the temple of Hercules in the morning, and in the afternoon..."

"Wait!" Quintus held up a hand. "I thought that was meant to be a surprise."

Lucia made a face. "Surprises are like tickling. Not everyone can stand them. Let's give Aunt Shifra the chance to decline."

***

The surprise proved to be a visit to Ostia's magnificent theater, which dated back to the reign of Augustus. When Dacia learned that the next day's outing would include not only a synagogue and a pagan temple, but a stage play as well, she begged to be excused.

Quintus showed off the immense red brick structure with a proprietary pride.

"Not many cities the size of Ostia can boast a theater this grand. The emperor Commodus enlarged it back in his day and actually fought here as a gladiator."

They passed through the huge red brick entrance and took seats in the first tier, which offered an excellent view of the stage and ornamented back wall.

Lucia led the way, clearly excited at the prospect of the play they would be seeing. "I can't believe your woman not wanting to come. Did you tell her it was a play by Terence? And it's in Latin, not Greek."

"A priest told her that theater performances are wicked and that Christians who go to them should be forbidden the sacraments." Shifra smiled. mischievously. "If such is the case, how is it that you and Quintus are here?"

Lucia straightened primly in her seat. "We're Christians, but we're not fanatics. We don't go to displays that feature naked women or sexual performances, but there's nothing wrong with a good play that teaches us about the human condition."

The play, *The Self-Tormentor,* told the story of two fathers and their disobedient sons. The title character was a father whose controlling behavior had driven his only son away. To punish himself, the father sold all his possessions, including all but one slave, and bought a farm on which he did daily hard labor. Supposedly a comedy, the play left Shifra in a melancholy mood, thinking about her own son and wondering if she would ever see him again.

***

That evening, at dinner, word came that the *Queen of Heaven* was ready to depart. Shifra thanked her hosts for their gracious treatment during her stay.

"It has meant more to me than merely passing time in a pleasant way. After the way Albina and Caleb treated me as an inconvenience, leaving me alone for hours and hardly exchanging a word about anything but the weather, I didn't expect such a welcome here as you have given me. Caleb acted as if he couldn't bear to look at me." Hot tears stung her cheeks. "I'd always considered them close and dear friends. Caleb especially. He lived with us when he was a boy." She paused, looking from one to the other. "I arrived here certain that you, who barely know me, would see me as a nuisance."

Lucia hurried to her side and gently wiped her tears with her napkin. "Don't be silly, Aunt Shifra. You were an important part of my childhood. I remember how you and Mira and Mother spent time together and took turns looking after us children. Those were lovely times. I feel so fortunate that I've had the chance to take care of you for these few days. And Quintus..." She smiled at her husband. "Quintus says he's glad to finally meet the 'aunt' I'm always talking about."

Quintus nodded. "We'd been married a year before I realized that you weren't really her mother's sister. If you knew how many times Lucia has quoted you about any number of things—your likes, your dislikes, what you think about Bishop Ambrose—you wouldn't say I barely know you."

Shifra laughed, and they resumed their meal, Lucia recalling childhood highlights and Quintus telling funny stories about his work as manager of the warehouses. The humbling experience with Albina and Caleb finally dissipated in intensity and Shifra basked in feelings of familial acceptance. As the meal ended and they stood to go to their rooms for the night, she again expressed bewilderment about her cold reception in the home of Albina and Caleb.

Quintus spoke close to Lucia's ear. She nodded and resumed her seat. Quintus motioned for Shifra to sit. "I can see that the way your old friends treated you is going to continue to gnaw at your peace of mind. I believe I can help you understand Caleb's behavior."

Shifra sat. "How do you know Caleb?"

"My work. Your friend Caleb moves a great deal of textiles through the warehouses here and in Portus. I'm not well acquainted with him, but I know him by sight, and his troubles a few years back made for hot gossip on the wharfs." He paused and studied Shifra's face. "You said that he didn't seem to want to talk to you."

"He barely said hello. When he did speak to me, he looked everywhere but at me. The one time he joined us for dinner, he left early, 'to attend to business.' This was so unlike the Caleb I had known. 'Magpie Caleb,' Benjamin called him during our visit, because he never stopped talking."

Quintus spoke slowly, quietly, as if choosing each word. "Caleb's weaving business is one of the largest in Rome. His factory is staffed with thirty skilled weavers, three dyers, and ten all-purpose slaves. His production rivals some of the state-run facilities." He pushed around a walnut that had not been cleared from the table. "Do you remember how surprised you were that the temple to Hercules is still standing, despite the law forbidding pagan worship?"

Shifra nodded. "The only temples I saw along the way were in a ruined state."

"The Empire is a big place. The emperors and the bishops can issue their edicts, but not every law can be enforced everywhere. There's a law that forbids the building of new synagogues. Yet, many a crumbling synagogue has been 'restored' like new. There's a law that forbids Jews to own slaves. In some places, the authorities interpret that as Christian slaves and permit Jews to own non-Christian slaves."

Shifra nodded again. "That was our case in Milan. But what has any of this have to do with Caleb?"

"His business depends upon slave-labor. Four years ago, one of his slaves became a Christian and converted almost all of the others. Almost immediately, other weaving companies—owned by Christians—clamored for the weavers Caleb could no longer own by law. The authorities told him that the only way he could keep them would be to become a Christian himself."

Shifra stared. Her heart pounded and her mouth went dry. She felt as she had once when walking on a dark street and heard footsteps behind her.

"And did he? Did he become a Christian?"

Quintus shrugged. "It was convert or lose the business he'd spent thirty years building."

Shifra's thoughts flew to her father. He'd taken Caleb under his wing as an orphan of fourteen, taught him the import business, loved him like a son. She sighed and nodded. "He was ashamed to face me."

Quintus spread his hands as if to placate her on Caleb's behalf. "He made the only decision possible. They would have lost everything, the factory, their villa, everything."

Shifra's lips tightened. She could not agree that Caleb had made the only decision possible. Hadn't she given up financial independence rather than apostatize? She shook her head to clear it of the memory. Another twelve days or so and she would be safe in the home of her brother, Akiva. A Jewish home that kept to the faith of its fathers.

Chapter Twenty-Two
Isidore

Shifra took her leave of Lucia at the house, but Quintus accompanied her and Dacia to the ship to see them settled with their luggage—and a generous supply of food, fresh and dried—for the two-week voyage.

Quintus embraced his departing guest with assurances of her safety. "The captain has sworn to check on you several times a day. He has instructed the deck crew to be on the alert for anyone who might linger suspiciously around your tent. I've paid him a bonus and told him he can take possession of the tent, beds, and water containers when you disembark at Alexandria. Go with God, Aunt Shifra. Lucia and I will pray for your safe arrival."

***

Four days after leaving Ostia, the ship, *The Queen of Heaven*, anchored at Messina to take on more passengers and cargo. They'd had ideal sailing weather, but Dacia had been seasick the whole way. She lay inside their tent, moaning and praying, a large basin beside her. The erratic motion of the ship at anchor had not helped. Shifra left her lying with a wet cloth over her face and walked over to the ship's side and found a place where she could look down at the activity on the quay.

Below her on the shore, crowds of people of every race and, pre-sumably, every religion, busied themselves about the business of load-ing and unloading cargo and buying and selling at the carts lined up along the far edge of the docking area. Near-naked slaves hauled bales and amphorae, Christian monks in black robes accosted travelers for alms, soldiers girt with short swords broke up scuffles and eyed the people who did not seem to be engaged in any type of business. Shifra leaned further over the side, attention caught by a figure in a bright blue tunic—a dark brown man with a shiny shaved head. He stopped just below her, laid down the pack he carried, removed a string of bags from around his neck and knelt.

From the pack, he drew a small flask and removed the stopper. Holding the flask in his left hand, he raised his head toward the sky, eyes shut, lips moving. The din from the crowd and the clanging of metal fittings on the ship's rigging was such that Shifra probably couldn't have heard him if he'd been next to her. She certainly couldn't make out his words, but his closed eyes and the way he raised and lowered his head several times led her to believe that he was pray-ing. Transferring the flask to his right hand, he poured some of its contents onto the earth beside him, replaced the stopper and returned it to his pack.

Before he could rise, four or five black-robed monks surrounded him and yanked him to his feet. One slapped him across his face, send-ing him into the arms of another who pushed him back to the first. As the monk prepared to strike him again, a soldier emerged from the crowd and grabbed the uplifted arm. Clearly demanding to know what was going on, one of the soldiers questioned first the monks, then the man they'd accosted, who pointed up at the ship. As one, all the faces in the group turned upward and Shifra realized with a start that they were looking at her. Feeling her face grow hot, she backed away from the railing. In a matter of minutes, the group had boarded the ship and were coming toward her, one of the soldiers in front.

"Pardon, Domina," he called. "We need your testimony."

Shifra waited. The man in the blue tunic stared at her, an expression in his eyes that seemed to be begging for something. He stood as close as he could to the soldier. Behind him, the monks shouted. "Blasphemer! We saw him. He was making a demon-offering and must be flogged." The monk snatched at the man, who moved to the other side of the soldier.

"Back off. I'll handle this." The officer turned to Shifra. "I just need to know what you saw, Domina. Was this man making a libation?"

Shifra looked at the man. She could not tell how old he might be. His face was lined, but not from age. A scar over one eye and another at the side of his neck suggested that he knew what suffering was. She had no doubt that he had been making an offering to some god before boarding. At a distance, she'd imagined that the bright blue tunic must be new, perhaps bought for the trip. Close up, she saw that it had been torn and patched. The tunic ended just below his knees. The sandals he wore had also been mended.

"Well?" The officer slammed his staff impatiently against the deck. "Could you see what he was doing down there?"

Shifra considered. Bearing false witness is a sin. On the other hand, the rabbis taught the importance of *pikuach nefesh*: "Watching over a soul." Preserving a life took precedence over religious law. She looked past the officer at the monks behind him. Their intention was clear. A flogging delivered in hatred could result in the man's death. She turned to the officer.

"Yes. I could see him from where I stood. I saw him kneel to fasten his sandal."

181

"Nooo!" The monks cried out as one. The one who had struck the man shouted at the soldier. "She's lying! It was a libation. I saw the spilled wine on the ground."

The soldier looked at Shifra. She repeated her testimony. "He knelt to fasten his sandal. Nothing else."

The soldiers marshalled the protesting monks from the ship. Shifra realized that she was shaking and moved to sit on a stool outside her tent. The man for whom she had lied came to stand before her.

"My humble thanks, lady."

The man's bald head shone in the sun. Thick black eyebrows met above his nose. His smile revealed teeth as yellow as turmeric, one of the front ones missing. His person emitted the odor of sweat, olive oil, and stale wine. The smell caught at her stomach and she tasted bile. With effort, she composed a smile. "I did nothing." She expected him to go on his way, but he laid his pack beside the tent. From it, he drew a rug and spread it at one side of the entrance.

"My name is Isidore, lady. I am your servant."

***

Isidore quickly made himself indispensable. Because of Dacia's indisposition, Shifra had been the one to fetch water from the barrel located at some distance from their tent. Carrying the heavy pails across the rolling deck was an ordeal. She welcomed Isidore's offer to take on the task.

When Isidore learned that Dacia suffered from motion sickness, he prepared a potion from his string of bags of herbs and powders. Next morning, Dacia came out to sit on a stool in front of the tent, pale but improved.

"The Blessed Virgin has answered my prayers, Domina. I no longer feel like death."

Shifra smiled. "Isidore's potion may have had something to do with your cure."

Dacia lifted a lip in disgust. "Him! How can you bear to have him near us? He smells of sweat." Shifra frowned. Fortunately, Isidore was out of earshot, having gone to help crew with a fouled line.

"Bathing is not always a possibility, Dacia. Washing out of a basin for five days hasn't improved the way we smell either, I'd wager."

They sat in silence for a time. Shifra thought of what she had learned of Isidore since he'd attached himself to her in gratitude for saving him from a thrashing. He'd removed his tunic to help the sailors and she'd seen his back, latticed with the scars of many lashings. When she'd asked him about it, all he would say was that he'd been sold into slavery at the age of twelve and had finally saved enough money as a healer to buy his freedom.

Dacia never warmed to Isidore, but Shifra enjoyed chatting with him in the evenings, seated by the tent, gazing up at the stars. He told her that he'd been born in a village not far from Alexandria, that his mother had named him for the goddess.

"What goddess is that?" Shifra had asked.

"Isis, of course, Mother of the Gods, Star of the Sea, Queen of Heaven. My name, *Isidore*, means 'Gift of Isis.'"

Shifra laughed. "You mean that this ship is named for Isis?"

Isidore nodded, his face suddenly set in a frown. "Yes," he said slowly, "that is why I chose it for my return to Egypt. It is a propitious name."

Shifra could tell she'd hurt him with her laughter.

"I'm not laughing at you or your goddess, Isidore. I laughed because Dacia was delighted when she heard the name of the ship because she assumed it was named for a goddess in her religion."

Isidore's face relaxed. "Ah, yes. I have heard of the Christian goddess, Maria. Like Isis, she is the mother of a god. Perhaps they are the same."

Shifra was glad that Dacia had gone to bed.

The remaining days of the voyage passed without incident. The seas were calm and the winds reliable. The captain told the passengers that they would soon make land.

On the tenth day, Shifra was at the side of the ship, looking for the famous lighthouse of her home city.

Isidore saw it first, as a tiny speck. Together, they watched it grow until it seemed to fill the horizon, the lighthouse of Alexandria, its huge limestone blocks still standing, solid and eternal in a changing world.

Her stomach gave a little leap as she thought of her brother Akiva waiting somewhere at the docks, perhaps watching for her ship the way she'd been watching for the lighthouse. Would he recognize her after more than thirty years? Would she him? She reached into the purse she wore at her waist and pulled out a necklace. From the fine gold links hung a double locket, delicately hinged. She stroked it gently with her fingers. Father had commissioned the locket as a wedding present. How like him, thoughtful and self-effacing. Likenesses of her mother and beloved brother, but none of himself.

"Nearly there, lady!" Isidore stopped beside her, smiling broadly, showing his uneven yellow teeth. He smelled of garlic.

"Yes," she said, stepping back in spite of herself. "I'll be glad to feel the earth beneath my feet again and sleep in a proper bed. Will you be staying in Alexandria?"

"No. I'll be traveling on to Menouthis to give thanks to the goddess for my freedom and safe passage. When I've completed my pilgrimage,

I'll look for a place where I can earn my living. I hope I can stay and make my home there."

A flurry of activity drew Shifra's attention. Sailors were rushing everywhere. The ship was too close to land to worry about shipwreck. It must be pre-docking activity. A small boat approached from the city. She knew from her childhood escapades with Akiva that this was a pilot boat come to guide the ship to its moorings.

Akiva.

She wondered if he had become like their father. Certainly he had looked like him from birth. "As like as if struck from the same mold," their old nurse was fond of saying. The soft brown eyes, the nose that spoke of the family's origins in Judea, the mouth so quick to laughter.

Shifra sighed. How she prayed that Akiva would be as she remembered him. Although he was the younger by two years, he'd always taken the part of a big brother, protector and counselor. They'd gone everywhere together in the old days, they and their patient, secret-keeping pedagogue, Atlas, exploring the docks, peeking into the pagan temples, sampling the wares of the street vendors without worrying about whether or not they were ritually clean. Atlas could be trusted to keep their secrets.

A sudden violent shudder went through the ship, causing Shifra to stagger and reach out for the railing to keep her balance. The ship had docked. Her heart thudded in anticipation of seeing her brother after so many years. She hurried to the tent to see if Dacia was ready.

Settling Dacia on a folding stool against the railing, Shifra scanned the crowd for Akiva. The quayside scene at Alexandria recalled the one at Messina, but bigger—what seemed total chaos as the laborers, vendors, soldiers, and disembarking passengers pursued their goals. She noticed a group of black-robed monks, moving in unison, an ominous dark patch like a ray fish in shallow water. One, at the front, stood head and shoulders above the others. Then, among a press of men waiting for the sailors to throw down the gangplank, she saw Akiva. Even after all the passing years, she knew him. He had their father's build, tall and broad shouldered. And, like their father's in his later years, his shoulders were slightly hunched. Father's stoop had been the result of long hours spent over accounts for his successful importing business. Akiva's came from secretarial work in the imperial governor's office.

The gangplank struck the dock with a huge clang and Akiva, followed by two husky men in short tunics, was one of the first to mount to the deck. Shifra ran to him, ready to throw herself into his arms, but when she reached him, he kept his arms at his sides. She stopped and looked up at his face, trying to read the expression that met her. He had the look of a man looking at a stranger. "Shifra?"

"Yes, Brother," she said softly in Latin. "It is I, your sister, Shifra."

Something flickered in his eyes, his arms moved, but he did not raise them to embrace her. He glanced at Dacia who had risen from the stool and stood unsteadily beside her mistress.

"Your maid?" He spoke in Greek and Shifra responded in kind.

"Yes. Her name is Dacia. She has not been well."

"I can see that," he said. "Her face is as white as the underside of a mackerel. Come, I'll get you home as quickly as possible. I expect she'll recover quickly, once she has solid ground under her feet."

Akiva motioned to the men who had followed him on board and sent them to fetch the luggage from the tent. Shifra looked around for Isidore. Only a few feet away, he moved toward her quickly when their eyes met.

"The time has come for farewell, Domina. May the protection of the goddess guard your steps."

Dacia recoiled at the words and made her cross sign, but Shifra smiled. Reaching into her purse, she closed her fingers around one of her remaining coins. "Thank you, Isidore. And thank you for your many services that made the voyage safer and more pleasant than it might have been." She proffered the coin. "Please take this small token of my gratitude."

Isidore did the recoiling this time. He held up both hands, palms outward. "Please, lady! Do not think to pay me for my small effort to repay you for saving my life at Messina." Tears started from his eyes and Shifra felt shame wash over her. She slid the money back into her purse. "Please, Isidore, forgive me, Isidore—my friend."

"What's going on here?" Akiva stepped between Shifra and Isidore. "Is this person troubling you, sister?"

His servants, who had returned with the luggage, put it down as they eyed their master for instructions.

"No, not at all," Shifra said quickly. "This man has been most kind to me, helping with meals and guarding Dacia and me from unwanted advances. Isidore, this is my brother, Akiva. Akiva, Isidore—my friend."

Akiva gave an almost imperceptible nod of acknowledgement and sent his servants on their way. With a final bow toward Shifra, Isidore followed the luggage carriers down the gangplank.

Dacia swayed and seemed in danger of falling.

"We'd best get on either side of her," Akiva said. "Let's go."

As they made their slow way down the gangplank, Shifra looked ahead at the area nearest the point of descending passengers. Isidore had reached the landing place and was kneeling at one side. Oh no. Surely, he wasn't going to risk another libation. She looked around for the group of monks, who might pose a threat to the little healer. They were moving towards him. She willed Isidore to hurry.

Chapter Twenty-Three
Family Reunion

Akiva's men loaded the luggage into a small mule-drawn cart and climbed in after it. The cart moved away, revealing a white carriage, the door bearing a colorful painted design. Shifra looked inquiringly at Akiva.

"That's the insignia of the Roman Prefect of Egypt. I have the use of the prefect's coach as needed." He and Shifra maneuvered Dacia into the coach, where she leaned limply into a corner. They got in after her and Akiva signaled the driver.

The closed carriage moved slowly across the crowded quay. Shifra raised a corner of the curtain, but all she could see were people and the wheels of other carriages. In a few minutes, they reached a road and Shifra looked eagerly for familiar landmarks. She saw with a thrill of recognition the bases of the two huge obelisks that stood in front of the Caesareum. Like the lighthouse, she thought, with a comfortable feeling of satisfaction, they would always stand in Alexandria. She laughed to herself, struck by a silly thought. As big as they were, they'd been moved from their original places at the command of the Roman emperor Augustus many years in the past. Who knew, but that at some time, hundreds of years from now they might be moved again. She laughed again at the ridiculous thought.

Assuming that Akiva still lived in the family home in the Delta, the prosperous Jewish quarter where they'd grown up, Shifra was surprised when the carriage turned right at the Theatre and entered the imperial neighborhood that housed Hadrian's Palace and the Temple of Saturn. She frowned. "You said you were taking us straight home," she said.

"I am."

"You don't live in the Delta anymore?"

Akiva shook his head. "The Delta isn't what it was," he said sadly. "When we were children, Father could live in the Jewish quarter and still have the respect of the highest citizen in Alexandria. Nowadays, I'm sorry to say, an address in the Delta is the kiss of death to anyone who wants to get ahead in the imperial service."

"What about our old home? Have you sold it?" Her voice caught on a sob. She'd so looked forward to seeing the garden and the fountains. The rose arbor where she'd read so many books, far from the household bustle.

"No." He paused. "Do you know about Callinicum?"

The name stabbed. "Oh yes. What Jew doesn't?"

"One Sunday, about two months after the emperor withdrew his punishment from the bishop at Callinicum, our own bishop—old Theophilus, uncle of the bishop we have now—delivered a sermon on the iniquity of the Jews. The same night, a mob descended on the Delta to burn a synagogue in sympathy with the Christians at Callinicum. They picked the synagogue that stood next to our house. House and hall burned together. The best I could do was save the servants."

The carriage drew to a stop. Akiva's apartments were within the precincts of the old palace. Servants hurried to open the carriage doors and help the occupants descend. Then, he escorted his sister and her woman into an airy foyer painted with vines and flowery arbors. The household servants, four men and six women, waited in a line to welcome her, each stepping forward, bowing, and stepping back.

Shifra turned delightedly to her brother. "It's lovely, Akiva." Her brother was frowning and looking around.

"Where's Aella?"

The servants gazed silently at the floor. The sound of light footsteps preceded a young girl who came scampering down a marble staircase.

"Here I am, Father! I'm so sorry I'm late, but I sat down to read just a little and…"

The girl jumped from the bottom step and ran towards them, sliding to a stop in front of Shifra.

"Aunt Shifra!" The girl threw her arms around Shifra and hugged her tight, not at all like someone greeting a previously unknown and unseen relative. "I'm so happy that you are here! I hope we shall be good friends."

Shifra staggered back a step, and not just from the force of the embrace. The girl's face was not that of a stranger. It was the very same face that occupied the righthand side of her locket.

"She looks just like Mother," she breathed, glancing at her brother. He was looking at his daughter with an expression of immeasurable love and pride.

"Yes," he said. "Doesn't she just?"

Aella conducted Shifra to her room, chattering all the way.

"I've had the servants put you in the room next to mine," she said. "That way you'll be near me and the library. Father told me that you love to read. We have nine hundred and seventy-three scrolls," she said. "I've counted them, you see. And we even have six of the new kind of book that the Christian writings come in. They're called *codices*. One is a *codex*, two are *codices*."

Shifra found herself smiling without stop. The girl was a delight.

"How old are, you, Aella?"

"Twelve," she said promptly. Suddenly her face flushed scarlet. She looked earnestly at Shifra and embraced her again. "I'm so glad you've come to live with us, Aunt. Now I'll have you to tell when my menses begin. I so dreaded Mother's not being here for that."

Shifra sat on the edge of the bed and drew her weeping niece down beside her. She stroked the girl's hair and no longer wondered if she'd done the right thing by coming to live with her brother.

***

As young as she was, Aella was clearly the lady of the house. As soon as she recovered from her emotional episode, she directed the servants to bring refreshments for her aunt. She put Dacia in the care of two of the women and told them to send for the palace doctor to check her over. One of Shifra's trunks was not with the rest of her luggage, so Aella dispatched a servant back to the docklands to retrieve it. She accompanied her aunt to her room, ascertained that she had refreshments and warm water for washing, and then left her alone to rest until supper.

***

Supper was spread in an exquisitely furnished dining room, like the entry painted with flora and architectural motifs such as arbors and trellises. Nowhere did Shifra see the depiction of an animal or human being.

Before they began the meal, Aella lighted candles and gave the prayer that Shifra remembered her mother recite every Friday to welcome the Sabbath. Shifra sighed contentedly. After all she'd been through—losing her husband for no better reason than that he was a Jew, losing her inheritance because she was a Jew, losing her livelihood as a healer because she was a Jew—now she could relax in the cozy security of her brother's Jewish home.

"This is just wonderful, Akiva. The Sabbath candle ceremony is the perfect way to make me feel that, at long last, I've reached a refuge from the constant message that the customs of the Jews must be erased from the Earth. It is such a relief to be in a Jewish home again."

Aella, who was spreading honey on a roll raised her head. She looked toward her father and seemed to be about to speak, but Akiva preempted her.

"The times are difficult for the Jewish people," he said. "No question about that. But let's talk about more cheerful things, Sister. You're here at last! Aella and I are so glad to have you with us. Tell us about the voyage. Was it insufferably tedious?"

Shifra wondered what her niece had been about to say, but Aella's attention seemed to be back on her meal and Akiva's manner had become warmer than it had been on the way from the harbor. She smiled and gave herself up to the feeling of the first happiness she'd felt in months.

"Some of the time, yes. The noise of the wheels could be maddening and some of the places we stayed were unpleasant, but we stopped at interesting places, and I had long talks with people I had never been around in my old life." She gave a brief wondering laugh. "I even became fond of the barbarian slave who was our driver."

Aella spoke through a spray of bread crumbs. "Hypatia says that man is a social creature and that love and friendship is what binds the world together and that because souls do not exist in a hierarchy, friendship is possible across class lines."

Shifra stared at her niece. Akiva laughed.

"You will find that your niece is replete with opinions about many subjects."

Aella bubbled on.

"Hypatia says that a person without opinions is a person who never thinks. She says that it's all right to change your opinion when new information presents itself, but it's better to have a wrong opinion than no opinion at all." She looked earnestly at her aunt. "Father says you and he knew Hypatia when you were children. What was she like then? Was she as beautiful as people say? Did you ever talk to her?"

"Hypatia? I remember the name, but…"

"Theon's daughter," Akiva prompted.

"Oh, yes. She was older than us. And a bit stuck-up, as I recall." Aella's mouth opened in a look of astonishment.

Akiva stood. "I think your aunt must be very tired from her sea journey. We should give her all the time she needs to rest before bombarding her with questions and opinions."

Aella leapt to her feet and placed a hand under Shifra's elbow to help her rise. "I'm so sorry, Aunt. You're probably too tired to remember the things I want to know. Come, I'll take you up to your room and help you get comfortable. And then I'll leave you alone until you are absolutely ready to endure all the questions I have for you!"

Charmed by the child's artlessness, Shifra kissed her brother and allowed her niece to lead her to her chamber.

Chapter Twenty-Four
Aella

The following days drifted by as a pleasant dream. Shifra had not realized just how exhausted she'd been. Gradually the sensation that her
bed was moving passed. The servants came and went, bringing her
food, bathing her limbs with warm cloths, carrying away the chamber
pot, repositioning screens throughout the day to keep the sun from
disturbing her sleep. Each time she woke, it was to the scent of fresh
flowers and the sound of a distant flute or lyre. Finally, on what must
have been her third morning to wake in Alexandria, she opened her
eyes ready to sit up and rejoin society. The first face she looked upon
was that of Aella, seated by her bed with a scroll in her hand.

"Good morning, Aunt," she said. "Do you feel ready for a proper
tub bath today?"

"Yes, please, Niece," Shifra replied.

As the servants brought a brass tub and filled it with buckets of
heated water, Shifra suddenly remembered her own servant. "Dacia!"
she exclaimed. "Whatever has happened to my maid? Is she still ill?
She didn't...she didn't..."

Aella laughed. "No, she didn't die of her sea sickness," she said.
"She's recovered quite nicely and has been helping the housemaids
and learning Greek."

"Dacia?" Shifra exclaimed. "Dacia may have a Greek name, but, apart from her native tongue, she has never spoken anything but Latin."

"That may be, but Father said that if she's going to live in Alexandria she is going to have to be able to get along in Greek, so he's assigned me to devote two hours a day to teaching her. We've already had our morning lesson."

"How is she doing?" Shifra asked.

Aella shrugged. "The best she can, I suppose."

After her bath, Shifra put on the new clothing that Aella had laid out for her, a white tunic with a blue stola and a mantle of darker blue. "This is just beautiful," she said to Aella, "much finer than anything I brought with me."

"Father says, now that you will be living with us, I'm to see that you dress like an Alexandrian lady."

Shifra was sure that her brother meant well, but she couldn't help feeling a pang of humiliation to think that her own clothing didn't come up to the mark of Alexandrian finery.

"Would you like to have your breakfast brought, or would you like to go down to the cenarium today?" Aella asked.

"Oh, by all means, let us go downstairs. This room is lovely, but I am ready to get out of it for a while."

***

Akiva had left for work, so Aella and Shifra had the cenarium to themselves. Shifra gazed with admiration at the food before her, oat cakes, grapes, apples, smoked fish, and something white that looked like cubes of solidified milk and tasted like honey. She tried everything set before her. Realizing that Aella was not talking, she looked up to see if she was still in the room.

Shifra's niece was sitting quietly across from her, not eating, but returning her look. She seemed tense, her arms held stiffly at her sides, her brow slightly ridged, as if she might be on the verge of speaking, but couldn't decide whether or not to do it.

Shifra looked down at the multitude of plates in front of her, most of them empty. Could it be that she had shocked her niece by making a pig of herself? She looked back at Aella.

"Is there anything the matter?" she asked.

Aella inhaled deeply. "No, Aunt. You just go on with your breakfast."

Shifra felt herself blush and pushed back from the table, dabbed at her lips with a napkin and set it down. "I've finished, thank you. It was all very good."

Aella continued to stare at her as if on the verge of speech.

"Are you all right?" Shifra asked. "You look as if you have something on your mind."

"Well," said Aella, "I was just wondering. Do you think you're rested enough for me to start asking you questions again?"

Laughing, Shifra stood and held out her arms. "Come here, Niece," she said and Aella jumped up and ran into her embrace. "I'm ready for all the questions you can ask me."

***

As it turned out, the questions poured from aunt and niece in about equal measure. Aella was more interested in books and academic subjects, while Shifra wanted to know about her niece's mother and her life with her father.

"She's been dead for more than a year," Aella said of her mother, "Father acts like it just happened. I've told him it's all right if he wants to marry again, but he says I run the house to his satisfaction so he doesn't see why he'd want to spoil anything by bringing another woman in."

"What about me?" Shifra asked. "Your father has told me that I may pass the rest of my life in his house if I wish it."

"Oh," Aella scoffed, "you're not another woman. You're my aunt. I'll expect to look after you the same as I do Father."

Shifra laughed. "But what will happen to us when you marry?"

"I'll never marry," the girl exclaimed. "I'm going to be a great scholar like Hypatia. I won't have time for a husband and children."

Aella immediately launched into her plans to become like her heroine Hypatia. As soon as she had read every work of the ancient Greeks, she would proceed to those of the most admired contemporaries. She would fit in the works of Plato as she read the literature, but she was finding his theories rather difficult to follow and was looking forward to hearing Hypatia explain them. She'd also begun writing epigrams of her own, would Shifra like to read some?

Shifra kept up with the quicksilver chattering of her niece to the best of her ability. She surprised herself with how much she remembered of her own youthful reading and was able to match Aella quote for quote from Homer and some of the playwrights. When it came to contemporary literature, however, and the classic works of Plato, she was at a loss.

"Your grandfather Elad didn't think that Plato was suitable reading for a young Jewish girl," she told Aella. "He wanted me to be acquainted with Greek literature so I could hold my own with the wives of the men my theoretical husband would be doing business with, but he did not think that the study of philosophy was suitable for a woman."

"How awful," Aella wailed. "Philosophy is the queen of all studies. Women are just as capable of understanding higher thought as men. And the works of Plato are the basis for all thought and spiritual development."

Shifra gasped. Her disapproval echoed in her voice. "I'm really shocked, child. Even Christians revere the holy scriptures of the Jews above all writings."

Aella jumped up and ran to her aunt, throwing her arms around her neck and talking into her hair. "Don't be displeased with me, dear Aunt, please don't be. I revere the holy books, truly I do. Hypatia says that the universal truths of Plato are to be found in all the holy books in the world, that all the religions teach some part of God's truth and that all should be respected for that reason."

Shifra was beginning to feel very tired of her niece's constant references to Hypatia.

"Excuse me, child," she said. "I'm feeling tired. I think I'll go lie down for a while."

Chapter Twenty-Five
An Unanticipated Revelation

Heart pounding, Shifra lay down in the privacy of her room, stunned to have heard the works of a pagan philosopher equated with the words of scripture. How could an observant Jew countenance such views in his house? As she stared at the ceiling, other uneasy thoughts stirred in her mind. Upon her arrival, on the previous Sabbath eve, she'd noted with approval the floral motifs in the portico murals. No Jewish house would have paintings that depicted living creatures. Her first impression of the dining area had been that its walls also depicted only growing things, but this morning, she'd noticed the image of a standing figure similar to the one on the atrium in the house of Vibius and Iris—a shepherd carrying a sheep on his shoulders. Still, Akiva's living quarters were in a wing of what had been a pagan emperor's palace. It was possible something may have been overlooked in redecoration.

She rolled onto her side. She was tired. Even after a week, the weariness of the journey had not completely left her. She'd speak to Akiva about it this evening. At the lighting of the Sabbath candles.

This time, after Aella had lighted the candles and read the prayer, Shifra wondered if Akiva even knew that his daughter valued the works of Plato above holy scripture. She didn't want to cause a rift between them. Better to wait until they could speak without Aella in the room. Her glance fell on the part of the wall where the painted shepherd stood with his sheep. She shuddered. This, she could mention. Akiva, however, spoke before her.

"So, sister. You begin your second week in Alexandria. What do you think of your new home?"

His words stifled the criticism she'd been preparing. How trivial to chafe at a picture that was in her power to ignore. Her new home was a vast improvement on her steadily decaying status in Milan. Here, she had every comfort, safety, no need to scrabble for a livelihood.

"I think the Lord is good, to bring me to my brother's home, to bless me with a loving niece, to rescue me from the harsh judgement of the Christian bishop who robbed me of my inheritance. I can think of nowhere that I'd rather be than at this table with you and Aella, sitting in the glow of the Sabbath candles." She smiled warmly at him and Aella. "And now that I'm rested from my journey, you can take me with you to synagogue tomorrow."

Akiva and Aella exchanged glances. Akiva sighed deeply.

"If I could avoid this any longer, I would. But there's something you must know, my sister. A thing that grieves me to tell you." He looked at Aella, who nodded encouragingly.

"As long as you were in Milan," he went on, "I saw no need to tell you. Now that you are here, a member of my household, you must be told."

Shifra's eyes fixed on his mouth, followed the formation of his words, while her mind resisted what she knew she was about to hear.

"I waited until father died. But I had to do it, Shifra, if I was to get anywhere in the imperial service. I'm not a merchant. I didn't have the right kind of mind to take up father's business. And to tell the truth, his business had been in decline for years. I'm a good secretary. And, at least some of the time, my position enables me to protect Jews from the worst oppression."

Shifra's mouth had gone dry. Her heart thudded as it had after Aella's paean to Plato. Her own brother.

"You apostatized. You betrayed the religion of your fathers."

"I'm sorry, sister. I don't expect you to do as I have, but if the bishop learns that you are a Jew, the pressure for you to convert will be more than either of us can bear. I must ask you to dissemble."

Blinded by tears, Shifra left the table and fled to her room. She threw herself on the bed and wept as she had when first she viewed the murdered body of her husband.

**

Dacia followed the pot girl up the dimly lit stairs from the kitchen to the family quarters. Finally, she was being allowed to rejoin her mistress.

She recalled little of the first two days of their arrival at the brother's home. She barely remembered being taken to the servants' quarters. They'd put her to bed and cared for her in every way, even praying over her in Jesus' name. As soon as her wits returned, she asked to be taken to her mistress. The housekeeper told her that the master had given instructions for her to remain below stairs until further notice. On no account was she to speak to the lady Shifra until he gave her leave.

Finally, today, exactly a week since their arrival in Alexandria, the housekeeper instructed the lowliest kitchen slave to take Dacia to her mistress.

Entering the chamber, Dacia saw Shifra lying face-down on the bed, her body shaking from the force of weeping. She hurried to her side and leaned over her to stroke her hair.

"Domina, dear Domina, I am here. Dacia is here. What is it that troubles you so?"

Shifra struggled to a sitting position. Dacia sat and took her in her arms.

"He apostatized, Dacia! My brother. My own brother has betrayed his heritage and become a Christian." Her sobs broke out afresh. Dacia patted her comfortingly. To her, the fact that Akiva had left his benighted Jewish ways for Christianity was a good thing, even if it was the Nicean variety of the faith. But, she knew how much Jewishness mattered to her mistress. She didn't understand it, but she loved the woman and her departed master for having rescued her as a child from the abusive household of Faustus Ulpius, treating her wounds and bringing her up almost as a daughter.

Shifra pulled away and fixed Dacia with an accusing look.

"Where have you been all this time? Why haven't you been here to tend to me?"

Dacia recoiled, stung by the suggestion that she'd somehow betrayed her mistress.

"They wouldn't let me come to you."

"But why?"

"When did you find out that your brother is a Christian?"

Shifra frowned. "Just this evening."

Dacia nodded. "I knew from the beginning that this was a Christian household. Most of the slaves are Christian. Your brother feared I would tell you before he was ready."

Shifra's mouth dropped open. "Of course. Jews may not own Christian slaves." Anger drained from her face into an expression of helplessness. "What am I to do, Dacia? What am I to do?"

Dacia rose and looked around the room. The washing basin had not been removed. She wet a cloth and wiped her mistress's tear-stained face. As a woman and a slave, she knew the answer to Shifra's pathetic question.

"All anyone can do when things do not go as we wish, Domina. You must do the best you can."

Chapter Twenty-Six
Cyril's Church

On Sunday, Shifra, Akiva, and Aella were carried to the Caesareum in chairs.

Conceived by Cleopatra as a temple to commemorate her lovers, Julius Caesar and Marc Antony, the building had been completed by Augustus Caesar and dedicated to his family cult. That's where the name Caesareum came from. Since the closing of the temples by the first Theodosius, it had been transformed into the Cathedral of Alexandria.

Dacia, who had walked, awaited her mistress at the entrance. There, worshippers separated as they entered, men to the left and women to the right. Aella led the way to the front, where they had a clear view of the bishop's throne, the altar, and the lectern. Shifra was glad to see that Dacia had thought to bring a folding stool for her. She was also glad to be wearing a veil, so that no one could see that she did not know the words when the congregation responded to prayers led by the lector.

Before the service began, Aella identified the men who had already taken their places in the area front of them.

"The bushy-haired man sitting next to the lectern is Peter the lector. His job is to read from the scriptures and lead the prayers and singing."

Shifra made a quiet scoffing sound. "With those thick arms, he looks more like a laborer than a cleric."

"He acts like one too," Aella agreed. "He's loud and rough. Once I saw him grab a boy by the ear and give him a thrashing for almost hitting him with a ball in the street."

To the far left of the lectern stood an elaborate empty chair. Two men in white sat on each side.

"That's the patriarch's throne," Aella whispered. "The service starts when Pope Cyril comes in and sits in it. Those men on the left of it are the deacon and subdeacon."

"Who is the little rat-faced man on the right side?"

Aella tried to stifle a giggle. "That's Hierax. He's the *grammaticus*. He instructs new converts and keeps a school for boys who want to become clerics. Mostly, he runs errands for Archbishop Cyril. He does look like a rat. His pointy little pink nose practically twitches."

The entrance of the patriarch forestalled further information. Shifra settled in for her first Christian service.

Cyril, a tall, gaunt man, no stranger to fasting, stood behind the altar, facing the congregation, and performed the ritual, slowly and deliberately. Peter the lector did the readings in a voice that Shifra guessed could be heard by the people at the very back. Shifra recognized more than one prayer and hymn that echoed the words of the Tanakh.

Cyril delivered the sermon while sitting on his throne. The subject was worldly wisdom compared to the wisdom of Christ. "Beware lest any man spoil you through philosophy and vain deceit." When Cyril declared in a voice almost as loud as the reader's, "Abstain from all heathen books!" she whirled to look at Aella.

Her niece stared straight ahead as the patriarch explained that no other books were needful to Christians because everything was in the scriptures: history, poetry, songs, laws and statutes, and the origin of the world. As Cyril went on about the dangers of non-Christian writing, Shifra's attention wandered.

Across the aisle, on the men's side, Akiva stood next to a tall man in a white tunic edged with purple. She guessed he must be the governor, Orestes. On the women's side, just past Aella and slightly in front of her, a woman dressed in a deep red stola, elegantly embroidered with gold thread, held something in her hand. Every so often, the woman lifted the object devoutly to her lips.

Grateful to be sitting, Shifra spent the remainder of the service rapt in her own thoughts. She loved her brother and she knew that her motherless niece needed a caring woman in her life. But, what of her own needs? She had believed her brother's home would be a refuge from the injustices of the outside world. Instead, she found herself in a situation in some ways worse than the one she'd fled. In Milan, at least, her religion had been no secret. There, she could belong openly to a community of believers. Akiva had made it clear that he expected her to conceal the fact that she had not converted. As the people around her voiced their closing prayer to their three gods, Shifra prayed silently to the one God for strength and guidance.

Outside, Akiva stood beside the tall man he'd been beside in the church. Shifra had guessed correctly.

"This is my sister, Excellency," he said to his companion. "Shifra, this is His Excellency Orestes, colonial governor of Egypt."

Shifra bowed her head respectfully before looking up at her brother's employer. A handsome face, even features and a pleasant, confident look in his eyes. He bowed slightly.

"Welcome to Alexandria, lady. Your brother is fortunate in your presence."

"Thank you, Excellency. And thank you for lending him your coach to fetch me from the harbor."

As they exchanged polite comments, the scent of expensive unguents wafted toward them with the approach of the elegant lady in red whom Shifra had noticed inside.

"Greetings, Your Excellency," she fluted in a high, piercing voice. "And Secretary Akiva." She turned to Shifra. "This must be the sister everyone is talking about. Throwing her arms wide, she lunged to embrace Shifra and kiss her on both sides of her veiled face. "God be praised for your safe arrival," she said. "I know we shall be great friends in Jesus."

Shifra disentangled herself from the embrace and stepped back. An appropriate response eluded her. Akiva came to her rescue.

"Greetings, Clio," he said. "Yes, this is my sister Shifra. My daughter and I are pleased to welcome her to our household."

Clio nodded enthusiastically, her uncovered face beaming happy enthusiasm. "I know you will want to join me in good works for the Lord."

Shifra looked helplessly at her brother. He took her elbow and made a show of moving away.

"Thank you so much, Clio. You and my sister must talk some time. For now, even after a week, she is fatigued by the long journey from Milan. Perhaps later…"

"I'll call tomorrow," Clio interjected. To Shifra, she said, "I can tell you what it is I do to help the poor unfortunates of the Delta. As soon as you have rested sufficiently, I know you will be eager to help in this holy work."

Safely back in the chair with Aella, Shifra burst into laughter. "Who IS that woman and what did she keep kissing in the church?"

"That is Clio. She is a recent pagan convert and she's more Christian than the Christians. What she was kissing is the finger of Saint Menas. A very powerful relic."

A taste of bile rose in Shifra's throat. These Christians and their cult of death!

Aella went on. "Her husband is Herculanius, a wealthy land owner. Because of their great wealth, Clio has become a favorite of Pope Cyril. He's the one who gave her the saint's relic."

Shifra shook her head. "Do I really have to see her again?"

"You can laugh at her affectations," Aella said, "But I'm afraid you will have to see her again. You'll probably have to agree to help her with her charity work."

Dread overcame any inclination to laugh as her niece continued.

"If she wants you to go with her on her errands of mercy, you had better get ready to go."

True to her word, Clio called mid-morning next day, accompanied by two maids and a muscular young slave bearing a huge basket of fruit. Such was the recent convert's enthusiasm, Shifra's excuses fell one by one and she agreed to accompany her to the Delta a week from the day. That evening, at supper, Akiva made an announcement that drove her anxiety about Clio's plans completely out of her mind.

"The governor has invited us to dinner tomorrow. It will be your chance to meet some of the people we work with in our efforts to keep Alexandria from its habitual factional demonstrations."

Shifra's lungs suddenly struggled to pull in air. "Must I go? I wouldn't know how to behave, what to say."

Akiva smiled. "Certainly you must go. The dinner is in your honor, Orestes's way of welcoming and introducing you to your new home."

Jumping up from her place, Aella hugged Shifra from behind. "Don't worry, Auntie, I'll help you dress. Not even Clio will be lovelier, if she's there."

"Clio is not on the guest list," Akiva said.

Shifra sighed mightily. "That, at least, is a relief!"

A mischievous gleam showed in her brother's eyes. "There will be one other woman." Aella and Shifra looked at him expectantly. Keeping them in suspense for a few beats, he finally spoke. "Hypatia has accepted."

A piercing squeal erupted from Aella. "Oh, Father! Take me with you! Please, take me too."

"Sorry, my dove. This one is for grown-ups only. "Your aunt can give you a full report afterwards."

Chapter Twenty-Seven
Dinner with the Governor

A small army of servants greeted the dinner guests of Orestes, decking them in garlands and filets of fresh flowers before leading them to a flower-filled dining room.

Expecting the usual arrangement of groups of three couches at separate tables, Shifra gaped at an arrangement she'd heard about but never seen.

"It's a *stibadium!*"

A semicircle of six couches surrounded one table, like spokes radiating from the hub of a wheel.

"What a clever idea!" Shifra whispered to her brother. "This way, everyone can share in the same conversation."

Orestes guided his guests to their couches, placing the two women guests side by side.

Intensely curious to know more about her niece's heroine, Shifra turned to the woman on the next couch and found her looking back at her.

Even in her mid-fifties, Hypatia was a fine-looking woman. Her nose descended in a straight line from her brow and her still abundant eyebrows met above it. Her black hair had only a few grey strands among the curls. She wore a simple unbleached tunic under a rough scholar's cloak. Evidently her well-known standards of simplicity took precedent over such social niceties as dressing for dinner. The object of her scrutiny smiled and spoke.

"Hello. My name is Hypatia. I understand that you are the sister of the governor's secretary."

Shifra felt the heat rise in her face. "Yes, my name is Shifra. I've been living in Milan for the past thirty years, but I grew up here in Alexandria. I don't remember ever having met you, but my father was acquainted with yours."

As soon as the words were out, Shifra regretted them. Sure enough, Hypatia asked the obvious question.

"What was your father's name?"

To name him was to reveal her Jewish origins, but there was no help for it.

"Elad ben Eleazar. He was a merchant."

Hypatia nodded, as if the name were familiar and said, "I see."

The well-dressed man at the other side of Hypatia leaned into the conversation. Orestes had introduced him, but she didn't recall his name, just that he'd been some kind of envoy to Constantinople.

"If I may intrude. I am Synesius of Cyrene. I heard you say that you have been living in Milan for thirty years. You must have been acquainted with the renowned Bishop Ambrose. Was he as eloquent as I've heard?"

Ambrose. The hated name sent shudders down Shifra's arms. Akiva, on the couch beside her, gave her a warning jab with his elbow. He knew her feelings about the late bishop. She breathed deeply to control her emotions and tried to sound indifferent.

"I can't say. He preached at the basilica. My place of worship was in a different neighborhood."

Synesius persisted.

"What about the equally renowned Augustine of Hippo? He spent some years in Milan. Had you any acquaintance with him?"

Shifra frowned. "My husband and I were acquainted with an Augustine and his family, but they were from Thagaste."

Synesius smiled broadly. "The very same. Augustine had an estate in Thagaste, but he sold it not long after his return and is now the Bishop of Hippo. An amazing man. Never have I known such a prolific writer. How he does it and performs his preaching and other duties is beyond me. Tell me, did you know him before his conversion to Christianity?"

The memories of those early days in Milan came rushing back. Happy days, when her children were young and she and Benjamin enjoyed the friendship of Vibius and Iris, Augustine and Mira.

"Before," she said. "He and Mira and their son came to Milan when my husband and I had been there for about four years. Augustine was a Manichean at the time. Their son—my children called him Datus—was already quite grown, fifteen, as I recall. A sweet boy, he was, always willing to amuse the little ones."

Recollections of Augustine's crisis of faith clouded over the happy memories. Everything changed when he began studying with Ambrose. And then, when his mother arrived, he agreed to become a Christian and sent Mira back to Africa. Shifra would never forgive their shameful treatment of Mira. Again, she tried to keep emotion out of her voice.

"We didn't see much of them after his conversion. I have never heard what became of him and his mother after they left Milan."

"Ah," said Synesius, "I can help you there. His mother took ill and died at Ostia, before their departure for Africa. She was buried there. Augustine and Adeodatus—that was the boy's full name—returned to the family estates at Thagaste." He frowned and his voice broke as he continued. "The son—promising young man—died not long after their return."

The news struck at Shifra's heart like a fist. Dear Datus. Gone from the world. Mira must have been devastated. "What of Mira? Where is she now?"

Synesius frowned again, this time in apparent puzzlement. "Mira?"

"Augustine's wife."

"Wife? To my knowledge, Augustine never married."

Shifra controlled the urge to scream at the man and forced herself to speak in a modulated tone. "Of course he had a wife. Mira was the mother of his son. They'd been together for nearly twenty years when they came to Milan."

Synesius shrugged. "I expect she was just a concubine."

Heart pounding, Shifra fought to control the helpless anger Synesius's dismissive words roused in her. Mira, one of the kindest, cleverest, most loyal women she'd ever known—*just a concubine*. Augustine had adored her. And then Monika came to Milan. Mira once intimated that Augustine made the move from North Africa to Italy in part to get away from his mother's constant nagging about the two desires she had for her son: to become a Christian and to take a "proper wife." Between Monika and Ambrose, the curious, tolerant, fun-loving man who had come to Milan with Mira and their son, morphed into an inflexible religious enthusiast who could be persuaded to send away the only woman he'd ever loved.

As the red rage in her mind cleared, Shifra became aware that a different topic was being discussed. The guest beside Orestes was speaking.

"It's humiliating," he was saying, "and absolutely wrong that Pope Cyril can confiscate a man's property for no other reason than that he worships as his fathers taught him. As if Christians are the only ones who know the mind of God!"

Shifra turned to her brother and whispered. "Who's he?"

"Herculanius." He grinned. "He's your friend Clio's husband."

"Really! I wonder if he'd talk like that if she were here. Isn't he a Christian too?"

Akiva shrugged. "I've never been able to tell for sure. I've seen him in church with her, but he spends most Sundays at his country home. His mother lives there."

Synesius, his bald head gleaming in the lamp light, spoke. "Sorry, I didn't catch the name of the man who has been denied his rights. Is it someone I may have heard of?"

"Memmius Symmachus. He came to Alexandria from Rome to take possession of a villa his father owned."

"Ah," said Synesius, "I have heard of him. He's the son of the Symmachus who was prefect of Rome when Valentinian was emperor." He frowned in thought. "Must be nearly thirty years since Symmachus Senior petitioned the emperor to restore the Altar of Victory to the Senate House."

"Yes," said Herculanius, "and was treated shamefully for his efforts. Symmachus wrote to the emperor and traveled to Milan for an audience. The emperor sent the letter to Ambrose for his advice. He cast an accusatory look toward Shifra. "Your most holy bishop urged Valentinian to deny the prefect's request. Not only that, Symmachus, the most important man in Rome and leader of a still sizeable pagan party, was hurried from the imperial presence and set down at the hundredth milestone from Milan to make his way home."

Shifra bristled at hearing Herculanius refer to Ambrose as "her" bishop. She knew she should remain silent, but every word he spoke prodded old wounds. She could contain herself no longer.

"Never *my* bishop." She ignored Akiva's warning hand on her shoulder. "He hadn't been bishop long when my husband and I settled in Milan. We could never understand how he became a bishop to begin with. He'd been an imperial governor before, not a priest."

Shifra recalled what they'd been told. According to Vibius, the old bishop of Milan had belonged to the Arian faction of Christians, but the candidate in line to succeed him belonged to the Nicene faction. Ambrose had a reputation for fairness as governor, so the Arians saw him as a neutral choice. The emperor supported the idea, so the former governor was baptized, ordained, and consecrated bishop, all in the same week.

She couldn't keep the bitterness out of her voice. "It wasn't long before the new bishop showed that his sympathies were with the Nicene Christians. He not only favored the Nicene faction, he forbade the Arians the use of any churches in the city." She knew she should stop, but the sense of injustice pulled the words from her.

"Ambrose's legacy lives on with his current successor. Only one set of beliefs is acceptable. What happened to the son of Symmachus is not so different from what is happening in Milan."

She shrugged off Akiva's hand. She would have her say. "Just last year, a Jewish widow of my acquaintance had her inheritance confiscated because she refused to become a Christian." She knew that her brother was willing her to stop, but she could not withhold one more comment. "Please don't call that government official turned bishop 'my bishop.'"

For a time, the only sound was the rustling of tunics and clink and clatter of dishes and utensils as the servants went about their work.

Orestes looked from Shifra to Synesius, his expression a mixture of amusement and embarrassment. "My apologies, Domina Shifra. I regret that I failed to mention that Synesius is not only a former envoy to Constantinople, he is the bishop of Ptolemais."

A frisson of fear coursed through Shifra's body. She had abused Ambrose in the hearing of another Christian bishop. She stared at the table, too frightened to meet the eyes of anyone, waiting for the ax to fall. Surely, she'd brought ruin on her brother and herself.

In the moment of silence that followed the revelation, Shifra felt a terrible sinking in her abdomen. What had she done to her brother? The tense silence was broken by the explosive laughter of Synesius.

"Fear not, Lady," he said. "You have a right to your opinion." He nodded briefly toward Hypatia. "As my teacher might say, 'Reserve your right to think, for even to think wrongly is better than not to think at all.'"

Shifra was speechless. Never would she have expected a Christian bishop to be so tolerant. Her incredulity must have shown on her face. Herculanius, silent until now, roared with laughter.

"Synesius, I think you have done what many a man would dearly love to do—struck a woman dumb!"

Hypatia cleared her throat. For the merest fraction of second, silence gripped the company. Then, as if at a signal, everyone burst into laughter, even Shifra.

"Well," said Herculanius, looking at Hypatia, "I can see that my remark was not at all appropriate in present company."

"Indeed it was not," Synesius said. "And not just because of Hypatia's presence. You will find in me a great defender of female wisdom. Never did I wish my wife's silence."

"Your wife?" Shifra spoke without thinking. Instantly, she shut her lips tightly and looked around. Amusement showed on every face. "I, I'm sorry," she said. "I thought that bishops were not allowed to marry."

"An unnatural and unnecessary rule, in my opinion," said Orestes. "And one that not all bishops observe or insist upon."

"Maybe not," Herculanius said, "but Cyril does. When Synesius was made bishop by the old pope, Theophilus, I wondered about the situation." He smiled at Synesius. "At first, I believed that you must have taken a vow to live with your wife as brother to sister, but when your third son was born, a little counting showed him to be a bishop's child."

"God gave me my wife," Synesius said. "Maia and I had been married for six years when the old bishop of my province died and the people clamored for me to succeed him. They'd been beautiful years, filled with mutual love and affection and the birth of two fine sons. When Theophilus summoned me to Alexandria, I told him first thing that I would not be separated from my wife. Neither would I sneak around like an adulterer in my own home. And I certainly would not become her brother and avoid her bed."

Synesius wiped his lips with an embroidered napkin and folded it into careful rectangles. His face seemed to have lost all color. "I never sought to be a bishop. A bishop should be a man of God, a model to his flock. I told Theophilus that I was a poor choice. I told him that I am a philosopher, not a theologian. From my childhood I have been a lover of literature. And when I was not at my books, I was a lover of sports and the convivial company of friends." He made a slight scoffing sound. "For all my reading, I'd never read the Christian scriptures."

"Then why?" Shifra exclaimed. "That's like Ambrose. He was a Roman official, not a priest. That makes no sense to me."

"It makes perfect sense," Orestes said. "Effective leaders are in short supply. Bishops are not only spiritual leaders. They must also deal with civic matters. No one is more qualified to lead in these troubled times than a man who has received a Roman education, knows how to organize large groups of people, and can navigate political quagmires.

"Synesius spent three years at the imperial court in Constantinople, negotiating tax relief for his home district. When he returned home, he managed the defenses against endless raids from the desert barbarians that inhabit near Cyrene."

Synesius held up his hands, palms outward. "I understood that my education and experience qualified me—indeed, obligated me—to serve the people in non-spiritual matters. I made it clear to Theophilus that I would not abandon the Divine Truth." He glanced at Hypatia, as if for approval. "I know that false ideas may be beneficial to the populace. Not everyone is able to look directly upon the Divine Truth. The vulgar need a different system, suitable to their level of understanding. I told the patriarch that I would allow believers to remain in their already acquired convictions, but that he could not expect me to share them. For example, the image of the Resurrection is a powerful spiritual allegory and a source of comfort to one who takes it literally, but any educated person knows that such an event would be a physical impossibility."

Frowning, Orestes addressed himself to Hypatia. "What do you say, Didaska? Should not Synesius make an effort to enlighten the people who look to him for spiritual guidance?"

Hypatia pursed her lips in thought. "Fables should be taught as fables, myths as myths, and miracles as poetic fancies. To teach superstitions as truths is a most terrible thing. The child-mind accepts and believes them. Only with great pain can the adult rid himself of them. Indeed, men will fight for a superstition as quickly as for a living truth. More quickly, in fact." She paused, as if to give her listeners time to digest her words.

Shifra protested. "But, as a spiritual leader, didn't Synesius have a responsibility to teach them the beliefs of his church?"

Hypatia smiled gently. "Superstition, once accepted, is difficult to refute. Truth is a point of view, a way of looking at the world. Truth changes as perspective changes. Superstition exists apart from the realities of the world. Intangible, it is almost impossible to get at. Synesius has done nothing to deceive. He left the people in the comfort of their beliefs."

Emotionally depleted, Shifra paid no attention to whatever conversation followed. When Akiva indicated that it was time to go, she rose from her couch eagerly. She stood quietly by the entrance as her brother made their farewells. He spoke to Hypatia last. Shifra couldn't be sure, but they seemed to look in her direction several times.

Despite the lateness of the hour, Aella was awake and waiting for them and refused to go to bed until Shifra told her every detail of what Hypatia was wearing and what she said. Shifra relayed as much as she could remember. When she was finished, Akiva, who had sat up with them, embraced his daughter. "I don't know if this is anything that would interest you, my dove, but you and your aunt have been invited to attend Hypatia's lectures tomorrow."

Chapter Twenty-eight
Undercurrents of Unrest

Aella was up before dawn, racing in and out of Shifra's room, each time wearing a different outfit, asking her how she looked. The fifth time her whirlwind of a niece rushed in for another opinion, Shifra sat up in bed and laughingly told her to sit down.

"Aella, Aella, don't you remember my description of what Hypatia was wearing last night? An unbleached tunic and a worn Spartan cloak. Do you think that even if she notices what you are wearing, she'll approve of its richness and cut?"

Aella sank onto the stool by the bed, her exuberance suddenly quelled. "I didn't think," she said.

Shifra slid out from under the covers and sat on the bed's edge, her knees touching Aella's. She grasped the girl's hands. Aella looked at her through tears. "I didn't think," she said again.

Shifra leaned forward and kissed her forehead. "Not to worry, my dear. Now that you have thought of it, you'll go back to your room, put on your least remarkable outfit and give me time to make my own selection." She glanced across to where the maid had laid out the blue stola, Akiva's gift. "To begin with," she said, getting to her feet, "I'll have to see if you've left me anything that I brought with me from Milan." She fingered the rich robe that had been laid out for her. "This gorgeous thing will never do."

When they were ready to leave the house, Aella wore a white linen tunic and Shifra one of pale blue. The girl's spell of dejection had been short-lived and she was again bubbling with excited anticipation. Akiva handed them into the carriage. Cronus, a former wrestler, sat next to the driver. Shifra wondered briefly why he would be going with them.

"Hypatia's first lecture is at the Mouseion," Akiva said. "There's a library and a few shops and eating places. I'll meet you there for lunch and you can tell me what you've learned."

Something about the way he said it made Shifra look closely at her brother. She detected a gleam of amusement in his eyes.

"I suppose you think I won't understand a word of what she says."

"I didn't say that."

"You didn't have to."

As the carriage moved off, Shifra inhaled the pleasantly crisp breeze. "We could have walked."

"Oh no," Aella said. "Father won't let me walk anywhere. Not even with Cronus to go with me. He says that Alexandria is like Greek fire in the hands of amateur pirates. You never know when it's going to burst into flames."

Shifra shuddered as a sudden frisson of fear swept over her. As far away as Milan, the uncertain temperament of the Alexandrian mob was proverbial. She remembered how relieved her servant, Haluk, had been when he knew he would not have to go there. How could it be that a city renowned for its learning and sophistication could at the same time be rocked so often by violence born of mindless anger and ignorance? Perhaps that was a question for Hypatia.

The carriage slowed as it passed the Caesareum, the former temple that Shifra had been in for the Sunday service. Pedestrians clogged the street. A knot of several burly young men dressed in black made their way past their stalled carriage. One was especially tall, perhaps the man she'd seen from the ship as she waited to disembark. Shifra couldn't be sure, but it seemed that the men slowed their pace as they crossed in front of them.

"I wish those horrid monks would hurry up," Aella whispered. "I think they're taking their time deliberately to keep us from going forward."

Shifra laughed. "Surely not, Aella. They're just preoccupied with their own concerns. You mustn't put your thoughts into the minds of others."

At that moment, the tallest of the monks moved alongside and spat. Shifra heard the splat connect against the carriage door. The monk followed his spitting with a remark. He spoke Greek with an abominable accent, but Shifra recognized the word "Orestes." The monks finally passed, and the carriage moved forward.

"I suppose that spit was my imagination," Aella said.

"Who are those men?" Shifra asked.

"They're monks from a monastery at Nitria. That's about thirty miles from here, to the southeast. Not far enough, in my opinion."

Shifra remembered what Akiva had told her about the events that followed the death of Theophilus, the previous patriarch. "Oh. They're the ones Cyril used to seize the office of patriarch when his uncle died."

"Yes. Father says that whenever they show themselves in Alexandria, the prefect Orestes doubles the patrols."

The carriage came to rest at the Mouseion. The original building was long gone, but its replacement and the area retained the old name. Cronus helped the women descend and accompanied them to the entrance. A tall pimply youth in a ragged scholar's cloak blocked the entrance. "This entrance is for the lecture. You'll find the shops further down."

Aella stared indignantly up at the young man. "We are here for the lecture."

With an air of extreme reluctance, he permitted them to enter. The limestone lecture hall contained several rows of stepped benches in the form of a semicircle. At the center stood an elevated seat on which Hypatia was already seated. The rows were about half-filled, but at the rate people were filing in, the area would soon be packed. A few of the incomers were as shabbily dressed as the young doorman, but the clothing of most of the growing audience shouted wealth and privilege. And they were all men. No wonder he'd questioned their right to enter.

He led them to a place near the front, but to the side, where a thick pillar blocked them from the main section. Aella was too excited to settle, but Shifra sat and studied the audience. She recognized Synesius at once. He must have come early to secure a place in the front row. His crimson tunic gleamed with gold thread. His servant had set up a small table furnished with wax tablets and a stylus. Synesius was clearly planning to take notes.

A high-pitched humming rose above the sound of conversation and Aella finally sat down. "That's the sound of Hypatia's water clock," she said. "She designed it so that it makes a sound to signal a time."

Without the usual polite remarks with which many lecturers begin, Hypatia launched directly into her discourse. It was on the topic of conic sections, whatever that might be. Shifra had wondered about the purpose of a huge dark board the size of a dining table, set on edge to the right of Hypatia's lectern. As the lecture proceeded, Shifra realized that the board was a giant wax tablet. The wax had been colored nearly black, so when Hypatia wrote on it with a stylus to illustrate a formula, the writing showed white and easy to read. Synesius and others wrote furiously to keep up. Aella leaned forward in rapt attention. The topic apparently held great fascination for Hypatia's students, but Shifra found her mind wandering to the thought of food. She was glad when the lecture finally ended and Cronus met them in the street to join Akiva for lunch.

"Well, ladies," Akiva asked as they waited to be served at a clean cantina on the side of the agora closest to the Caesareum. "How did you enjoy the lecture?"

Shifra looked from Akiva to Aella. The girl looked back at her, eyes sparkling. Shifra considered lying.

"Well?" Akiva prompted.

"I didn't understand a word of it," she admitted. "Not a single word."

Akiva threw his head back and laughed. Aella frowned.

"I thought she was very good," Aella said.

"So did I," Shifra said. "I thought it was wonderful how she kept all those men fascinated for two hours. I just didn't understand what she was talking about." She turned to Akiva. "It's not going to be mathematics again this afternoon, is it?"

"No. This afternoon it's philosophy. At Hypatia's house."

The waiters brought their food and Shifra thought of nothing else until her hunger was satisfied.

As two hours remained before Hypatia would begin her afternoon lecture, Akiva suggested a walk around the Agora. They browsed the book stalls and Aella bought a treatise on conic sections. As they passed the twin obelisks that flanked the entrance to the Caesareum, Shifra stopped. She had not been able to see much of the interior on Sunday. "Do we have time to go in? I'd love to see the mosaics at the back."

"We have time," Akiva said, "but I'm afraid you're going to find the interior changed from what you remember. They've been remodeling ever since it was taken over by the Church. Even after all this time, areas are still under construction."

The smell of incense permeated the former temple. Shifra looked eagerly for the mosaic she'd admired as a child, a brilliantly colored depiction of Venus and Anchises in the heavens, looking down on their purported descendants, Julius Caesar and Caesar Augustus. She looked in vain. In its place stretched a huge blank swath of bare white plaster. Turning away in disappointment, she stumbled against something on the ground.

At the foot of the wall and piled untidily in a side aisle, leaned stacks of what looked like brightly colored roof tiles. She stooped to pick one up.

"Ow!"

Aella and Akiva whirled at the sound of her cry.

"What's the matter?" they asked at the same time.

Shifra dropped the tile and held out her hand. Small gouts of blood welled from her fingers where she'd grasped the tile. "I picked it up to see it better. I didn't know they'd be so sharp."

Aella pulled off her scarf to blot the blood. "There. That's not too bad, is it, Aunt?"

Akiva frowned. "What do you mean, child? There's no telling what kind of poison is on those filthy things. We'll go straight home to have the cuts tended properly."

The cuts had begun to hurt, but Shifra knew how much Aella looked forward to another lecture with Hypatia. Going home would mean missing the afternoon lecture. "Aella's right, Akiva. It's not worth missing the lecture over. I can clean my hand at the fountain near the place where we had lunch. Aella can ask inside for a little vinegar to cleanse the cuts." Grumbling, Akiva gave in. He, not Aella, returned to the cantina where they'd had lunch, emerging followed by a waiter carrying a cruet of vinegar and a clean cloth. Turning to his sister, he asked again, "You're sure you don't want to go home?"

"Absolutely not."

Aella gave her aunt a grateful hug before helping her wash the wound and wrap it with the clean cloth. Akiva dismissed the waiter with a silver denarius and they returned to where Cronus waited with the carriage.

***

On the way to Hypatia's house, Akiva opened the carriage curtains so that Shifra could look out. "Everything is so changed," she kept saying. "That's where a pretty little shrine to Hermes used to stand. And there's where Atlas would take us on holidays for Isis cakes. They passed a grassless space between houses. Shifra frowned and leaned out to look back. "Wasn't there a public garden there?"

Akiva nodded. "A children's garden, dedicated to Horus. Soon after Cyril succeeded his uncle as patriarch, the statue disappeared during the night. Then somebody sowed salt and now it is as you saw." As they turned into another street, Akiva signaled the coachman to stop. "Here's something else that has changed," he said. "Do you recognize these steps?" He helped Shifra out of the carriage.

Aella protested. "Must we stop, Father? If we're late, Hypatia's doorman won't let us in."

"We have plenty of time, Aella,"

Shifra stared upwards at the huge stone stairway. "The Serapeum!" She recalled climbing these steps with Akiva and their pedagogue Atlas when they were children. They never told their parents they'd entered the magnificent pagan temple.

As they climbed, the building at the top of the steps came into view. Shifra gasped.

"It's gone! I knew it had been closed and looted, but I never knew the building would be entirely gone. It was enormous. What is this that has replaced it?"

"A monastery. The Nitrian monks stay here when they come to Alexandria."

As they descended to the carriage, she recalled the old couple she'd met at the temple along the way from Milan. They'd walked so far, anticipating help in their distress, only to find the priests gone and the temple abandoned. The Serapeum! Like the Lighthouse and the obelisks that flanked the entrance to the Caesareum, the temple to Serapis had been solid, enormous, something magnificent and eternal that belonged only to Alexandria. Totally demolished, replaced by an insignificant home for monks. Shifra was no pagan, but she felt a surge of indignation wash over her.

"How unfair, Akiva! Think how important it was to so many people."

They settled back into their seats and Akiva gave the order to drive on. He shook his head from side to side. "Come now, sister. You're no longer a child. Surely you have learned that as the world turns, some people matter more than others. There was a time that pagans were the people who mattered. Now it's the Christians." He laughed mirthlessly. "Who knows. Maybe someday it will be the Jews who matter."

Chapter Twenty-Nine
Lectures with Hypatia

Hypatia's house was only a few stadia past the ruined Serapeum, in the once prosperous pagan quarter that still boasted some fine houses. She had probably been born in this house.

Carriages, chariots, and a variety of sedan chairs cluttered the street outside, guarded by their drivers and carriers. Akiva helped Shifra and Aella down from the carriage and looked at the crowd of conveyances. "Hypatia has quite a turnout today," he said. "I'd like to go in with you, but the prefect wants me to help him with an edict. Something to do with the Jews that needs careful wording. I'll send a man back with the carriage. Wait inside after the lecture until everyone has gone." He walked them to the entrance, introduced them to the porter and left. The porter turned them over to a page who led them to an airy upstairs room. From there, Shifra could see the former site of the Serapeum.

The page led them to a small couch near where Hypatia was seated chatting with Synesius. As in the morning, the bishop of Cyrene had set himself up as close to the teacher as possible. From the way Hypatia was smiling and nodding, it was clear that she was as fond of him as he was of her.

The room was sparsely furnished. Many of the students were seated on folding stools they'd brought, but others sat on a few couches that

Shifra assumed belonged there. Although spacious for a private house, the room was not big enough to accommodate everyone's servants, so they retreated as soon as they'd set up their masters' stools. Shifra quickly noted that she and Aella were again the only women in the audience. And, as before, many of the students wore rich clothing and symbols of office. Most interesting to Shifra was the fact that differing dress and haircuts showed the audience to be comprised of pagans, Christians, and Jews.

To Shifra's relief and pleasure, the afternoon lecture had nothing to do with mathematics. Hypatia spoke on the topic of the soul according to Plato.

"Every human soul exists before birth in a perfect world, knowing everything. At birth, the soul enters the body, forgetting everything it knew before and having to learn everything all over again."

A florid man seated at the end of the couch nearest Hypatia spoke.

"I am told that the Christians have a different view of the origin of the soul, do they not?"

Hypatia nodded. "They believe that in the beginning, God created only two souls: one for Adam and one for Eve."

The man frowned. "Adam and Eve?"

"According to Christian belief, Adam and Eve are the man and woman from whom all other human beings descend. Rather like Deucalion and Pyrrha, who restored mankind after the flood by throwing stones behind them."

"Ahh." The man nodded in understanding. "But, if these two people, Adam and Eve, possessed the only souls, what of their descendants? I am certain that Christians believe that every person possesses a soul. How do they acquire them?"

"They believe that the soul of the parent is somehow shared with the child." Hypatia's face did not change its serious expression, even when laughter arose from the audience.

Shifra did not join in the laughter, but the idea did seem strange. She had been taught—and believed—that the souls of every person who would ever be born had come into being with the rest of the Creation—in the beginning. The pre-ordained soul hovers, like the spirit of God upon the waters, until the baby takes its first breath upon leaving the womb and becomes a living soul.

A noisy discussion erupted, but Shifra did not try to follow. Instead, she struggled to understand how a parent could give this original soul to a child and at the same time continue to have a soul. At last, she developed a slight headache and gave up the effort.

When Hypatia concluded her lecture, Shifra and Aella remained seated. Most of the men left as soon as the lecture ended. Pages holding baskets stood at either side of the door and as the men exited, they dropped something into the baskets. A few of the students lingered around the teacher until she said something that caused them to bow and take their leave. Shifra elbowed Aella and rose. "Most of the carriages will have gone by now," she said. "Let's go outside."

Hypatia also rose, and walked over to them. "I'll walk out with you," she said.

Shifra saw Aella's face beam with hero worship as her idol fell into step with them.

"It must be very tiring to give two such lectures in one day," Shifra said.

Hypatia rolled her head this way and that, the way one does to loosen tired muscles.

"More so now than when I was younger," she said, "but it is so intellectually invigorating that I love doing it." She turned to Aella. "And you, little one," she said. "What do you have to say after two long lectures?"

Aella flushed crimson. "You were wonderful, Magistra," she gasped.

Hypatia laughed. "Many people tell me so," she said. "But what of the lectures? Did you gain anything from them?"

Aella nodded so energetically Shifra feared for the connection between head and neck. "Oh yes, Domina," the girl breathed. "I know that I want more than anything to understand the heavens and the works of Plato as you do."

Hypatia fixed the girl with a severe look. Shifra wondered if she had been offended by the girl's words. Standing there in her scholar's garment, taller than most women, Hypatia made Shifra think of the pagan goddess Athene. She recalled the story of the girl Arachne, who compared her skill at spinning to that of the goddess and was transformed into a spider for her temerity.

"Not many women can hope to acquire such learning as I have," Hypatia said.

Shifra moved protectively closer to Aella. "My niece is very young," she said. "Even the impossible seems possible to the young."

"I do not say that it would be impossible for Aella to acquire such learning," Hypatia said. "Only that as a woman, it would be very difficult. My father, Theon, treated me always as a son. The female frame of mind was never imposed on me." She reached out and took the fabric of Aella's stola between her fingers. "How soft and delicate to the touch is this." She took Aella's hand and drew it to her own garment. "Now, feel this, how coarse in comparison."

Aella did as she was told. She rubbed the fabric of the scholar's cloak between her fingers. "Indeed, it is very rough," she said.

"As is the female scholar's life," Hypatia said. "Women of your class are brought up to expect fine garments, soft beds, rich food. They are bred to make good marriages and produce fine children. There is no room for scholarship in the life of a woman."

"I think I understand now why I saw no women among your students," Shifra said.

They stood by the entrance. One of the pages held out his basket, but Hypatia waved him away. Shifra glimpsed the contents, a heap of gold and silver coins.

"I do not forbid women to attend my lectures," Hypatia said. "It is their menfolk who do that." She turned to Aella. "Not many men, especially Christian men, are as receptive to their women's intellectual interests as your father. Continue with your studies, Child. Read all of the works of Plato, Plotinus, and Iamblichus. Before understanding comes preparation. When you are older, you may come to me privately. We will see then if you have the makings of a scholar."

Their carriage was the only one left standing in front of Hypatia's house. On the return journey, Aella sighed and squealed by turn. Hypatia had spoken to her. Not only spoken, but told her what to read. Told her that she could come to her one day as a student.

"Don't work yourself into a faint over it," Shifra said. "Hypatia said 'we'll see.' In my experience, 'we'll see' often means 'not very likely.' Hypatia made it very clear that she doesn't think much of a woman's chances to become a scholar."

"Oh, I know what she meant," Aella said. "She was talking about how most women get married and have babies and don't have time to study. I've already told you. I'm not going to marry. I'm going devote my life to study."

Shifra smiled. "Have you discussed this with your father?"

"Not recently," she said. "But I have told him."

"What did he say?"

Aella frowned. "Actually, what he said was, 'we'll see.'"

Akiva was already home when Shifra and Aella got there. He greeted them both with hugs and kisses. Aella pulled away and ran to the stairs.

"Where are you going?" Akiva asked. "Aren't you going to tell me about the lecture?"

Aella drew herself up to her full height, one hand resting on the stair railing, the other lifted with one finger extended, rather like the pose of a Christian priest bestowing a blessing.

"I have some reading to do, Father," she said. "Preparation comes before understanding." With that, she turned and ran up the stairs.

"Well," Akiva said, "I take it that she enjoyed the lecture."

"Very much so," Shifra said. "Are you aware that you daughter plans to become a scholar rather than a wife?"

"I have been so informed," Akiva said, "but it's early days. I haven't yet started bringing home likely lads for her to meet."

Chapter Thirty
Charity Work in the Delta

The following Monday, Clio (she of the saint's finger) arrived with a small open wagon just as dawn broke. Without so much as a *"good morning,"* she cast an appraising eye at Shifra's feet. "I hope you are wearing comfortable shoes. Once we get to the Delta, you will be on your feet the whole time we are there."

"Good morning, Clio," Shifra said.

Two husky young men in bright green tunics, who had arrived seated in the wagon, dismounted to allow the three women to take the bench behind the driver. Bags and barrels crammed the wagon bed, leaving no room for them. When the driver flicked his whip over the mules and the wagon rolled on its way, the young men ran alongside, keeping pace all the way to the Delta, the neighborhood where Shifra had grown up. The clanging of the iron-shod wheels against the pavement made speech futile, so Shifra simply looked at the passing scene.

The previously well-kept streets had fallen into a neglected state. Holes gaped where paving stones had been pried up to be used for some other purpose. Broken jars and unidentifiable trash littered footpaths between houses.

The driver stopped the mules in front of an abandoned, half-demolished house.

"Here we are," Clio said.

The men in the green tunics helped the women descend.

"These are our parabalani," Clio said. "Seb and Laurus."

Shifra frowned. "Parabalani?"

"Perhaps you didn't have parabalani in Milan. We have a great many in Alexandria. Several hundred. They belong to a guild of men who care for the sick and dying during times of plague. They are under the direction of the patriarch. Papa Cyril has kindly assigned Seb and Laurus to help me with my charity work. You only have to look at them to know they are good companions to have in a dangerous neighborhood."

Muscular and broad-shouldered, the men looked able to stave off any number of ill-advised predators who might attempt to attack the women. The one called Seb presented a particularly threatening mien because of scarring that ran from his forehead above his left eye, surrounding it, and continuing down that side of his face, covering cheek and jaw, and disappearing at last beneath the neck of his tunic. Shifra had seen something similar in a child in Milan who had jostled his mother while she was holding a pan of boiling soup. In fact, Seb's bubbly flesh resembled Dacia's scar from the oil lamp.

Seb had the black curly hair and dark complexion of a native Egyptian, while the other man, Laurus, looked to be of Greek ancestry. Neither seemed winded by the run alongside the wagon.

In the brief time the wagon had been stopped, a crowd of shabby men and women carrying containers of every description surrounded it. Seb and Laurus stationed themselves beside the wagon, while the driver remained aboard and moved to the cargo area.

Clio gestured at the contents of the wagon. "Most come for the food we bring, but a few will be in need of medical help." Lifting an eyebrow in an unmistakable sneer, she asked, "You're not going to be put off by a few running sores, are you?"

Pressing her lips into an answering sneer, Shifra replied, "I assisted my husband with the wounded the year Visigoths attacked Milan and sent Emperor Honorius fleeing to Ravenna. I've seen worse than a few sores."

The people crowding up to the wagon seemed to know what was expected. Most of them formed lines leading to Seb and Laurus. A smaller number lined up where Clio had set up a small table.

Shifra watched as a withered man in a ragged tunic and no shoes said something to Seb. When he'd finished speaking, Seb turned and reached up to take a parcel from the driver. The old man took the parcel and made way for the next person, a woman with a baby in her arms. Again, the medicant said something to Seb and, when she'd finished, he turned to take another parcel of food from the driver and gave it to her. Shifra moved closer and when the third person spoke, she recognized the words of a prayer she'd heard at the Christian services. It began with the Latin word, *Credo*. She walked over to stand by Clio, who was binding a child's hand with a cabbage poultice. When she'd finished, she said, "Next," and a woman with her hands pressed against her stomach came forward.

"The cramps are terrible this morning," the woman said.

Clio held up a finger. "Are you forgetting something?"

The woman frowned in apparent confusion. Clio whispered, "*Credo?*"

The woman shut her eyes and gabbled out the prayer. Apparently satisfied, Clio chose a vial from the containers on the table. "Take six drops of this morning and evening for two days. And say a *Pater Noster* each time." She looked up and noticed Shifra.

"So, are you ready to help? Come over here and we can handle two at a time."

Shifra took her place on the other side of the table. "Why do you require them to say that prayer before you help them?"

236

Clio smiled. "You don't think I want to waste supplies on pagans or Jews!"

"What's to stop a non-Christian from reciting the prayer?"

Clio shrugged. "Anyone who will recite the Creed in order to get a little charity cannot care very much about their own religion, now can they? If we force them to say the words often enough, they'll come to believe them."

Shifra felt the heat rise along her neck. She could not recite the words and had no intention of learning them, but she would hear them spoken every Sunday from now on if she continued to conceal the fact that she was a Jew. How was concealment any better than apostasy?

Clio looked at the next person in line, a woman with a rag wrapped round her hand. She directed her to Shifra with a gesture and called out, "Next."

The woman thrust out her hand to Shifra, while rapidly saying the Credo. Shifra unwrapped the filthy rag. Her stomach lurched as she viewed the flesh at the base of the thumb. "How did this happen?" The woman kept her eyes cast down. "Rat bite, lady."

Shifra studied the materials on the table. The vials, flasks and boxes were carefully labeled. What she needed was boiling water to cauterize the wound. Lacking that, she expressed the pus and cleansed the wound with vinegar. Then, she applied a poultice of macerated willow bark and bound the thumb and adjoining hand with clean linen. The woman said she had vinegar at home, so Shifra gave her some linen strips and sent her on her way.

***

As weeks gathered into months, Shifra achieved an uneasy peace in her brother's house, clinging to her Jewish identity in secret, but otherwise conforming to his expectations in public. Despite the presence in the house of her brother and niece, she grew lonelier day by day. Even her long, affectionate relationship with Dacia had changed. The old comfortable rapport seemed to have diminished. Shifra longed for a friend with whom she could share uncensored thoughts.

***

After several closely supervised visits, Clio allowed Shifra and Dacia to make house calls without her. Sometimes, she sent Seb with them, sometimes Laurus. About a week after Yom Kippur, in the fall of her first year in Alexandria, Shifra left a patient's house ahead of Dacia and Seb, who were still putting things in order. As she stood out front, she saw what looked like a large bundle of laundry in the street. Going closer, she heard a moan and recognized the bundle as an elderly man, who must have fallen and injured his head. Quickly, she knelt beside him. A small pool of blood glistened beside his head, and his right arm lay twisted unnaturally beneath him. She looked back at the house she'd just been to, wondering how best to deal with the situation. She needed water and vinegar to cleanse the head wound and would need help to turn the man over to inspect the arm, which was probably broken. Dacia and Seb had still not emerged, so, when someone suddenly knelt beside her, she cried out. "Who?" Turning, she saw a gray-haired man perhaps ten years her senior. Smiling, he spoke in a deep pleasant voice.

"Pardon the intrusion, Domina, but I think you could use some help."

He slipped off the large bag that hung from his shoulder and placed it on the ground. "He needs to be turned. Could you…"

Before he could finish, Shifra shook off her surprise and helped turn the injured man onto his side. He moaned.

"Apologies, Simon. We tried to be gentle."

"You know this man?"

"Yes. He's one of my regulars. Lives with his son a few houses over from here. Shouldn't be out alone. Gets confused." He delved in the large bag, which seemed to contain medical supplies. "Good, I still have some boiled water." Working swiftly and surely, he cleaned and bandaged the wound. "Now—" He nodded at Shifra as if she were a regular assistant. "We need to stabilize the arm. Lucky he's wearing a short-sleeved tunic." He palpated the arm. "It's broken, all right. Take hold of his wrist and hold the arm steady while I wrap it." As she had countless times for Benjamin, Shifra assisted this stranger as if accustomed to it.

"There. He needs to rest a bit before we get him back home." He smiled at Shifra. "Well done, by the way. Having demanded your assistance, it's time I introduced myself. My name is Gideon ben Ezra."

Startled at the Jewish name, Shifra responded without thinking. "Shifra bat Elad."

Mutual astonishment showed in Gideon's face. He stood and extended a hand to help Shifra up. "You seem to be accustomed to tending the injured."

"My husband was a physician. I often assisted him."

"Was?"

"He died."

In a rush, Shifra told Gideon about Benjamin, his murder, her return to Alexandria, her brother's apostasy, and her own masquerade as a Christian do-gooder. Gideon, in turn, told her something of his background—the loss of wife, children, home, and medical practice to anti-Jewish violence. By the time that Dacia and Seb emerged, Simon's son had come looking for his father and helped Gideon take the old man back home. As for Shifra, she had found the confidant she had been longing for.

239

Chapter Thirty-One
A Surreptitious Plan

Having met Gideon, Shifra took a new interest in the trips to the Delta. However, few opportunities to pursue the friendship presented themselves on the days she visited the Delta because of Clio's presence. She began to wonder if Akiva might make it possible for her to visit the Delta on her own.

One evening, about three weeks after the meeting with Gideon, Aella, as usual, had gone from supper to her books, leaving her aunt and father to enjoy a hot drink in the tablinum before bed. Some days, Akiva returned home from work tense and irritable, but tonight he seemed relaxed and genial. She decided to make her case.

"I had something of an adventure the other day," she said, and told him about the old man fallen in the street and the kindly doctor who had come along to help.

Akiva harumphed. "I wouldn't expect a doctor to be roaming the Delta, giving out free medical assistance. Sounds odd to me. All the doctors I know are busy making money in the better parts of Alexandria."

Shifra proceeded to explain what was different about this particular doctor. "I tell you, Brother. I have not felt that helpful and satisfied with myself since I used to help Benjamin back in Milan. I do so want to be a part of Gideon's work with the poor Jews of the Delta. Helping our people would relieve much of the guilt I feel in hiding my religion."

***

Akiva gazed at his sister. He had not seen such hopefulness in her face since the day he met her at the ship. He knew she'd been disappointed in him. He'd not made the decision to convert lightly. As long as their father was alive, he attended synagogue and performed all the rituals their religion required. Even now, he retained the Friday night lighting of the Sabbath candles because they reminded him of childhood and comforted his soul. If he had been able to have a career in the imperial service and remain a Jew, he would have. A man had to go with the times. Once, it had been possible to be a Jew and serve the empire. They even had an ancestor who had risen to be procurator of Judea during the reign of Claudius. But now—

He spoke as noncommittally as he could.

"The Delta is a dangerous place. When you and Clio go there, you have the protection of two trained parabalani. Who would protect you?"

"Perhaps you could let Cronus go with us."

"Us?"

"I would expect to take Dacia with me."

"Does she know about your Jewish doctor?"

"No. She wasn't with me when we met. But I trust her. She hasn't revealed my secret in the three months we've been here."

"I wouldn't be too sure of her, Sister. This is a Christian household. She's in daily contact with Christians and, though she is not orthodox, she is more in sympathy with other Christians than with Jews."

She made a face that Akiva knew well. No use pursuing the point.

241

"Say that I could do without Cronus and a driver one day a week, what would keep Clio from finding out?"

"I could go on Thursdays. On Thursday Clio volunteers at the patriarch's palace. It is the crowning point of her week. She never misses it."

Driven as much by guilt as by love, Akiva permitted himself to be persuaded. "Very well, Sister. We shall try it. I'll let you have Cronus and one of the grooms to drive you there in the two-wheeler. Don't make me regret it."

***

Shifra put off telling Dacia of her plan. On the next Wednesday, when Clio brought them home after their day in the Delta, she decided that she would tell her as soon as they got inside. Before they descended from the wagon, however, Clio detained her with a hand on her arm.

"Before you go, I've a favor to ask."

Shifra waited, dreading what might be coming. Another day with her in the Delta? They already went every Monday and Wednesday.

Clio inclined her head in Dacia's direction. "I'd like to borrow your ancilla to help me at the palace tomorrow."

Hearing Dacia gasp, Shifra whirled, expecting to see a horrified look. Instead, she saw unconcealed joy.

Clio went on. "Herculanius transferred my usual woman to the farm to help his mother, and I don't have anyone else suitable at the moment."

Shifra knew Dacia well enough to read her face. The girl was hoping for her to approve the request. She'd planned to take Dacia with her to help Gideon, but Akiva's warning came into her mind. What if he were right about not trusting her? If Dacia spent her Thursdays with Clio, she would remain ignorant of Shifra's friendship with the Jewish doctor. Perhaps that would be a good thing after all.

"Very well, Clio. Dacia has my permission to accompany you tomorrow. We'll see how it works out for both of us."

Chapter Thirty-Two
Dacia Finds a Friend

The opportunity to accompany Clio for her Thursday service in the patriarch's palace filled Dacia with joy. She knew that Clio took only one parabalanus with her on Thursdays and that was Seb. Dacia had been fascinated by Seb from the beginning. First and most intriguing to her was the scar that covered the left side of his face from forehead to neck. Even his left eye was disfigured by it, the skin around it puckered, shrinking it smaller than his right eye. Her own disfigurement paled in comparison, yet he made no effort to conceal his. He seemed, in fact, completely unaware of it. The right side of his face was unmarked. Viewed in profile from the right side, he was quite good-looking, even more so than Roderick. Her breath caught. Until recently, Roderick the Goth had been daily in her thoughts. To forget him seemed disloyalty. Their acquaintance had been brief, and, except for one tender kiss, without physical contact. Yet, knowing him had changed her, made her see herself apart from her enslaved status, taught her to see herself as a person with an origin and an identity. *Amalia.*

During the first weeks of helping Clio in the Delta with the delivery of supplies, Dacia had not exchanged words of any kind with the male helpers. When Clio assigned either Seb or Laurus to accompany them on house calls, Dacia assumed that their only duty was to protect them in the rough neighborhood. She soon learned that the men were there to enforce Clio's rules.

Seb had gone with them the first time that Shifra visited a house without Clio. A ragged, stooped woman opened the door.

"Hello. We have come to help you," Shifra said.

The woman stared from rheumy eyes. Before she could answer, Seb shouldered forward and asked her to recite the Credo. When the woman produced the required formula, Seb stepped back and allowed Shifra and Dacia to enter, where they bathed the woman's feet and applied a healing balm between her toes.

After that, Seb insisted upon being the one to knock on the door. If residents were unable to recite the Credo, he offered to teach them. If the householder declined instruction, he used his huge bulk to nudge Shifra back into the street. The first time that happened, she shouted at him. "These people need help!" Seb merely shrugged and said, "The mistress's orders."

One day on their rounds, Seb asked Dacia what name he should call her by. She looked at his handsome dark features, so different from Roderick's northern complexion, and found herself hoping that they might become friends and that she might have the easy conversations with him that she'd had with Roderick.

"*Amalia*," she said. "You may call me *Amalia*." Her birth name, the name that had sounded so sweet on Roderick's tongue.

Seb smiled, his scar crinkling up on the left side of his mouth. "*Amalia*. That's a pretty name."

After that, when their duties permitted, they talked. About his life, about hers, about the teachings of Christ. She did not tell him that she followed the Arian form of Christianity. She feared it would be the end of their friendship.

Once, she asked him why Clio refused to help people who did not say the Credo. He shrugged. "If they are unwilling to seek the Light for the sake of their souls, they must seek help elsewhere for their bodily ills."

Dacia remembered that her Jewish master, Benjamin, had never turned anyone away who came to the house in need of medical help, never asked their religion. She remembered the night the bedraggled man came begging for help for his wife, how, despite the mistress's pleading, the master had gone with him. He'd gone and been killed for his trouble. Perhaps Clio's approach made sense. People who didn't accept Christ were going to Hell, so there wasn't really much point in wasting resources on them.

***

As it happened, cutting Dacia out of the Thursday charity mission in the Delta worked out very well. Shifra and Gideon made an efficient team, and they could converse freely on any topic. He did not chide her for her deception, but did warn her of its dangers.

"Hiding your religion has its advantages," he acknowledged, "but you risk being found out. Your friend, Clio, for example, would be enraged to discover she welcomed you as a Christian colleague, only to discover that you belong to our despised religion. If she wished to punish you, she has the ear of the patriarch himself."

Shifra smiled. "If she were to find out, then, yes, I could expect retribution. But who besides my brother and serving woman—and now you—know that I have not converted? Only three people in all of Alexandria, and none of them would betray me."

Part Four

Alexandria

August 413 – March 415

Chapter Thirty-Four
Aella Becomes Eligible

And so, Shifra settled into the fabricated life of a well-to-do Christian lady, doing charitable works among the poor and attending services at the former Caesareum on Sundays. After what Clio had said about the effect of repetition, she avoided listening to the recitation of the Creed that ended the service. When time came for the congregation to recite the Credo, she blocked the words by reciting the Shema three times in her mind. *Hear O Israel, the Lord is our God, the Lord is one. And as for you, you shall love the Lord your God with all your heart, with all your soul, and with all your strength.*

She continued to soothe her conscience by telling herself that concealing her religion was still better than renouncing it in a public show of conversion. Like Mordecai. Like Albina and Caleb. Like her own brother.

Inspired by Hypatia's promise to evaluate her scholarly potential in the future, Aella gladly left more and more of her former duties to her aunt. She viewed the commencement of her menses as an intrusion on her academic goals and a monthly tax on her time. Her father, on the other hand, when Shifra told him the news, clearly perceived their arrival as a signal for him to begin looking around for a suitable husband. Dinner guests became more frequent and inevitably included at least one eligible young man.

The first such dinner occurred on a July evening shortly after word came from Constantinople that thirteen-year-old Emperor Theodosius II had proclaimed his eldest sister Augusta. Fifteen-year-old Pulcheria now had administrative powers. According to Shifra's Delta ally, Gideon, the announcement was bad news for Jews. "She has two great hatreds," he told her. "Jews and Nestorians. Jews, because she blames them for Jesus' death, and Nestorians, because they don't show sufficient respect to the woman who bore him."

The topic of Pulcheria's ascension to rank of Augusta animated Akiva's first husband-seeking dinner that July, almost a year to the month of Shifra's return to Alexandria.

"A fifteen-year-old—and a female into the bargain—advising our thirteen-year-old emperor." The speaker was Herculanius. He'd come without his wife, Clio, but with her young nephew, Philip. "That ought to make for some interesting legislation."

Shifra observed the faces of the diners. Aella with a vacant gaze, doubtless pondering some Platonic truth; everyone else contemplating Herculanius's cynical comment. The nephew, a tall lean blond in an exquisitely embroidered tunic, frowned in evident disapproval. The other two guests, a lawyer named Marcellus and his young assistant, Justus, a dark stocky young man with an untidy mop of black hair, displayed neither approval nor disapproval.

The nephew spoke. "Aunt Clio says that the Augusta Pulcheria has God's blessing and will therefore advise her brother most holily. She says that Papa Cyril approves most strongly of her elevation in rank. Already, Pulcheria has instituted daily prayer and scripture reading in the palace. She and her sisters have taken vows of perpetual virginity and no man is permitted to enter the palace living quarters."

Herculanius scoffed. "I suppose that means she doesn't count monks and priests as men. From what I hear, there are plenty of them attending on her." He took a drink of wine. "What do you think, Marcellus? All that power to a girl?"

Marcellus rubbed his jaw thoughtfully. When he spoke, he reminded Shifra a little of Benjamin, conveying an air of tolerance and neutrality. In appearance, he was nothing like her late husband, but in manner, he exuded the same sense of calm and kindness. He chose his words carefully before speaking, including both Herculanius and Philip in his response.

"Of matters imperial or divine, I have little experience. It is not my place to pass judgement on the decisions of imperial personages or prelates. Therefore, I must decline to offer an opinion on the matter."

Nothing in his expression or tone of voice suggested disagreement with either Herculanius or his nephew. As Shifra continued to look at Marcellus, he briefly caught her eye. It may have been her imagination, but it seemed that the look he turned on her contained a hint of conspiratorial delight.

Herculanius turned a sour look on his nephew. "So, Philip, are you saying that you think women have the capacity to make rational decisions on matters of state?"

Color rising, Philip drew back sharply. "I was speaking of the Augusta Pulcheria, not women in general. I think it possible that God might make use of a woman when circumstances demand. The Lord works in mysterious ways, His wonders to perform. The late emperor left only one male heir and, at present, he is below his majority. He requires a strong religious guiding hand free of self-aggrandizing politics. The Lord has provided this in the person of a pious older sister. Females in general are, of course, a different matter."

This comment pulled Aella out of her contemplation of higher things.

"What are you saying, Philip? Are you saying that women in general are not capable of rational thought?"

Philip smiled indulgently. "I'm saying that the woman's sphere differs from that of the man. Scripture tells us that God created woman to be a help to man, to bear his children and to nurture them. Those duties do not require lofty thought. Such thinking belongs to the male sphere."

Face flaming, Aella turned to the other young man. "What of you, Justus? Do you share Philip's thoughts about the function and purpose of women?"

Justus, apparently having modelled his professional behavior on his mentor, mirrored the older man's gesture of rubbing his chin as he thought. When he spoke, his voice was steady and modest. "The holy scriptures tell me that the Lord God made all of mankind in his own image, *male and female created He them*. And the worthy Saint Paul, he also teaches us that in Christ, *there is neither male nor female, for all are one in Christ Jesus*. It seems to me that women, having been created equal, must possess the same intellectual abilities as men."

Shifra noted the change in Aella's angry expression. She stared at Justus in wonder and admiration. Glancing at Akiva, Shifra saw a look of paternal satisfaction.

Chapter Thirty-Four
An Old Acquaintance

Because of Aella's positive reaction to his comment at that first dinner, Justus became a frequent guest and—with him—the lawyer Marcellus.

Shifra, not naturally inclined to feel comfortable at meals with nonfamily members, found herself looking forward to dinner when she knew that Marcellus would be among the guests.

A widower of about Shifra's own age, Marcellus had retired from a lucrative practice in Constantinople, where his clients had included members of the imperial government. In Alexandria, he practiced sparingly, mostly serving as teacher and mentor to Justus and two or three young men like him. About a head taller than Shifra, he still had a full head of curly hair, a mixture of gray and black, which he wore short. He had a droll sense of humor. Most of the time, she could not be sure when he was joking. He gave an opinion only when asked for it. Shifra liked the way his eyes crinkled almost shut when he laughed. She supposed he was a Christian. She'd never seen him at Cyril's church, but Alexandria had more than one place of Christian worship. One evening, when she told him that she attended Hypatia's lectures from time to time, he expressed an interest in hearing more, but dinner conversation did not permit prolonged discussion. After the guests had gone, Akiva stopped her on her way to bed.

"I have a message for you, Sister. Marcellus wishes to know if you would give him the pleasure of taking you for a ride in the country tomorrow afternoon."

Shifra felt her face burn. "And why could he not ask me himself?"

Akiva grinned. "I expect he wants to give you the chance to refuse without embarrassment."

"What do you think I should do? I mean, he's a Christian. Would I be risking my secret?"

Akiva laughed. "My dear, I'll say what has often been said to me— you don't *look* Jewish."

Shifra swatted her brother. She often wished she and Marcellus had more time to talk than was possible at dinner. "Very well. Tomorrow is Friday, so both Dacia and I are free."

"Dacia? If I know Marcellus, he will want to take you in his cisium. I believe you know that a cisium seats only two."

Again Shifra felt the heat rise in her face. Akiva bent to give her a quick kiss. "Let me know in the morning what you decide, and I'll send a boy to tell Marcellus whether or not to fetch you."

***

Marcellus called for Shifra at the ninth hour. A black horse with unusual white markings by his eyes drew his stylish lacquered cisium. He stroked the animal's nose before helping Shifra to her seat.

"I call him Argos, because those round markings make it look like he has more eyes than he needs."

After the midday break, shoppers began filling the streets as shopkeepers reopened, so Marcellus drove carefully to avoid pedestrians. Once they reached the outskirts of the city, he picked up speed.

Shifra loved the pleasant force of the breeze against her face as she sat in the uncovered cisium.

"This is lovely, Marcellus. What is our destination?"

"I wish to show you my country house. It's about an hour's drive from the city. We can stop there for a cooling drink and then make the return journey—if you find that agreeable."

"That sounds delightful."

Road noise and the wind kept the conversation to occasional exclamations about the scenery. Shifra relaxed in the intervening silences, finding them comfortable and not at all awkward.

The approach to Marcellus' villa wound through a planting of cork oak that provided welcome shade.

"It's small as villas go," Marcellus said, as they came to a stop under a portico attached to the main house. "But it has been a pleasant retreat from affairs of law. We—my wife and I—bought it when I retired from my practice in Constantinople. She loved the sea view."

Servants hurried from the house and grounds in a flurry of helpfulness. Argos was unhitched and led off to equine comforts as Marcellus and Shifra entered the house.

'Small' it might be, but the rooms and furnishings bespoke quality. Beautiful mosaics decorated the floors and fine murals the wall.

"I won't bore you with a complete tour," Marcellus said, "but I do want you to see my library." He led her to a room lined with shelves on which resided hundreds of scroll boxes. Shifra exlaimed in admiration.

"My niece would want to live in this room. She adores reading and fancies herself a future Hypatia. She has a fair number of scrolls, but I notice that she has been buying books in the codex format."

Marcellus shrugged. "I do have a few of the codices, but most of what I like to read still comes on scrolls. So far, most of the texts available in codex form are on Christian topics."

Stung by surprise at what seemed a less than pious attitude in a Christian, Shifra spoke impulsively. "I thought you were Christian!"

He laughed. "I'm a Christian now, but I worshipped the old gods most of my life. I find most Christian writing lacking in interest. Give me Homer, Vergil, Livy, Tacitus, and Pliny any day."

"If you don't mind my asking, what prompted you to become a Christian?"

"To please Flavia. My wife. It was her dying wish." His eyes lost focus for a moment. "I never could refuse her anything." With another lightning change of expression, he put his finger to his lips and made a show of looking around conspiratorially. "Don't tell your friend Clio, but I keep a shelf for the Penates in my bedroom here."

Shifra laughed. "Your secret's safe with me." She felt a warmth between them. A new sense of comradeship. When Marcellus had shown her the dining room and tablinum, he led her to the garden, where servants had laid out refreshments. From the vine-shaded table, they had a magnificent view of the sea.

"Flavia's favorite place," he said. "We were sitting here when she died."

Shifra reached out and touched him briefly on the wrist. "It's perfectly beautiful, Marcellus. Being with you in her favorite place must have been a great comfort to her."

Marcellus quickly recovered his composure, waved away the servant and served her himself. "The wine is from our own grapes. Pliny claimed that our part of Africa grows nothing but grain, but we have grapes and olives enough to supply the villa and my house in town. The real income comes from fish-processing." He grinned. "Luckily, the wind is right today, or I'm afraid you might be getting a noseful of fish odor. The 'crop' that supports the estate is *garum*, the all-purpose fish sauce that no Roman cook can do without. We ship most of it to Italy."

They spent a pleasant hour that passed all too quickly.

"Time to go," Marcellus announced, "I promised your brother to have you back by the twelfth hour."

As they re-entered the city, Marcellus slowed again to avoid pedestrians carelessly crossing the streets. Among the bright tunics favored by most Alexandrians, Shifra noticed a sprinkling of black. She mentioned it to Marcellus, who nodded vigorously.

"Monks from Nitria. Never a good sign."

After nearly a full year in Alexandria, Shifra had learned enough about local politics to know that the Nitrian monks were an unofficial army for the patriarch. When the old pope lay dying, everyone expected the deacon Timothy to succeed. Instead, Cyril summoned the black monks of Nitria. With their help, and that of the parabalani, he barricaded the palace and summoned an archbishop from Constantinople to consecrate him. The religion-ridden boy emperor in Constantinople approved the succession, and Cyril took the throne of Saint Mark. Since then, he had set himself up as the equal—if not the superior—of the civil authority. Many a day, Akiva came home from the governor's office worn out from the conflicts between Orestes and the patriarch.

As they neared the neighborhood in which Marcellus had his town house, they noticed some kind of altercation in progress. Marcellus reined Argos to a walk, for a better look. Three or four black-garbed monks stood around a small figure in a yellow tunic. Something familiar about the figure caused Shifra to frown. The monks seemed to be interrogating him. When the man responded, one of the monks slapped him across the face. With an angry cry, Marcellus pulled Argos to a halt, handed the reins to Shifra, and leapt down from the cisium. By now, a second monk had struck the civilian, knocking him to the ground and now all three were kicking him. Marcellus grabbed one monk, placed a foot against his ankle and tossed him to the ground. Two large men in aprons came out of adjacent shops and placed themselves between the monks and their victim.

"Explain yourselves," Marcellus shouted. "Is this man your slave that you abuse him?"

One of the monks, a short, skinny man with a pock-marked face and gaps where his front teeth should be, answered. "He's a devil-worshipper. We heard him invoke Isis. It's illegal to pray to the old gods."

"It's also illegal to attack the person of a free Alexandrian. The governor will hear of this."

The monk spat, insolently close to Marcellus' sandal. "Much good it will do him. Pope Cyril is the only authority we answer to." Glaring, the three monks moved off. Shifra got down from the cisium and bent over the prone body. A glistening of blood indicated that at least one kick had landed against the man's head. Shifra knelt to see how bad the wound was. She gasped in recognition.

"Isidore!"

Before her lay her former ship's companion, the little healer whom she'd lied for to save him from a beating in Sicily. She looked up at Marcellus.

"I know this man. Please, we must help him"

***

Without demanding an explanation, Marcellus sent a shop boy to his house, which was not far. The boy returned with two servants and a small wagon, into which they loaded the injured man. By then, he had regained consciousness and burst into tears when he recognized Shifra.

"The goddess be praised! Again she sends you to my aid."

Shifra made a hushing sound. "This is not the place to mention goddesses, Isidore. Please, it will only bring you trouble."

Marcellus sent his servants back, with instructions to tend to Isidore's hurts and put him to bed in the servants' quarters. He thanked the shopkeepers for their help, gave the shop boy several denarii, and took Shifra home.

"So, how is it you know that fellow? Clearly, he is not of your class, nor even the sort of servant you may have had in the past."

Shifra studied the face next to her, a good, kind, honest face. Even before he knew that Shifra had an interest in Isidore, he'd gone to his rescue. Then, without explanation, he had taken the stranger under his protection, sending him to his own home to be cared for. She decided that she could tell him what she had told no one—how she had lied to save a pagan from a beating.

***

That day's outing forged a friendship between Shifra and Marcellus as satisfying in its way as her bond with Gideon. A more stringent Christian would have judged her harshly for telling the authorities that Isidore had been fastening his sandal, not pouring a libation. Marcellus laughed. She still did not want to risk telling him she was not a Christian. Other than that, she found him easier to talk to than her own brother. And, from time to time, he accompanied her to lectures with Hypatia.

Chapter Thirty-Five
A Lesson in Politics

The new year dawned cool and rainy. Clio cancelled the usual mid-week visit to the Delta in order to spend the day in prayer and fasting. The day marked a year and four months since Shifra's return to the city of her birth, and she found herself spending the day in reflection.

She'd come with expectations of a safe, comfortable Jewish existence with her brother and her niece. Safety and comfort she had found, but her religion remained as much a liability here as it had been in Milan. Because her brother worked in the governor's office, Shifra had first-hand knowledge of a growing clash between the civil authority and the Alexandrian patriarch.

For Papa Cyril, as Clio called him, the new year marked two years and two months since his seizure of the patriarchy. He'd spent the past years stamping out Christian heresies, but now, according to Akiva, he was turning his destructive attention to the Jews.

Because of the holiday, Shifra planned a more festive dinner than usual, ordering her brother's favorite dishes, plus an outrageously expensive amphora of Falernian wine. As the meal ended, Akiva sighed a deep, appreciative sigh.

"A dinner fit for the emperor, Sister. It makes me dread returning to the mundane world of government work tomorrow."

"I'm pleased that you enjoyed it, Akiva. Only I'm surprised to hear you say you dread going back to work. I thought you loved your work."

"Time was, I did. Lately, though, the political and religious currents so much a part of Alexandria seem to be intensifying. Seems that every day, Cyril sends some sort of complaint to Orestes by way of that rat-faced Hierax or Peter, that officious, bull-throated lector of his. More often than not, the complaint targets the Jews." He took a lingering sip of the Falernian and sighed again. "I've seen so many black monks of late that I can only wonder how many are left to run the monastery at Nitria."

"Wasn't it like this with the previous patriarch?"

"Theophilus was a brutal man in his religious beliefs. He destroyed the magnificent Serapeum, sacred to the god Serapis, protector of Alexandria, which had stood for two hundred years. He led his parabalani and black monks against the Origenist monks, killing 10,000 of them. Nevertheless, he knew how to get along with the civil authorities. And he maintained lines of communication with pagans and Jews. I can recall dinners in the papal palace where guests included Hypatia and Karsas ben Levi. I can't imagine Cyril sitting at the same table with a pagan philosopher or a Jewish merchant."

***

Next day, dreading what new clash between Cyril and Orestes might be awaiting him, Akiva had Cronus drive him to the governor's office. He could have walked the short distance, but gave in to a sense of impending menace. Before leaving home, he'd cautioned Shifra and Aella not go anywhere without Cronus to escort them.

The office of the governor occupied a building next to the Mouseion in the central part of the city. The scene that greeted Akiva when he entered his workplace was worse than anything he could have anticipated. Apparently today's complaint from the patriarch's palace had not come via Peter or Hierax. Cyril himself and the governor stood face to face, in an attitude of intense confrontation, oblivious to Akiva's entrance.

Orestes, clearly trying to hold his temper, said, "I believe that is the Theatre's purpose, to provide entertainment to the people who desire it."

"Perhaps," Cyril sniffed, "but when the raucous entertainment impinges upon holy services and observances, then entertainment becomes an impediment to worship and therefore a religious matter."

"The Theatre was there when the Caesareum—now your church— was still a temple," Orestes pointed out.

"That means nothing," Cyril said. "Paganism ruled this empire before God opened the eyes of the blessed Constantine. What used to be is no more."

"So what are you asking me to do?"

"I want you to close the Theatre on Saturdays. After all, that's the Jewish Sabbath so Jews shouldn't be cavorting at a place of entertainment. They should be in their homes, observing whatever Satanic rites their religion calls for."

"I will take your concerns under advisement," Orestes responded. "Good day to Your Excellency."

"Damn the man," Orestes spat, when Cyril was gone. "He can't bear to let others live their lives as they see fit. First the Novatians and now the Jews."

"Things do get pretty wild at the Theatre on Saturdays," Akiva observed.

"That's a fact," Orestes said. "But you know as well as I that it's because the Christians shout insults at any Jews they see coming out or going into the Theatre. I hardly think that constitutes a religious matter."

Orestes confessed to Akiva that his first impulse was to ignore Cyril and permit matters to continue as they were, but upon reflection he knew that if he didn't act, the new patriarch would complain to the emperor at Constantinople. He decided that he would draft an edict to govern behavior at the Theatre in an effort to reduce the contact possible between the Jews and the Christians. He dictated the edict to Akiva, who then assigned slaves to make copies.

The next day was Saturday. Orestes and Akiva took the copies of the edict to the Theatre in person. Although the next performance would not begin for another three hours, the foyer was crowded with patrons, most of them—as Cyril had complained—Jews. Akiva scanned the crowd and recognized the merchant Karsas's dour countenance. Then, with some surprise, he saw Hierax. The man turned quickly away when their eyes met, but Akiva was certain it was the rat-faced Hierax and that he was up to no good.

Orestes took up a position just inside the main entrance. Akiva read the edict, stopping after each article to allow Orestes to explain it at length. The Jews, who regarded Orestes as their protector in an increasingly hostile atmosphere, listened quietly, if sullenly. As Orestes finished explaining the final item, a shrill voice called out.

"Let that be a lesson to you impious Jews!" Hierax. The unmistakable high-pitched whine was heavy with contempt. "Even the imperial prefect knows that Jews are animals to be controlled by rules. He's being too lenient. This filthy place of promiscuity should be closed down, yea, burned to the ground and all of you Christ-killing Jews with it!"

A roar of anger erupted from the crowd. Karsas lunged toward Hierax, but was restrained by others in the crowd.

Orestes shouted, "Bring me that man!"

Two Roman soldiers pinioned Hierax's arms and brought him before the prefect.

"Who sent you?" Orestes demanded.

Hierax's voice quavered, but he answered defiantly. "I serve the Patriarch of Alexandria."

"Did he send you to stir up this crowd?"

The cleric pressed his lips together and said nothing further.

Orestes sent for ropes and Akiva sensed what was coming. When the soldier returned with the rope, the governor ordered the patriarch's man to be strung up by the wrists from a beam outside the Theatre entrance. "Leave him there until the next performance begins," Orestes commanded. To Hierax, he said, "Tell your master, when next you see him, that the regulation of public spaces does not concern the Church."

***

Shifra could tell when Akiva walked through the door that he'd had a more enervating day than usual. Quickly, she sent a servant for wine and walked with her brother into the atrium, where they sat on the low wall that enclosed the impluvium.

"Do you want to talk about it?" she asked.

Akiva drew a huge sigh.

"It wasn't enough that yesterday he went to the governor's office and demanded that we shut down the Theatre. Today he sent that toady Hierax to stir up the Jews about Orestes's edict."

Shifra knew who "he" was. She had been in Alexandria long enough and had attended enough dinners with Akiva's friends and colleagues to know that the governor's archenemy was Cyril the patriarch.

The servant brought a tray with pitchers of wine and water. Akiva waved away the water and took a deep draft of the undiluted wine. He looked at Shifra and turned quickly away. "Orestes had to do something. Thanks to Hierax's hateful words, the Jews in the Theatre were that close to rioting. Karsas was raging like an aurochs in the arena and had to be held back."

Shifra gasped. "You mean there were Jews in the Theatre on the Sabbath?"

Akiva shrugged and took another drink. "Not every Jew is observant. Some are Jewish in politics only."

"That's terrible!"

Akiva laughed. "You're new to the affairs of state, little sister. You still imagine that calling yourself a Christian or a Jew or a pagan is a solely religious matter. Sometimes, it's just a convenient label. Politics and religion are two fish swimming in the same ocean. Any kind of label will do to distinguish factions."

Shifra sighed. The scholar Mordecai's nominal apostasy to keep his library had shaken her, but he still observed the Sabbath in the privacy of his home. The idea of Jews watching mime shows on the holiest day of the week stupified her.

Akiva patted her on the shoulder. "If Cyril were a rabbi, he'd have some excuse to complain to the unobservant Jews. But Cyril is a Christian prelate. What Jews choose to do on Saturdays has absolutely nothing to do with him. Breach of peace is a civil matter, not a religious one." He stood. Shifra remembered the odd way he'd looked at her when he said that Orestes had to do something.

"What did Orestes do? About Hierax, I mean."

Akiva answered without looking at her.

"He had him hung up by the wrists for a couple of hours. So the Jews and anyone else could pelt him with whatever came handy." At the door, he paused. "The Jews were pacified. Cyril's response remains to be seen."

Chapter Thirty-Six
The Limits of Philosophy

That night Shifra lay in bed, unable to sleep. Hierax's ratlike face swam in her mind's eye, shifting with the face of Isidore, the kindly pagan pilgrim who had been so helpful on the voyage from Messina. She'd noticed the scars on Isidore's wrists. She'd wondered about them. Now she knew how he must have come by them. Poor Hierax. Regardless of what he'd said, surely no creature deserved to have his limbs wrenched like that. How could an educated, civilized man like Orestes give such an order?

She tried not to think of the connection between Orestes and her brother. Would Akiva, the Akiva of her childhood, have given such a command had he been in charge? A sudden scream caused her to sit up in the bed, heart pounding. Her window overlooked the enclosed garden. Some small animal had been snatched up by an owl. She did not want to believe it, but perhaps all creatures, including human beings, shared the savage reality of the small and weak snatched up by the big and powerful.

On the Sunday that followed the torturing of Hierax, the patriarch preached against the Jews. On Monday, a crowd of Nitrian monks waylayed Karsas, the Jewish leader, and beat him to within an inch of his life.

On Tuesday, Akiva had Cronus and another burly slave walk him to the office and wait outside the door. Akiva had not had time to sit down before the governor stalked into his work area and glared at him from bloodshot eyes. "Karsas spent the night at my house. My physicians have been with him all night."

"Will he live?"

Orestes shrugged. "The doctors think so, but he may not want to. He's lost an eye, and it's not certain when or if he'll be able to walk again." He sank wearily onto Akiva's chair. "Without Karsas to rein them in, I dread what the Jews may do after this."

"Have you spoken with the patriarch? Shouldn't he discipline the monks who attacked him?"

"A plague on the patriarch! Those monks do nothing without his approval. He's determined to push the Jews to the edge of their patience. First the Novatians and now the Jews. He won't be satisfied until he has pillaged every synagogue and driven every Jew from Alexandria."

Orestes got unsteadily to his feet. "I'm afraid the Jews may go after the churches. We haven't enough men to guard them all, but I've set a watch over Cyril's. They may target the Caesareum both because it's his church and because it is next to the Theatre. Meanwhile, I must get some rest. My instinct tells me that worse is coming, and I am too tired to make decisions. I'm going home to sleep for a few hours. Alert me at once if there's more trouble."

Akiva remained in the office for about two hours, catching up on some routine correspondence, but his fears of what mischief might follow the attack on Karsas prevented him from concentrating on anything more demanding. Glad he'd brought Cronus and Verus for protection, he left early. Tension hung like a cloud over the streets. Several ordinarily busy shops were shuttered in midafternoon. He noticed that the few pedestrians he passed were men, and he tried to remember if this was a day Shifra visited the Delta. He quickened his footsteps and relief flooded over him when he reached home and found both his sister and daughter were there.

"Good! You're both here. I don't want you going anywhere for the next few days."

"Really, Father! What have we done?" Despite her words, Aella ran to her father and kissed him. "I promise, I haven't been stealing the neighbor's pears."

Akiva laughed and hugged her. When she was eight, she had indeed stolen some pears from a neighbor's tree and been confined to her room for a week.

"The streets are not safe just now. I told you what happened to Karsas yesterday. The governor is afraid that the Jews may be planning to retaliate. He has set a watch on Cyril's church. I'll feel better if you both stay close to home for the next few days."

That night, Akiva slept fitfully. Every time he woke, he strained his ears listening for sounds that might signal an attack on the Caesareum, which stood only a few streets over. He had finally fallen asleep when he was waked by a pounding on the street door. He'd gone to bed in his clothes, so all he had to do was pull on his boots. He reached the door as the porter opened it. A man from the watch stood on the doorstep. Behind him, in the dim early light, two horses breathed little clouds into the cold morning air. "The governor sent me, Sir. He said you should bring writing materials."

Akiva fetched a wax tablet and stylus and hurried outside. With the help of the porter and a mounting block, he climbed onto the horse that had been brought for him.

"What has happened? Is it the church? I didn't hear anything in the night."

"You wouldn't have heard anything from here, sir. The disturbance was in the neighborhood of Saint Mark's."

As they approached the church reputed to have been built on the site where the evangelist Mark had breathed his last, Akiva searched in vain for signs of damage. Because his attention was fixed on the church building, he almost slid off when his mount shied violently. His escort grabbed the horse's bridle and calmed it to a halt.

"We'd best dismount here, sir. The horses won't go further."

During the ride, the morning light had strengthened and Akiva could make out shapes on the ground ahead, what looked like heaps of discarded laundry. An unfamiliar odor rose from the scene. He looked around for Orestes and saw him speaking to a man in a light-colored tunic with dark uneven splotches of color on it. As he walked toward them, he saw that the splotches were red. He looked more closely at one of the shapes on the ground and saw that it was a man with what looked like a dark band around his neck. He gasped in horror and recognized the odor—the coppery smell of blood mixed with the stench of excrement. The piles of laundry were dead men. He scanned the street and saw that the bodies stretched beyond his line of sight. A wagon stood to one side and figures moved among the bodies, kneeling beside them briefly before rising and moving to the next.

"What has happened here, Orestes?"

"What I feared. The Jews' revenge for the murder of Karsas."

"Murder?"

"He died in the night, although the men who did this couldn't have known it yet." He nodded at the man in the bloody tunic. "Tell my secretary what happened."

Shaking, the man spoke in spurts. "I was sleeping. Everyone was sleeping. It must have been the seventh hour or later. The noise woke me, clanging—like pots knocking together—and men shouting. 'Saint Mark's! Fire! Fire! Saint Mark's is on Fire! Help!' I put on my sandals, grabbed a bucket, unbarred the door, and ran to help." The man stopped, breathing heavily. He staggered, as if standing was difficult. Orestes prodded him to continue.

"The moon gave hardly any light. Clouds. People filled the streets, like crowds on feast days. A man came at me and grabbed my hands—first one, then the other. It was like he was feeling for something on my fingers. Then, he raised his hand and I saw the glint of his knife as he thrust it toward my neck. I dropped my bucket and grabbed his wrist. The blade cut me alongside my neck as I pulled it down, but it was worse for him." He staggered again and Akiva put out a hand to steady him. He groaned. "Please, sirs, can I go home now?"

Orestes motioned to a soldier. "First go with this man to the medic's wagon. A field surgeon will see to your neck." He nodded at Akiva.

"Make a note of all that. Then, go with Marcus and take a count of the dead." He indicated the man who had brought Akiva to the site of the massacre. "The medics are checking for signs of life, so start the count where they've already been."

News of the massacre reached Shifra before Akiva returned home from his grisly day's work. Dacia brought it to her from one of the servants who had been to the market.

"He said that the streets by Saint Mark's are covered with the dead bodies of Christians." She made the cross sign on her forehead. "Please, mistress, please save yourself and become a Christian before it's too late!"

Shifra stared at her maid. In all the years they'd been together, never had Dacia urged her to change her religion. Had the woman been within arm's reach, she would have slapped her.

"How dare you! It was my husband—a Jew—who rescued you from the abuse of a Christian household when you were ten years old. In all the years since, when have you suffered a moment's insult or abuse in our Jewish household?"

Dacia ran from the room. Shifra stood and paced the room, furiously at first, and then slowing uncertainly. She needed to talk to someone about the massacre wrought by Jews. Was it true? Could a mob of her coreligionists do such a heinous thing? Dacia's role as confidant was clearly at an end.

Gideon was who she wanted to talk to, but going into the Delta was out of the question. She couldn't go alone. Who else could she talk to without restraint? She continued to pace slowly. And then it came to her. Hypatia! In the year and a half that she had lived in Alexandria, she had often chatted with the philosopher at dinners and while waiting for her ride home after a lecture. Although she'd never told Hypatia that she was an unconverted Jew, Shifra felt certain that the information would be of little consequence to the pagan philosopher. Her students came from every religion and school of thought. Devoted to the Platonic Truth, to her, all other beliefs were merely copies or pale imitations of that truth.

Hypatia's house was not too far to walk. She knew that Akiva did not want her going even short distances alone and on foot. Slipping out today would double her brother's wrath, as he'd already told her and Aella to stay in. A scratch at the door caused her to look up. A housemaid stood there.

"If you please, lady. Marcellus Bursio is below and has asked to see you."

"Ask him to wait in the tablinum," she told the maid. "I'll join him shortly."

The servant left and Shifra changed her shoes to an outdoor pair. Since his rescue of Isidore from the black monks, Marcellus had made Isidore a gardener at his town house, permitting him to sleep in one of the sheds. Surely, she could tell him anything, without fear of recrimination or exposure. She warmed at the genuine concern she saw in his eyes as he rose at her entrance.

272

"Greetings, Shifra. I don't know if you have heard about last night's disturbance. I only heard of it myself when I went to the Mouseion for this morning's lecture."

"Greetings, Marcellus. I have heard. Terrible news." If she wanted to persuade him to take her to find Hypatia, she had to be careful not to let him know that Akiva had instructed her to stay at home. "Was Hypatia at the Mouseion when you were there?"

"No. A librarian's assistant stood at the entrance telling everyone that today's lectures have been cancelled because of the disturbance. That's how I learned of the massacre."

She chose her words. "They say it was the Jews that did it."

Marcellus made a scoffing sound. "Not surprising they should reach a breaking point. Cyril has done nothing but goad them."

Shifra stared. Even from Marcellus, she'd expected a more negative response. Perhaps she spent too much time with Clio. She could imagine her saying something like, "What can you expect from Christ-killers?" or "The sooner they're rounded up and executed, the better."

"You don't think they did it out of pure Jewish malevolence?"

Marcellus shrugged. "I think the act was evil, of course. But I can understand the feelings of persecution that made it possible. The last straw was the attack on Karsas. Poor man. I don't believe for a moment that this would have happened under his leadership."

"You don't think their religion makes them do evil things?"

Marcellus laughed. "Of course not. No more than I think pagans worship demons." He smiled. "I've told you that, although I'm a Christian now, I worshipped the old gods most of my life. As far as I was concerned before my conversion—and to speak truth, now—the Jews have as much right to their god as we have to ours."

Relief flooded over her. The words came almost of their own volition. "Would you do something for me?"

273

Standing to attention, he struck his chest with his fist, reminding her of Marius, the centurion who brought her safely to Rome from Milan. "At your service, Domina."

The streets were strangely empty. Many shops remained shuttered, and the area in front of Hypatia's house was empty of the usual array of carriages that surrounded the place when she gave lectures at home. Marcellus walked Shifra to the door and remained outside when the porter admitted her.

Hypatia received her in a small, dimly lit chamber on the upper level of the house. A paper, perhaps a letter, lay on her lap. She did not waste time with social greetings. She motioned for Shifra to sit on the chair opposite her. She didn't even prompt her with a word like "Well?" but waited for her to speak first.

"Have you heard?" Shifra asked.

"Of the killings in the night?"

Shifra nodded. Hypatia was nothing if not direct. No round-about expressions such as "uprising," "disturbance," or even "riot," but straight to the heart of the matter with "killings."

"They say the Jews instigated it," Shifra said.

"They did," Hypatia said. "And now the Christians will retaliate. It will continue thus because neither side has any notion of the Truth."

"Can you do anything to stop it?" Shifra tried to make eye contact with Hypatia, but her head remained bowed. "Can you talk to Cyril and the Jewish leaders and get them to stop this senseless feuding?"

"I am a philosopher, Shifra. Not a diplomat. I teach the Truth. I'm not schooled in the ways of negotiation and compromise. I am able to reason with reasonable men, but Cyril is not a reasonable man. The Jews who planned last night's murders are not reasonable men. Their quarrels will continue because their minds are closed to reason."

"But when will it end?" Shifra cried. "When will Cyril stop stirring up his poor ignorant followers against Jews and pagans and even other Christians who disagree with him?"

Hypatia shrugged. "It will never end," she said, eyes fixed on her lap. "The only way to end such senseless conflict is to turn every human being into a philosopher. Unfortunately, not every human being is capable of accepting the Truth. As a result, men will continue to kill over false ideas."

A silence fell between them. For the first time in Hypatia's presence, Shifra felt uneasy. Usually so direct and focused, Hypatia had not, except briefly, met her eyes. And she showed no inclination to intervene with the patriarch. Shifra had another thought.

"What about Synesius? He might have some influence with Cyril. He is a Christian bishop, but not one who hates the Jews. Perhaps you could ask Synesius to appeal to the patriarch."

Hypatia looked up and Shifra saw that her eyes looked red from weeping. "Synesius is dead." She indicated the paper in her lap. "This letter is from his brother. My friend of so many years is gone."

Shifra's mind flew to a recent lecture in which Hypatia had talked about Plato's teachings about the inevitability of death and the appropriate attitude to have about it. Aella had repeated one of Plato's quotations so many times that Shifra had memorized it. *Birth and death are not two different states, but they are different aspects of the same state. There is as little reason to deplore the one as there is to be pleased over the other.* Hypatia had said that, because the soul is immortal and life a repeating cycle. Ergo, it is foolish to mourn the dead.

Shifra looked at Hypatia's tear-stained face and understood the limits of philosophy.

On the ride home, Shifra told Marcellus about Synesius.

"Sorry to hear it. Synesius was a good man for the times. Took on the job of bishop because it enabled him to protect his region. Never let religious dogma override his responsibilities to the public good."

"He wasn't very old," Shifra said. "I didn't ask what he died of."

Marcellus halted the carriage in front of Akiva's house. "My guess is he died of grief. During the past three or four years, he's lost his wife and all three of his sons. Family was everything to Synesius. He died because he hadn't anything left to live for."

Chapter Thirty-Seven
Worse and Worse

Rather than bring the stench of death home with him, Akiva stopped at the public baths and sent Cronus to fetch him a clean tunic. He passed gratefully from the tepidarium into the hot room, permitting the steam to relax muscles that had been squeezed rigid by the events of the day. By the time he was done in the square of Saint Mark's, he'd recorded the deaths of thirty Christians and three Jews. He'd left the rows of corpses to the red-clad public mortuary workers to clean up and stitch as necessary to make it easier for relations to identify them. For now, he wanted to empty his mind of the steady building of events that was sure to erupt into something still worse in the coming days.

***

Dacia anticipated her mistress's return, wondering where she had gone with Marcellus Bursio. She was tidying Shifra's bed chamber while she waited, sorting out clothing ready for the wash. She knew that the master had forbidden the women of the house to go out until he felt it was safe. Dacia had looked forward to going to the Delta today as they did every Monday. She longed more than ever for the freedom that would permit her to act on her desires. The days she could see

Seb, speak to him, and work alongside him had become the most important part of her life.

"What are you doing?"

Dacia whirled, realizing that she'd stopped working and was sitting on the bed, lost in thought. She jumped to her feet. "Gathering clothing for the wash, lady."

"Be done with it then, and leave me."

The curt words stung. Certainly, in the years she had lived with this woman, this was not the first time Shifra had lost her temper. Nothing unusual about that, but this time was different. This time the anger had lasted beyond the moment. This time, the matter concerned more than a lost comb or cold water in the morning wash basin.

"Forgive me, lady. I know I have angered you, but I spoke out of fear for you. After what the Jews did at Saint Mark's, the Christians are sure to punish them terribly. I'm afraid of what might happen to you if you are found out." To herself, she added, *and I fear for your immortal soul if you do not accept the Lord Jesus.*

"How can you, of all people, urge me to abandon my religion? Did you not sacrifice your opportunity for full manumission rather than abandon the religion of your childhood?"

Dacia bowed her head. She could not avoid it any longer. She had to find the strength to tell her. Forcing herself to look at her mistress and benefactor, she found the words. "I am no longer an Arian, Domina. I have been shown the error of the teachings I received as a child. Seb has convinced me that Jesus is co-eternal with God the Father, and the Nicene church is the only true path to salvation. I beg you, save yourself and be baptized."

The look her mistress turned on her took Dacia back to the day they learned that Roderick had taken his own life. Horror followed surprise, and then Shifra made a gagging sound and ran to the wash basin and vomited into it. Dacia grabbed a cloth and ran to offer it.

Shifra snatched it from her, but backed away. Her eyes flashing, she wiped her lips before speaking, her voice low and heavy with disdain. "Leave me. I do not know you."

Dacia left the room, her heart heavy with sorrow and dread.

***

Before going directly to the office the day following the massacre, Akiva had Cronus drive him around the city. Unusual numbers of people seemed to be moving toward the patriarch's palace, but otherwise, stores had opened and daily activities had resumed.

Orestes greeted him with a snarl.

"Do you know what that wretched man has done now?"

Akiva did not have to wonder what wretched man he meant. He did not try to respond. The governor paced angrily and elaborated. "He sent a troop of his black monks to the synagogue nearest Saint Mark's, pillaged their ritual objects and barred the doors."

"He may be up to something else," Akiva said. "I saw crowds headed for his palace just now."

The sound of running feet drew their attention to the doorway. An imperial watchman burst in. "Sir, the patriarch has made an announcement at the palace and has sent runners through the city to repeat it." Coughing interrupted his speech and he stood gasping for breath.

"Out with it man! What announcement?"

"Every synagogue in Alexandria is to be closed and every Jew is hereby banished from the city on pain of death."

Orestes's face flamed scarlet and Akiva could swear his eyes bulged from their sockets.

"By God!" the governor shouted, "Again the man usurps the Imperial power. He will answer for this." He barked a series of orders.

He instructed Akiva to write a summons for the patriarch to appear before him at the town hall at the tenth hour that day—about four hours from then. Legionaires, not slaves, were sent to deliver it. Once they'd been dispatched, he told Akiva to look up several statutes related to the handling of religious matters and to meet him with them an hour before the scheduled confrontation at the town hall. Then he left the secretary to his work and strode out of the office.

As directed, Akiva reported to the town hall an hour before the time the patriarch was due to arrive. A crowd was already forming. He wondered what Orestes would do if Cyril refused to come. For the first time, he began to fear for his future. In the past, the Imperial Service offered security that non-government work rarely did. Since gaining the post ten years ago, he had served two emperors and five prefects, providing a smooth transition between each of the latter. During that time, Alexandria had weathered riots, disease, and destructive storms, but until two years ago, when the old pope died, Alexandria's religious and civic authorities rarely came into open conflict. Cyril had proved to be a different breed of prelate. He seemed to think that his religious authority was equal to or superior to that of the Imperial governor. Something else that had changed was the emperor in Constantinople. Theodosius II was a child, whose guardian was a religious sister only two or three years his senior, who was no friend to the Jews. Not long since, Pulcheria had altered the law regarding synagogues. Whereas, previously, no new synagogues were to be built, those already in existence were permitted to remain in use, the emperor's sister had decreed the destruction of all existing synagogues. Fortunately like most such edicts directed against Jews and pagans, their implementation depended upon local conditions. The Empire was vast.

Orestes joined Akiva on the steps of the hall. The governor ran his eyes over the edicts and laws the secretary had looked up regarding the treatment of Jews. He nodded, "As I thought," he said. "He has absolutely no right to do this."

As the appointed hour approached, the crowd in the street had swelled to hundreds of onlookers. A confrontation between the governor and the patriarch offered entertainment better than a pantomime. Akiva gazed above the crowd in the direction of the papal palace and saw movement that resolved itself into a procession of dark figures. As it grew closer, he could see ranks of Nitrian monks in their black robes leading the procession. Behind them, elevated to the level of a man's shoulders, Cyril sat in a chair, clad in gorgeous robes of state. As the procession reached the parvis in front of the town hall, the bearers lowered the chair and Cyril made his way up the steps to stand with the governor. He was accompanied by Peter the lector, who was carrying what looked like a book.

"As you see, Orestes, I have obeyed your summons. I stand ready to hear what you wish of me. But, first, it is my desire to present you with a gift."

Akiva could tell that Orestes had been nonplussed by Cyril's mode of arrival and, now, the offer of a gift, as if he were the plenipotentiary of some foreign power. Before he could respond to Cyril, Akiva leaned in to speak close to his ear. "Do not accept anything from him, Excellency."

Cyril motioned to Peter the lector, who knelt before the governor. He held up a book, a codex richly bound in red leather. "Please accept this copy of the holy Gospels."

Orestes shook his head. "Many thanks, Pope Cyril, but this meeting is not one for gift-giving. You are here because it has come to my attention that you have attacked and pillaged a synagogue. Moreover, you have issued a command of expulsion to the Jews of the city."

The patriarch nodded as if he were agreeing with the most mundane of assertions. "You speak truly. I have ordered these things done.

As your excellency must know, the Jews massacred a large number of Christians two nights ago. They have forfeited any right to live among peace-loving people. It is only right that they be banished and their property put to good use."

The governor spoke loudly enough for the onlookers in the front ranks to hear and pass on his words.

"Those who committed this heinous deed will be hunted down and punished as criminals, not as Jews. Since the great Alexander founded this city, the Jews have had their portion and their rights. Synagogues are private property. As such, they are protected by imperial law. You shall return what was stolen."

The monks who occupied the first ranks of the patriarch's followers shifted their weight from foot to foot and spoke among themselves. Akiva interpreted the murmuring as disapproval of the governor's words. He had seen what they could do on more than one occasion. First, when Cyril occupied the papal palace two years ago as his uncle lay dying, preventing the archdeacon Timothy from succeeding as patriarch. And again, when Cyril banished the Novatian Christians from the city and confiscated their churches. The Nitrian monks recognized only one authority, and it wasn't that vested in the imperial governor.

The patriarch turned to face his followers, but his words were addressed to Orestes. "I shall take your words under advisement." Without another look at the governor, he descended the steps and resumed his seat on the gilded wooden throne. The bearers lifted it to their shoulders and the procession headed back to the palace.

The onlookers moved off, perhaps disappointed in the lack of conflict.

Orestes turned to Akiva. "Why did you tell me not to accept the book?"

"The Church is big on symbolism. If you had accepted a copy of the gospels from a prelate, the act could be interpreted as the civil authority bowing to the ecclesiastical."

The two men stared after the departing prelate. Akiva couldn't tell that anything had been accomplished by the meeting.

Chapter Thirty-Eight
Civil Disobedience

When three days passed without violence, Akiva agreed that Shifra could resume her charity work with Clio.

As usual, Shifra and Dacia drove to the area with Clio and the two parabalani. This was a day for going house to house and, before the wagon rolled to a halt, they were surrounded by petitioners. First, they dealt with the people surrounding the wagon. Then, Clio sent Dacia and Seb with a woman whose husband lay at home in a fever, leaving Shifra to carry her bag to a house where a child had stepped on broken glass. Having cleaned and bound the screaming child's foot and dreading the next frantic petitioner, she came out to an unfamiliar street. She looked around for clues as to where she was in relation to the wagon, proceeded uncertainly to the end of the street, and turned into the next.

"Shifra!"

"Gideon?" She barely recognized the usually neatly dressed, confidently erect physician. Today, his shoulders slumped, his cloak hung awry, and the tunic under it was caked with what looked like blood. "What has happened to you, Gideon? Are you injured? Can I help you?"

Smiling wryly, he shook his head. "The blood isn't mine, Shifra. I've been up all night, tending to the wounds of poor unfortunates who happened to be on the streets following the funerals at Saint Mark's yesterday. Some of the mourners thought to comfort themselves by hunting down Jews and beating them unconscious."

"Has the governor been informed?"

Gideon laughed shortly. "Do you really think the governor cares what happens to a few Jews? Especially after the midnight massacre? And what if he did care? From what I hear, Cyril is the power in Alexandria now, not Orestes. And Cyril wants all Jews banished."

"You are mistaken, Gideon. The governor *is* in charge. Only yesterday, Orestes summoned Cyril to the town hall and chastised him for overstepping his authority. He told him that he had no right to banish the Jews. My brother was there. He said the patriarch tried to assert his authority by giving the governor a copy of the gospels, but, when Orestes refused to accept it, he went back to his palace and that was the end of it."

Gideon set his bag on the ground and stretched. "You are too sanguine, Shifra. The end is still to come. Many of the families I've been with in the night are already packing up their belongings and looking to sell what they cannot take with them. Mark me, Cyril will have his way, sooner or later. Be very careful who knows that you have not abandoned your faith."

Orestes increased daytime patrols and made a practice of touring the streets himself, accompanied by an armed escort. Akiva often accompanied him and felt some optimism regarding the future when he saw renewed commercial activity. The cantinas were busy. With warmer March weather, many had set up tables outside. In front of fabric shops, bearers lounged by their chairs, waiting for their mistresses to emerge. Not so reassuring were increased numbers of Nitrian monks, moving in gloomy black-robed eddies through the foot traffic. With Easter still two weeks away, Akiva wondered why they weren't at Nitria, observing Lenten penitential restrictions.

Today, Akiva rode with the governor on his daily circuit. Two guards stood in the carriage and six accompanied on foot. The governor's progress slowed as they neared Pompey's column. As the carriage turned into the avenue that led back to Hadrian's palace, they found the way blocked from side to side by a crowd that looked to be made up mostly of men in black robes. The foot soldiers moved to open a space for the horses to proceed.

One of the monks, a head taller than the rest, moved closer and shouted.

"You've no authority over us, Orestes! A pagan Roman prefect has no authority over those who serve the living god."

Akiva saw the blood rise in the governor's face as he responded.

"I'm as much a Christian as you, monk. Baptized by Chrysostom himself. I have the certificate."

"Chrysostom! A defender of Origen's spawn and no true Christian!" With that, the tall monk hurled a stone toward the prefect.

Akiva heard the crack as the stone connected with Orestes' head. Bright red blood sprayed from the wound, spattering the men in the carriage with him and flooding his face and neck. The other monks stooped for more stones. Akiva helped the guards in the chariot lower Orestes out of the line of fire. The guards in the street drew their swords and advanced towards the monks. At that moment, more monks appeared around the corner of a building and the foot soldiers fled. Stones rained on the carriage. Akiva and his two companions got as low as they could, shielding Orestes with their bodies. Then, the shouts took on a different message. In place of taunts and curses for Orestes, insults and aversions for the monks gained the ascendancy.

Back, traitors!

Back, filthy crows!

The tall one, get the tall one.

He's the one who struck down the prefect.

Get him!

Akiva got to his feet and saw help arriving from an unexpected source—the Alexandrian citizens.

The basket vendor shoved his wheeled cart between the monks and the chariot. The eel-seller tipped his vat of boiling water into the street, causing the nearest monks to dance horribly in their sandals and back away. Three of the waiting chair-bearers threw themselves at the tallest monk and brought him down to the cheers of bystanders. Orestes's scattered guards regrouped and took the fallen monk into custody. Akiva took the reins and drove the horses as fast as he could to get the blood-drenched Orestes to a doctor.

Chapter Thirty-Nine
Cyril Suffers a Defeat

That evening, Akiva told Shifra and Aella about the attack on the governor. The women had already eaten supper, but went with him to the dining room, where the servants served him the meal he had missed.

Aella sat close to her father. "Nestor told us that the black monks killed the governor."

Akiva laughed and quoted Vergil. *"And so the breath of rumor, scant and slight, is wafted down."*

"He's not dead?"

"No. Not even close. Mind you, the wound bled like the Nile in flood. All of us in the carriage were covered in it." He shuddered and made a shivering sound. "As soon as we got Orestes to the doctor, we headed for the baths."

"How badly hurt is he?" Shifra asked.

"Hardly at all. Head wounds are notorious for being big bleeders. This one was superficial. As soon as the doctor cleaned and bandaged it, Orestes stormed off to the prison to interrogate Ammonius."

"Ammonius?"

"The stone was thrown by a Nitrian monk named Ammonius. If he hadn't been so tall, he could probably have escaped in the crowd."

Recollections stirred in Shifra's mind. The tall monk advancing ominously on Isidore the day they disembarked in the Alexandrian harbor. And again, the tall monk who spat on their carriage as she and Aella went to attend a lecture by Hypatia for the first time.

"What will happen to him?"

Akiva finished chewing. "It already has happened. Orestes interrogated him for three hours solid. Asked him the obvious questions. *Who sent him? Was the intention to kill the governor? What other mischief is plotted?*"

"And?" Shifra wanted to slap him for the way he was dragging it out. "What did he say?"

Akiva stopped eating and looked at his sister. "That's the amazing thing. Three hours of the weighted whip, hot pitch, and the wooden horse, and all he did was sneer at us. Finally, as the carnifex began flaying his legs, Ammonius stopped breathing. Never told us a thing." He went back to his meal.

Shifra rose from the table, her stomach heaving. As she hurried out of the room, her brother's words followed. "Of course, there's no question but that Cyril was behind the attack on Orestes."

As soon as word spread that Ammonius had died under torture, a delegation of parabalani arrived at the prison to claim the body for the Church. As Orestes expressed no reason to deny the request, Akiva released the body. Cyril immediately scheduled a funeral and Shifra attended, together with others in the household.

The coffin rested on a stand before the altar. The church was not as full as it was on a Sunday, but the congregation included a diverse mix of citizens. The patriarch usually spoke while seated on the wooden throne, but today he stood beside the coffin. He praised Ammonius as a Christian martyr who had sacrificed his life in service of the Church. He announced that he would henceforth be known as Saint Thaumasius and be added to the Church calendar. As he spoke, Shifra became aware of people moving and then the sound of whispering and, finally, little bursts of laughter. The patriarch stiffened and stared out at the congregants. The deep-voiced lector, Peter, shouted "Silence!" The laughter subsided and Cyril brought the service quickly to an end. He left the altar without a final blessing. The exiting congregation resumed their conversations and ridicule.

"Ammonius, a saint? Ha!"

"Saint *Wonderful?* Saint *Bone-breaker,* more like."

The comments did not stop with the congregants in the Caesareum. As the news of the newly sainted Ammonius spread through the city, so did the murmuring and outright ridicule, not only from pagans, Jews, and humble Christians, but from secular Christian leaders. The tall monk had been too well known for his brutal and intimidating behavior for anyone to take his elevation to sanctity seriously. Three days after his announcement, Cyril annulled the canonization of the dead monk and sent his body back to Nitria, to be buried in obscurity.

Akiva and Orestes took great satisfaction in Cyril's humiliation, but Shifra knew it was only a local victory. The emperor in Constantinople had yet to be heard from in response to the warring letters sent by the governor and the patriarch.

Chapter Forty
One More Lecture

With still a week to go before Easter, life in Alexandria seemed to settle back into normal patterns of activity. One difference was a growing presence of the black-clad monks from the monastery at Nitria. They were everywhere again—in the town center, on the side streets, along the quayside.

As Akiva had anticipated, courtship diluted his daughter's scholarly interests. The field had shrunk to only two—Clio's nephew Philip and Marcellus's law clerk, Justus.

Hypatia, who cancelled her classes for a time following the death of Synesius, had resumed her lectures and Shifra was eager to attend. The Monday before Easter, as Shifra prepared to attend Hypatia's morning lecture, she was surprised when Aella said she wanted to go too. Not only had Hypatia's name dropped from the girl's daily conversation, Lent, that Christian season of deprivation of pleasures had another week to go. For Shifra, Hypatia's lectures belonged to the realm of pleasure. At least one of Aella's Christian suitors would surely object.

"What about Philip? I heard him say that Lent is for praying and fasting. Wouldn't he consider a lecture a wicked indulgence?"

Aella laughed. "Who cares what Philip thinks? He's not the only one courting me."

"But, what about the Church rules? Are you allowed?"

Aella laughed. "Of course, I'm 'allowed.' Not every Christian thinks that anything other than praying and fasting during Lent counts as wicked indulgence. Papa doesn't mind if I go to a lecture. He did say that he wanted us to take a servant along, in case we have to send him a message before Cronus gets back to pick us up afterwards."

Although the companionable intimacy of earlier times no longer existed between them, Shifra still employed Dacia for normal household duties, so she chose Dacia to accompany them. As they drove to Hypatia's house, the carriage moved slowly because of heavy foot traffic.

"They're everywhere!"

Shifra nodded. She knew that Aella meant the monks. "The monastery at Nitria must be empty." She recalled with a shudder the time she and Aella drove to their first lecture. Two years ago, the black-robed monks had presented an intimidating presence, but today, they seemed to have doubled in number.

Cronus left them at the door, saying that he would return in two hours. As she entered the lecture room, Shifra looked around for Marcellus and was disappointed not to see him. She enjoyed talking about the lectures with him. Unlike other men she knew, including her brother, Marcellus never displayed contempt for the female intellect. She continued to rebuff his offer of marriage, but the prospect did not present itself as intolerable.

After the lecture, Shifra took a seat on a bench in the vestibule. Aella and Dacia hovered near the door, watching for their carriage. At length, they were the only ones waiting.

Exasperated, Shifra went to the door and looked out. "Whatever can be keeping the man?"

Dacia went further toward the street. "Someone's coming," she called. Shifra and Aella joined her outside. A runner approached.

"It's Silas," Dacia said. "Something has happened."

After catching his breath, the runner delivered his message.

"The master needed the carriage. There's been a disturbance outside the city. The governor has called out the master and others. Master says if you can't get a ride, he doesn't want you to walk without an escort. Just stay here until he can send Cronus." Shifra thought of Marcellus. Too bad he hadn't come for the lecture. But, if he'd come in his two-seater, what would she have done with Aella and Dacia?

One of Hypatia's servants brought water. Silas drank it and turned to go.

"I have two more messages to deliver, Lady. Farewell."

A few minutes later, two vehicles, coming from opposite directions, pulled into the area in front of the house. One was Hypatia's carriage.

"Still here?"

Shifra looked up to see Hypatia. After the lecture, she had retired to her living quarters, but now was dressed to go out.

"Our driver has been delayed," Shifra explained. "Perhaps we can wait here until he comes?"

Hypatia smiled and gestured at her carriage. "I'm giving an afternoon lecture at the Mouseion. You are welcome to ride with me." The Mouseion was only steps away from Akiva's quarters in Hadrian's old palace.

"That would be perfect." Shifra looked around for her niece, but saw only Dacia. "Where's Aella?" Dacia pointed toward the door and Shifra went outside. The driver of the other carriage had dismounted and was engaged in earnest conversation with Aella. Shifra called to her.

"Aella, come. Hypatia is on her way to the Mouseion and we can ride with her."

Her niece had other plans.

"Look, Aunt Shifra, it's Justus. Would you mind awfully if I drove back with him?"

Shifra understood at once that the convenient appearance of Justus was no accident. "Hello, Justus. You just happened to be passing?"

The young man reddened, but kept up the deception. "I saw Akiva's boy, Silas, and he told me that Cronus had not yet come for you. I'll be glad to take you home."

Shifra looked at his vehicle, a two-seater. "I have already accepted Hypatia's kind offer. Come, Aella."

The look Aella turned on her aunt would have melted a gorgon's heart. Shifra understood that Aella craved time with Justus other than what was possible seated at a dinner table under her father's eyes.

"You know there's not enough room in that carriage for three of us plus Justus. And you know that I cannot approve of your going riding unaccompanied with a young man."

Hypatia ascended into her carriage and looked down at the others. "Come, Shifra. You were young once. The seat in that cisium looks wide enough for three bottoms thinner than ours. You come with me and send your maid with your niece."

Shifra sighed. "Very well. Go with them, Dacia. I'll ride with Hypatia." To Justus, she said, "I'll expect us all to get home about the same time."

Chapter Forty-One
An Abomination Unthinkable

Justus directed his carriage east, clearly intending to take the long way round. Hypatia's driver chose the northbound road that led directly to their destination. The further they went, the more monks materialized at the edges of the roadway.

Shifra turned to Hypatia. "Why have so many of them come to the city, do you think?"

"The patriarch wishes to intimidate the governor. It is his way to show that he commands more foot soldiers."

Among the black robes, Shifra glimpsed the green tunics of the parabalani. She wondered if Seb and Laurus were among them.

As they turned right on the Canopus Road, the monks moved from the sides of the road to its center. Within yards of the Mouseion, Hypatia's carriage was forced to slow and then stop. Shifra heard a voice shout from the crowd. Familiar, where had she heard it?

"Whore of Babylon! Pagan priestess. Enemy of the Faith!"

Shifra recognized the deep voice of the lector Peter. She searched the crowd and saw him, a white-clad figure standing out from the wall of black robes. By now, the crowd surrounded the carriage and Shifra felt a rocking motion that recalled her first frightening encounter with the Nitrian monks. This time, the rocking continued, becoming stronger, angrier.

Peter the lector pointed at Hypatia in a great sweeping gesture and harangued the crowd.

"People of Alexandria, good Christians of Alexandria, behold the woman who has bewitched the governor. The woman who defends the vile Jews and persuades her pagan followers to attack the people of God. Remember Ammonius. Avenge the holy monk Ammonius. Destroy this tool of Satan!"

The strong rocking of the carriage threw Shifra and Hypatia into a rough embrace. Arms like mighty claws reached up from the mob, grasping at both women. Clasping Hypatia with all her strength, Shifra felt herself being dragged in the opposite direction. With a terrific wrench, the connection between the women was broken, and Shifra felt herself yanked from the carriage onto the madly pulsing crowd of bodies. Shifra heard the voice of Peter the lector above the roar of his followers.

"Drag her to the church. Let God Himself witness the end of this pagan limb of the devil!" And then Peter's voice was drowned by a woman's scream that sent thrills of horror through Shifra's core.

***

The emergency that summoned Akiva to join Orestes outside the city had been a ruse. The governor had been warned that a villa belonging to a high-ranking Roman council member was about to be attacked by nomads. He'd sent for Akiva and told him to come in his carriage, with extra arrows and as many foot soldiers as possible. As soon as it became clear that the rumored threat was nonexistent, they'd hurried back to the city, only to find what looked like the aftermath of a battle in front of the Caesareum. A repeat of the midnight massacre, the street lay littered with piles of clothing that resolved themselves into bodies. Medics were already on the scene. A soldier, one of the men on duty at the governor's office, limped up to them. His uniform was torn and a needle-thin streak of blood ran from his ear to his chin.

"We could do nothing, Sir. There were hundreds of them. We tried to stop them, but they took her." Orestes stared.

"Her?"

"Hypatia the sage." The soldier gestured at the Caesareum. "In there."

Akiva followed Orestes into the church. The pile of roof tiles that had become a fixture against the back wall looked as if a large animal had tried to make a bed in it, scattered the hard sharp objects over the floor and then peed on them, making them and the floor glisten. Akiva looked more closely. The floor was wet. He lifted one foot. His boot came away with a sticky sound.

Orestes whirled on him. "Explain this, man. What happened here. Where is Hypatia?"

Haltingly, the man explained what the mob had done to the scholar.

"They dragged the lady from her carriage, Sir. They stripped her of her clothing. By the time she was inside the church, she was completely naked. The cleric, the one with the loud voice, told them to stand away from her. She'd stopped screaming by then, just making whimpering sounds, kind of." He gestured at the tiles. "Someone picked up one of those tiles there and threw it at her. Then everyone was throwing them. And then, I can't say who started it, but I reckon they saw how sharp those things are and went to cutting her with them."

Comprehending now what made the floor sticky, Akiva turned away and vomited onto a pile of shards.

**

297

Shifra opened her eyes and saw white clouds against a blue sky. She was alive, lying on the ground. She moved to get up, but a heavy weight lay across her. A body. The rocking carriage, the curses and tugging came rushing back into her mind. She screamed. "Help! Help! Somebody, help me!"

***

Akiva stumbled out of the church, wiping his mouth on the edge of his cloak. Not far from him, a woman was screaming, calling for help. He knew the voice. "Sister! I'm coming."

She lay beneath the body of a man. Akiva rolled the body off of her, thinking it was dead, but as it rolled, it groaned.

"Akiva, thank the Lord." She sat up into Akiva's embrace which lasted several minutes. Then, gently, he helped her to her feet.

"Are you all right? Did this man assault you?" Shifra looked more closely at the man who had been lying on her. Blood obscured his face. His tunic was torn and covered with road dirt. Akiva drew his dagger. "I'll dispatch him this minute if he assaulted you."

Shifra bent closer and wiped the injured man's face with a torn part of his tunic. "Isidore! This is Isidore. He didn't attack me. It must have been Isidore who pulled me out of the carriage when the mob took Hypatia."

"Come, sister. I'll take you home and fetch the doctor."

"What about Isidore?"

"The medics will tend to him."

Shifra planted her feet. "No. Isidore saved my life. He deserves the best care we can give him. I won't go without him."

***

Only when a doctor was brought and assured her that Isidore would recover did Shifra allow Dacia to take her to her room. It was from Dacia that Shifra learned the grisly details of Hypatia's final moments.

"Cronus says the blood in the Caesareum was up to the soldiers' ankles!"

Shifra frowned. Akiva said only that the mob had dragged Hypatia into the church, where they killed her. She'd imagined a sword thrust or blow to the head. "What are you saying, Dacia? Why would there be so much blood?"

"It was the tiles."

"What tiles?"

"You know, the pile of tiles stored at the back, for the roof or something."

Shifra nodded. "I have good reason to remember those tiles, Dacia. I picked one up once and slashed my fingers with it. What about them?"

"Cronus says the mob grabbed the tiles and started throwing them at Hypatia—like stoning someone in the Bible. But then, when they saw how sharp they were, they started using them as scrapers."

"Scrapers? Why on earth would they need scrapers?"

Dacia swallowed audibly and looked away. For the first time, she seemed less than eager to share her information.

"Well? Go on. Why did they want scrapers?"

Still not meeting her mistress's eyes, Dacia went on with her gruesome narrative. "To scrape the flesh from the philosopher lady's bones."

Shifra seized her right hand with her left, enveloped by a memory so vivid as to be physical. She felt again the sudden shock of the tile's razor-sharp edge slicing her flesh, followed by the aching pain that remained long after she'd cleansed her hand at the fountain. She saw the bright blood welling from her wound, the gash caused by the slight contact with only one tile. And then she imagined Hypatia's last moments, as hundreds of tiles scraped the skin and flesh from her naked body. Shifra's stomach heaved, spewing its contents onto her lap.

Chapter Forty-Two

Options

Three days after Easter, a messenger arrived from Constantinople with the Emperor's response in the matter of the Jews. As soon as he read it, Akiva knew that his life was about to change. The emperor agreed with Cyril that anything to do with the Jews was a religious matter and that the prefect must stand ready to assist as needed.

As Orestes raged up and down the office after reading the letter, Akiva pondered the likely outcomes for himself. As a converted Jew, he ran the perpetual risk of charges of recidivism from a disgruntled servant or ambitious colleague. And there was his unconverted sister. He could hardly claim ignorance should she be revealed as a practicing Jew. And what about his job?

Orestes threw the letter at Akiva.

"Even before this got here, did you hear what he said when I ordered him to send his bloody monks back to Nitria? He said that my orders to him are of no account. He said that the civil government has completed its role in God's plan. There he sat in his gorgeous robes surrounded by men like Peter the lector who might as well be back-stabbing courtiers and telling me that earthly power has shifted, that the Church—in the person of him and the other four popes—is the new governing body. He told me that I represent the emperor, but that he represents God."

Orestes threw himself onto a chair, breathing heavily. "I ought to resign." He looked up at Akiva. "By God, I will resign" He stood and drew himself up to his full height. "I am an imperial prefect. I refuse to be ordered about by a mere priest. Other postings can use a man of my experience and credentials. Besides, I've been here nearly thirty-six months. Under the old emperor, that was the usual term for Egypt. I'll remind the emperor and ask for a new placement somewhere else in the empire."

With feelings of personal dread, Akiva wrote the governor's letter of resignation. Cyril would be pleased. But, once rid of Orestes, what would prevent him from ridding himself of the secretary who had served him?

***

Shifra could tell something was troubling her brother during dinner, but she had to wait to ask him about it until after the guests had gone. She approached him in the tablinum, where he sat staring at a pile of papers.

"What is it, Akiva? You seemed preoccupied during dinner."

He looked up. "Orestes plans to leave Alexandria."

"I'm not surprised. He must be furious having his orders overturned by Cyril. I hope the next prefect will get along better with the patriarch." She smiled. "You'll be able to advise him."

Akiva stared at her. "You don't understand. Cyril is certain to influence the selection of the next governor and he's not going to want me advising him." He sighed. "I can probably find private secretarial work, but nothing that pays as well as a government posting. I'm afraid I will not be able to provide for you and Aella as in the past." He gestured at their surroundings. "For one thing, we'll have to leave this place. And we'll have to sell most of the servants."

Shifra's heart raced. Milan all over again. Still, Akiva had a profession. She could do without the luxuries of Hadrian's palace. She looked reassuringly at her brother. "We'll be all right. I certainly don't need all this luxury. And, I'm sure you've noticed that Aella is in love with Justus. It won't be long before he'll be asking for her hand."

Akiva got up and took several paces around the room. He stopped next to Shifra.

"He already has asked. I told him that I couldn't approve."

"But Aella loves him!"

"Justus is a fine young man, but he is not the match we need. Philip, on the other hand, has a future. As Clio's nephew, he has the favor of the patriarch."

Shifra started to speak, but Akiva held up his hand. "Please, don't. My mind is made up. Justus is still a student. His employment is uncertain. Philip already has a good income as a junior lawyer here in Alexandria. I'm certain that he will eventually gain a position at the emperor's court in Constantinople." He resumed his seat. "As for you, my sister, I take your well-being just as seriously." He pursed his lips. "How do you feel about Marcellus?"

***

Dacia and Seb were alone in the house with the dead man. They had sat with him for three hours before he passed, and then they prepared the body for burial. The man's daughter was out notifying other relatives. Seb performed the necessary tasks with his usual attention and efficiency, but as soon as everything was done, he seemed distracted. As they gathered their supplies, he seemed to be avoiding eye contact. Shifra had gone to meet Clio, leaving Dacia and Seb to stay until the family returned. Minutes passed and Dacia struggled to think of anything she could have said or done to cause this new distancing.

Everything packed and ready to go, Dacia sat on a bench and watched Seb move aimlessly around the small, poorly furnished room. When she thought she could no longer refrain from questioning, he suddenly came toward her and sat beside her on the bench.

"I have something to say to you, Amalia."

By now, he knew that her slave name was Dacia and he remembered to use it when others were near. When they were alone, he called her by her birth name and she felt her heart melt when he did.

"What is it, Seb?"

"I couldn't ask you before, because I had to have Papa Cyril's permission. As a parabalanus, I owe him everything. My parents were going to sell me because they couldn't feed me."

Tears flooded Dacia's eyes. Another way in which they were alike. He'd never mentioned that, just that his parents had been poor and that the patriarch recruited the parabalani from the poorest families. She looked at Seb, his face, so comely on one side and so horribly scarred on the other. The expressive dark eyes she'd seen so often turned on the dying, filled with compassion. She never wanted to admit her feelings for him. She told herself that he was her spiritual mentor only, that she loved him for bringing her into the true faith. But she lied to herself. The love she felt for him was that of a woman for a man. She shook her head to clear it of such thoughts.

"Amalia? Are you listening to me?"

"Yes, Seb. I'm sorry. You've been acting strange today and I'm confused."

He reddened. "I'm the one who's sorry. I didn't know it would be so hard to talk to you about it." He took a deep breath. "I love you, Amalia, and I want you for my wife."

Dacia gasped and threw a hand over her face as if making sure the veil was there. Seb pressed on.

"I don't know when I first knew, but when I was sure, I spoke to Papa Cyril about it. When you and your mistress came to Alexandria, I'd been in the order for ten years. I thought I'd spend the rest of my life with them." He stopped speaking and put out his hand as if to touch her face. She pulled away. He reddened again.

"As soon as I knew," he went on, "I spoke to Papa Cyril about it. I told him that I wanted to leave the order and marry."

Dacia shuddered. "Was he angry?"

"No, not angry. Surprised. He asked me how I expected to be able to support myself and a wife." He looked at her. "As a parabalanus, all my expenses are covered by the Church. But I had given it a lot of thought before speaking to him. I told him I could work at the military hospital. They hire civilians for some of the work. Like when the Jews killed all those Christians at Saint Mark's. They didn't have enough wound-dresser soldiers, so they hired some locals." He smiled for the first time. "There are other places, too, that need my kind of skills. I know I can provide for you."

Dacia's heart raced. Her emotions see-sawed from joy to fear and back. To be loved, by Seb. To be wanted as his wife. She touched the veil that concealed the scar left by the burning lamp oil, permanent reminder of that long-ago violation. He would have to see it. And once he saw it, how could he still want her? She looked at him. He was still smiling and she could see the love in his eyes.

"That was last year when I told him. He said that if I still felt the same after a year, he would give me permission to leave the order. He said he'd even marry us himself."

Dacia put both hands to her face and burst into tears. She sensed Seb stand and hover over her.

"Amalia, dearest. What is it? Don't you want to marry me?"

Dacia spoke through her tears. "Oh, yes, Seb. I love you. I have loved you for the longest time, but...you don't know what I look like." She lifted her head and looked at him over her veil. "You've never seen me without my face covering."

He laughed and rubbed a hand across the scarred side of his own face. "And you have seen me always with my face uncovered and still, you say you love me." He reached toward her face. This time, she permitted him to place his hands against the sides of her face covering. She placed her own hands over his.

"Let me see, Amalia." Together, they drew down the veil.

He replaced his hands against her now uncovered face. Lifting first one and then the other, he kissed each side.

"There, I have seen beneath the veil. I have seen the face of my wife."

Dacia sighed and lifted her face to his, to be kissed on the lips.

Chapter Forty-Three
The Ground Shifts

Shifra was always glad to have time in the Delta away from Dacia and Seb. Today the neighborhood showed the effects of Cyril's order of expulsion. Steady streams of families in wagons filled with bundles and furniture, or individuals on foot with packs on their backs, moved along the streets towards city gates and their unknown futures. As she'd hoped, she encountered Gideon in a side street, helping a couple get an elderly relative into a cart. She waited until he was free.

"Hello, Gideon. Still here, I see."

"Not for long. My goods are packed and I have booked passage on a ship to Palestine."

"Palestine!" The memory of her son's departure from Milan burned like a wound. "My son may be there."

"Really. You have never mentioned a son."

"No. He left us while my husband still lived. Alexander, a wonderful boy. We sent him to Rome to finish his studies and when he returned to Milan, he expected to rise in the legal profession, like our friend and his mentor, Atellus Vibius."

"What caused him to leave?"

"He was a Jew. Unlike Vibius, who had grown up pagan, Alexander was not willing to convert. After too many rejections to count, he said he would find a place where it was not an offense to be a Jew."

Gideon laughed humorlessly. "I'd call him an optimist."

"Is there nowhere like that in Palestine?"

"Oh, some places are better than others. I aim to settle along the coast in Galilee where the population is mostly Jewish. The Christians have pretty much taken over Judea."

"I shall be sorry to see you go, Gideon."

He looked at her closely. "And you? You feel safe in ignoring the expulsion orders?"

She frowned. "What do you mean? No one knows that I am Jewish."

"Surely, someone does."

"Not anyone who would betray me."

Gideon bowed slightly. "May that be. I have valued our friendship, Shifra. May God go with you."

"And you, Gideon, my friend."

As she watched him move away, she wondered at the aching in her throat.

***

The family finally arrived to tend their dead relative and Dacia and Seb sought the street where they'd arranged to meet Shifra. Seb observed the moving streams of Jewish exiles with a look of satisfaction.

"At last! Alexandria will be free of these demon Jews at last."

Dacia stopped and stared at her companion. Maybe her delight at being loved had softened her feelings today, but his remark struck her as unexpectedly cruel.

"Why would you call them 'demons' Seb? I know that Jews are unenlightened and that they must accept Christ if they are to be saved, but they're just people, same as anybody."

Seb shook his head fiercely. "Papa Cyril says that Jews think like the Devil because they are his children. He says that as long as we allow Jews to live among us, all our souls are in danger."

Dacia resumed walking. "Maybe some of them are bad, but not all of them are. My second master in Milan was a Jew and he saved me from some terrible cruel owners." As they continued on their way, she recalled how Shifra had sat with her and dressed her wounds. She remembered how, when she'd recovered, her mistress dressed her in nice clothing and taught her to read. She regretted that her effort to save her mistress's soul had damaged the bond between them, but she still loved her. She leaned in against Seb, her heart suffused with love. "And look how my mistress comes twice a week to help the poor and sick. You can tell how good a person she is, even if she's a Jew."

This time Seb stopped in his tracks.

"What did you say?"

***

A few Jews continued to make their way to the gates and the harbor. In another week, they would all be gone. The city was peaceful. That's more than Akiva could say about his household.

When he told his daughter that his preferred suitor was Philip, she locked herself in her room, declaring that if she could not marry Justus, she would starve herself to death. Tonight, three days later, Aella was in the dining room with her father and her aunt. Starvation had lost its appeal. The conversation labored, as it had for days, along the lines of matrimony. The aunt was proving as recalcitrant as the daughter.

"I'm too old to marry! I'm happy as I am, running your household and doing charity work. I'll no longer have the joy of Hypatia's

309

lectures, but I can read and discuss things with Marcellus. I don't have to marry him."

"Don't you understand? There won't be a household to run if I lose my job with the imperial service."

Shifra jutted out her chin. "There will be a household. It just won't be as grand as this one."

Aella sat beside her aunt. "Justus is not as rich as Philip, but why should that matter? We won't be poor. And maybe he'll become rich someday."

Akiva sighed. How many times and ways had he already tried to explain the difference to her? "Justus is a fine lad, but Philip has influence. Marrying Justus does nothing for your family. Philip is the nephew of Clio and Herculanius. He has cousins and uncles who serve at the palace in Constantinople, are close to the emperor and his sister. Marrying Philip preserves my place in the imperial service. The patriarch would not be tempted to push me out." He sighed. "Philip is good-looking. And young. It's not as if I were asking you to marry an ugly old man."

Aella wailed and ran from the room. Shifra looked at him and shook her head.

"Young men are not interchangeable, brother."

"Perhaps not. But marriage is a serious family matter, not something to be decided by individual female whim. Aella is young. She must make a good match. Philip meets all the criteria—wealth, good family, imperial connections. And according to his parents, he is completely besotted with her. It would be irresponsible of me to tie her to Justus when Philip is available."

Shifra smiled. "Whereas, your sister is old. What is your responsibility there?"

Akiva sighed. "Not so urgent as in my daughter's case, but I still must provide for you. If Aella marries Philip, my position is safe. Cyril would not move against the in-law of his esteemed Clio. The Secretary's unmarried sister in that case could comfortably live out her days as a useful widow in her brother's house."

"But?"

"But Marcellus has spoken to me more than once. He much enjoys your company and, as he had a good marriage, he is desirous to have another." They sat with their own thoughts for several minutes. "He's a wealthy man, Shifra. I've been to his country villa. It is superb."

"He is a Christian."

Akiva shrugged. "Nominal. He converted to please his wife on her deathbed."

Shifra considered. "We would have to be married in a Christian ceremony."

"True. But we could go to a rural priest somewhere out of the city and get it done with a minimum of ceremony."

"I'll think on it."

Chapter Forty-Four
Aella Decides

Philip's parents asked that the betrothal ceremony take place without delay in the Caesareum. Without further persuasion from her father, Aella had agreed to marry Philip.

"But why?"

It was the day of the betrothal and Shifra looked forward to the ceremony for her niece as she would a death sentence. They had finished dressing and were waiting in her room before going down. Dacia moved silently about her work of putting things away.

"You don't even like Philip. He's officious and controlling. He scorns your interest in philosophy and literature. What can you be thinking?"

She tried to embrace her niece, but Aella pulled away. Beneath the eye makeup, clearly, the child had spent hours weeping.

"If anyone can understand, it should be you, Aunt Shifra. Family is more important than individual feelings. I'm doing it for my family. For my father. You told me once that when you were faced with converting to keep your inheritance, you could see your own father in your mind's eye and couldn't do it. You said you couldn't bear to abandon his religion. Well, I can't bear to let my father lose everything he has worked for."

To prevent further speech, Aella left the room. Shifra sighed. Her heart ached for the girl.

***

The carnage from the day of Hypatia's murder in the church had been cleaned up. Stacks of roof tiles remained along the back wall, but not as many as before. Bile rose in Shifra's throat as she recalled Dacia's description of what was done to that lovely woman in the back of the church.

The betrothal proceedings took place in a small room off the sanctuary. Cyril himself presided, assisted by his own scribe and a lawyer, who served Philip's family.

Philip's entourage included Clio and Herculanius. Akiva had invited Marcellus to join them. The young couple stood side by side, their hands joined by a white ribbon, as business and spiritual arrangements were made for the rest of their lives together. Shifra fought tears as she looked at her niece's solemn, pale features.

Glancing at the patriarch, Shifra noticed a young man standing behind him and to the side. Dressed in a rather fine brown tunic, he seemed familiar, but strive as she might, she could not immediately place him. Dark hair, dark eyes. Then he turned his head and she saw the other side of his face. Seb. She'd never seen him dressed in anything other than his green parabalani tunic. What could he possibly be doing here?

Cyril gave the final blessing, the young couple embraced, Philip's parents embraced the bride-to-be, Akiva embraced Philip and his parents.

"Come," said Akiva. "Let us go back to my home, where a reception worthy of this occasion awaits us."

Shifra turned to Marcellus. "Thank the Lord that's over."

313

But it wasn't.

Chapter Forty-Five

Seam Crossings

As the guests moved out of the small room, the patriarch called Akiva back and said something close to his ear. Akiva nodded, urged everyone, including Aella, to go ahead, promising to join them shortly. Before Shifra and Marcellus could leave, he stopped them.

"You go on ahead, Marcellus. Cyril wants to speak to Shifra and me."

"I'll stay."

The lawyer and the scribe, last to leave, closed the door on their way out.

Cyril smiled without speaking. Shifra did not find it a pleasant smile, especially when it lingered on her. After what seemed minutes, Akiva broke the silence.

"You have something to say, Your Eminence?"

"Yes, Secretary Akiva, I have. But not to you, to your sister."

Cyril turned and nodded at Seb, who went behind a curtain and came back out with a woman, dressed in saffron and wearing a garland of flowers on her head. With a gasp, Shifra recognized Dacia, and saw that her face was uncovered. Beneath the garland, her hair was covered with a yellow net. Shifra realized that Dacia was dressed as a bride. From the way she and Seb now stood together, arms linked, it was clear that the wedding had taken place.

Cyril raised his right hand, pointed it at Shifra like Moses pointing at the Red Sea, and spoke in a thundering voice.

"There are laws in this Empire, lady. A Jew may not own a Christian slave."

Akiva cried out. "What has that to do with my sister, Eminence?"

Cyril turned his glare from Shifra to her brother. "Your sister has lived in your home for two years and more. Be thankful that I do not choose to inquire how you did not know the truth about her."

Shifra put hand on her brother's arm. "Do not endanger yourself further, Akiva. I will answer." She stepped forward. "Dacia has not been a slave since my husband's death. He freed her in his will. The money he left for her use in setting herself up as a freedwoman was confiscated by your Church. She stayed with me of necessity."

"You don't deny that you did hold her as a slave?"

"No, I do not. But at that time, her religious beliefs were what you call heretical. For that reason her inheritance was kept from her by your Church."

Dacia rushed forward and threw herself on her knees before Shifra. "Please, Domina, forgive me. I never meant to betray you. Seb told me that all Jews are demons and I told him… I told him that you have never been anything but good to me."

Shifra drew the weeping girl to her feet and embraced her. "I do not blame you, Dacia. It was a heavy burden that you bore well for a very long time." She held her at arm's length. "And see? Didn't I tell you that you would find love one day?"

Dacia smiled through her tears. "You did." She touched the damaged side of her face. "Seb says he loves my scar because it makes us match."

Shifra kissed her former slave. "Be happy in your new life."

Seb reclaimed Dacia's arm and together they hurried out of the room. Cyril, his face and posture no longer set in Biblical mode, approached the remaining members of his audience. His voice, when he spoke, was convivial.

"It was Seb who told me, not the girl. She begged him not to, but he knew it was his duty."

Marcellus, who had remained in the background, moved to stand beside Shifra. She could feel his shoulder against hers.

Akiva glared at the prelate. "What now? What do you intend to do to my sister? Her life is blameless. For two years she has been helping Clio with her Christian charities. Surely you do not intend to drive her from the city."

Cyril spread his hands. "Not at all. What happens is entirely up to her." He smiled at Shifra. "No need to disrupt your life. You can begin instruction at once and go on with your activities as usual." The avuncular smile dissolved. "Or you can leave the city with the rest of the Jews by the end of the week."

With a rustle of silk, the patriarch swept past them, on his way to the door.

"Wait." Marcellus called after him. Cyril stopped. Marcellus drew Shifra and Akiva out of earshot. "Marry me, Shifra. We can live at my country estate. The only time you will have to go to church will be at Easter and Christmas. The rest of the time, you can worship as you wish."

"Do it, sister. It's the only way."

Shifra looked from one to the other, two men who cared about what happened to her. This time she wouldn't have Dacia. She would be completely alone. She wouldn't have a destination with her brother at the end. She thought of Mordecai and his library. *Sometimes dissembling is the price of survival.* She felt the weight of fear and dread lift a little. Her limbs felt as if they'd turned to pasta. She looked at Marcellus. He must have seen something in her eyes, because he walked back to where Cyril waited.

"The lady has agreed to be my wife. We will do what is necessary."

Cyril beamed his delight. "Excellent, excellent. As you know, I do not approve of the remarriage of widows, but in this case, I cannot object. The previous marriage is of no consequence, as both parties were Jews." He turned to Shifra. "It is as if you had never been married, my dear."

The words struck Shifra's ears and mind like a dagger of lightning. *As if she had never been married.* She breathed deeply and felt her back straighten, as if her breath were inflating her flaccid muscles. *As if Benjamin never existed.*

"No! I cannot do it. I will not do it." She turned to Marcellus. "Please forgive me, Marcellus. I admire and respect you more than I can say. I would be honored to be your wife, but I will not behave as if my first husband, my beloved Benjamin, the father of my children never existed, that our marriage counted for nothing. And I cannot insult the faith of my fathers by going through a sham conversion."

Cyril shook his head. "Go then, into the fog of unbelief. I have done all that charity requires."

Akiva stared in disbelief. "You have sealed your fate, sister. There's no turning back now. You must leave Alexandria by the appointed time. There's not a thing I can do to prevent it." He took a deep breath. "We'll talk tonight. For now, I'm wanted at my daughter's betrothal celebration." At the door, he looked back. "It's probably best if you don't come home until it's over."

Alone with Marcellus, Shifra let the tears come. He led her to a chair and stood over her until she regained control.

"Do you have any idea where you want to go?"

She looked up. "If it hasn't left yet, there's a ship in the harbor bound for Palestine. Perhaps there I can find a place where I can live without deception."

Margaret Joan Maddox, aka Maeve Maddox, has published six non-fiction books and three novels. She holds a PhD in comparative literature. Her interest in the religions of the Roman Empire dates from ninth grade Latin class. The topic of how a minor Jewish sect originating in an imperial backwater displaced the Empire's long-established religions continues to fascinate her. She finds it disquieting that first-century techniques of religious domination are alive and well in the twenty-first century.

www.ingramcontent.com/pod-product-compliance
Lightning Source LLC
Chambersburg PA
CBHW030603180626
46816CB00005B/1660